ACCLAIM FOR GAIL BOWEN AND
THE JOANNE KILBOURN MYSTERIES

"Bowen is one of those rare, magical mystery writers readers love not only for her suspense skills but for her stories' elegance, sense of place and true-to-life form. . . . A master of ramping up suspense." — *Ottawa Citizen*

"Bowen can confidently place her series beside any other being produced in North America." — Halifax *Chronicle-Herald*

"Gail Bowen's Joanne Kilbourn mysteries are small works of elegance that assume the reader of suspense is after more than blood and guts, that she is looking for the meaning behind a life lived and a life taken." — *Calgary Herald*

"Bowen has a hard eye for the way human ambition can take advantage of human gullibility." — *Publishers Weekly*

"Gail Bowen got the recipe right with her series on Joanne Kilbourn." — *Vancouver Sun*

"What works so well [is Bowen's] sense of place – Regina comes to life – and her ability to inhabit the everyday life of an interesting family with wit and vigour. . . . Gail Bowen continues to be a fine mystery writer, with a protagonist readers can invest in for the long run." — *National Post*

"Gail Bowen is one of Canada's literary treasures." — *Ottawa Citizen*

D0365826

OTHER JOANNE KILBOURN MYSTERIES

BY GAIL BOWEN

BURYING ARIEL

A Joanne Kilbourn Mystery

GAIL BOWEN

McClelland & Stewart

First M&S paperback edition published 2001
This edition published 2011

Library and Archives Canada Cataloguing in Publication

Bowen, Gail, 1942-
Burying Ariel : a Joanne Kilbourn mystery / Gail Bowen.

ISBN 978-0-7710-1309-6

I. Title.

PS8553.08995B87 2011   C813'.54   C2011-900310-4

We acknowledge the financial support of the Government of Canada
through the Book Publishing Industry Development Program and that
of the Government of Ontario through the Ontario Media Development
Corporation's Ontario Book Initiative. We further acknowledge the
support of the Canada Council for the Arts and the Ontario Arts
Council for our publishing program.

Published simultaneously in the United States of America by
McClelland & Stewart Ltd., P.O. Box 1030, Plattsburgh, New York 12901

Library of Congress Control Number: 2011925601

Cover art: © Grapix | Dreamstime.com
This book was produced using recycled materials.
Typeset in Trump Mediaeval by M&S, Toronto
Printed and bound in the United States of America

McClelland & Stewart Ltd.
75 Sherbourne Street
Toronto, Ontario
M5A 2P9
www.mcclelland.com

1 2 3 4 5   15 14 13 12 11

With thanks to Dr. David Barnard, who introduced me to the poetry of Denise Levertov and whose gentle presence ensures that the memebers of our univeristy community treat each other with collegiality and respect. Thanks as well to Drs. Lee Hunter, Joan Baldwin, and Linda Nilson for their extraordinary care. And as always, thanks to Ted for more than even he can imagine.

BURYING ARIEL

CHAPTER

1

The nails on the fingers that reached out to grab my arm as I left the Faculty Club's private dining room were bitten to the quick, and the cuticles were chewed raw. The hand belonged to a man whose rage was so fierce he had taken to ripping his own body, but it had become as familiar to me as my own. It was ten minutes to one on the Thursday afternoon before the Victoria Day weekend. The celebration of the old Queen's birthday may have been a signal to the rest of Canada to unbutton and unwind, but Kevin Coyle's private demons didn't take holidays.

"I thought I was going to have to go in there and get you," he said. "I have news."

"Kevin, there's a celebration going on, remember? Today's the luncheon for Rosalie."

Behind the Coke-bottle lenses of his horn-rims, his eyes glittered. "Does a party for an old maid who's finally managed to snag herself a man take precedence over murder?"

By his own assessment, my former colleague in the Political Science department hadn't drawn a wholly rational breath since a group of female students had accused him of attitudinal harassment two years earlier. I removed his hand from my arm. "Put a sock in it, Kevin. It's a holiday weekend. I'm declaring a moratorium on tortured metaphors. I don't want to hear how your reputation as a gentleman and a scholar has been murdered."

He shook his head. "This murder is no metaphor, Joanne. It's real, and I'm certain it's connected to my case. A young man from the library just came up to the Political Science office. He'd been sent to find Livia. Of course, our esteemed head wasn't there; nor were any of the rest of you. As usual, I was alone, so he delivered the news to me."

"And the news is . . . ?"

"A woman's body has been found in an archive room in the basement of the library."

I felt my nerves twang. "Was she a student of ours? Is that why the man was looking for Livia?"

Kevin took off his glasses. I'd never seen him without them. He looked surprisingly vulnerable. "Not a student, Joanne. A colleague. It was Ariel Warren."

For a moment, I clung to the grace of denial. "No! I just saw her this morning. She was wearing that vintage band jacket she bought to wear to Rosalie's party."

"The jacket didn't protect her," Kevin said flatly. "I wish it had." He swallowed hard, as if empathy were an emotion that had to be choked back. "Our profession is a cesspool, but she was a decent young woman."

Kevin's reference to Ariel in the past tense had the finality of a tolling bell. I felt my knees go weak. "She was only twenty-seven," I said.

"Too young to die," he agreed.

On the other side of the door, there was a burst of laughter. I closed my eyes. I'd known Ariel Warren since she was a child. My first memory of her was at a Halloween party we'd had for my daughter Mieka's sixth birthday. Ariel had come as a sunflower, with a circle of golden petals radiating from her small face.

"There could be a mistake," I said, but my voice was forlorn, bereft of hope.

Kevin put his glasses back on and peered at me. "Are you going to cry?"

"Not yet," I said. "Right now, I'm going over to the library to see what I can find out." I looked hard at him. "Kevin, I don't think either of us should say anything more until we're sure we know the truth."

His laugh was a bark of derision. "*The truth*. You'll never find out the truth about this. Mark my words. They'll cover up the connection between this death and my case the way they've covered up everything else. Either that, or they'll rearrange the facts to implicate me."

On a good day I could pity Kevin, but this was not a good day. I had to struggle to keep my composure. "Try to look at this the way a person with an ounce of decency would," I said. "Someone has been murdered. This isn't about you."

"That's where you're wrong," Kevin said. "Ariel wouldn't be in our department if it weren't for me. And I know for a fact that she'd unearthed something that would exonerate me."

"Exactly what had she 'unearthed'?"

He shrugged helplessly. "They killed her before she had a chance to reveal what she'd found. That little coven that set me up will stop at nothing." He patted my arm. "Tread carefully. I had only three friends in this department, and now it appears that two of them are dead."

As I watched him disappear down the stairs, I felt the first stirrings of panic. Kevin might be obsessive, but there was nothing wrong with his math. When the charges against him had surfaced, I was one of two people in Political Science who had sided with Kevin Coyle; the other had been Ben Jesse, our department head. Ben was a thoroughly decent man who feared unsubstantiated complaints, however serious, more than confrontation and nasty publicity. It was an ugly time for our department and for our university; it pitted us against one another and ended longstanding friendships. A man governed by expedience would have thrown Kevin to the wolves, but Ben was a person of principle. He defended Kevin because he believed in fairness and due process. His refusal to cave in to political bullying cost him dearly. In the midst of a lengthy and rancorous encounter with a group of students, Ben suffered a heart attack. He was, they told us later, dead before he hit the floor.

Now there was another death.

I reached the library just as a half-dozen police officers were coming through the door from outside. I was in luck; one of the officers was Detective Robert Hallam, the fiancé of Rosalie Norman, our department's administrative assistant and guest of honour at our luncheon that day.

Robert was a small, dapper man with a choleric temperament and an unshakeable belief that the world was divided into two camps: the good guys and the bad guys. I was both a friend of his beloved and a woman who had chosen a cop for her own beloved, so I had made the cut. In Robert's estimation, I was one of the good guys, and as soon as he spotted me, he came over.

"You've heard about this already?"

"News travels fast at a university," I said. "I need a favour. Can you tell me the name of the woman who was killed?"

He shook his head. "I just got the call." Robert scanned the lobby, then pointed to a man in a grey windbreaker who was taking photographs of the area around the elevator. "Eddie will have some answers," he said. Robert walked over to the elevators. He and Eddie exchanged a few words; then Eddie handed him some pictures. Robert shuffled through them and came back to me.

"The identification in the dead woman's wallet belongs to Ariel Warren," he said. "The deceased died as a result of a knife in the back. One wound, but it was a doozy. We've already sent someone to talk to the next of kin."

"Are those photographs of Ariel?" I asked.

"They're of the dead woman," he said. "I never had the pleasure, so I can't say for certain that Ariel Warren is the woman in the pictures."

"Could I see them?"

He hesitated. "They're graphic, but there's one that's not too bad." He shuffled through the photos again, then held up a Polaroid. My throat tightened: the dark blond hair of the woman slumped on the table had fallen forward, but I could see the curve of her cheek and the shoulder of the scarlet band jacket she'd chosen to celebrate Rosalie's joy.

"It's her," I said.

Robert Hallam's face was grim. "I figured it was," he said. "But when the deceased is a friend of a friend, you always hope you're wrong. My Rosalie was very fond of that girl."

A thought occurred to me. "Rosalie still doesn't know. None of them do. Robert, is it all right if I go back and tell them what's happened, before the media get the story?"

"You can tell them. Nobody should find out news like this from some jerk with a microphone."

"I agree," I said. "This is going to be tough enough. Ariel had a lot of friends in our department."

"I'm sure she did." Robert looked thoughtful. "Joanne, tell people to stick around, would you? We'll need to talk to everybody who knew Ariel. She may have had a lot of friends, but she obviously had at least one enemy."

By the time I got back, the main dining room of the Faculty Club was deserted. The regular term was over, and people who taught in the spring session didn't tend to hang around past lunch. The door to the private dining room was still closed, but I could hear the stereo. During lunch, we had listened to show tunes about love and marriage. Ed Mariani, with whom I co-taught the class Politics and the Media, had made the selections, and they ranged from the sublime to the sappy. Now it was Stanley Holloway singing "Get Me to the Church on Time," and our ex-premier and newest department member, Howard Dowhanuik, was singing along in his tuneless, rumbling bass.

I looked at my watch. It was ten past one. Four and a half hours earlier Ariel had been alive. Not just living, but triumphantly alive. For much of the winter, she had looked thin and unwell, but when I'd seen her as I headed for my office that morning she had been radiant. She'd been sitting on the academic green surrounded by the students from her Political Science 101 class. It had been a scene for an Impressionist: a high, blue sky, air shimmering with light, new grass splashed by crayon-bright plantings of daffodils and tulips, and in the foreground, a woman wearing a brilliant scarlet jacket, her dark blond hair knotted loosely at the nape of her neck, her profile gravely beautiful as she listened to the earnest voices of a freshman class. When Ariel had called out a greeting, I'd felt a current of connection, not just with her, but with what it had been like to be twenty-seven on a soft spring day, doing work that I knew I was good at and looking forward to a future of illimitable possibilities.

There would be no more of those incandescent moments. Had anyone asked me that morning, I would have sworn that all of Ariel's colleagues would have felt her loss as keenly as I did. Now I wasn't sure. Kevin Coyle's accusation had brought only a pinprick of doubt. Since the advent of his case, Kevin had floated a hundred wacko theories. His claims were easy to dismiss; Detective Robert Hallam's observation wasn't. Suddenly, I was in uncharted territory.

The only thing I knew for certain was that for two people at Rosalie Norman's luncheon, the loss would be personal and profound.

Howard Dowhanuik's son, Charlie, and Ariel had been lovers. To the outside world, it seemed an unlikely pairing. Charlie, with characteristic edge, referred to their relationship as the non-Disney version of *Beauty and the Beast*. The allusion was cruel but not inaccurate. Ariel had the kind of delicately sculpted porcelain beauty found most often in illustrations to fairy stories. Charlie's face caused strangers to avert their eyes. He had been born with a port-wine birthmark that covered the right half of his face like a blood mask, and it had made his passage through childhood and adolescence an agony. Charlie's pain hadn't been eased by Howard's total absorption in politics or by the spotlight that shone on the premier's family in our small province. Through courage and a quick and acerbic wit, Charlie had made a life for himself, but until recently there had been no room in that life for his father. Loving Ariel and being loved by her had made Charlie generous. He had, at her urging, given Howard a second chance, and Howard had been humbly grateful.

The other person to whom I dreaded breaking the news was the young instructor who had been hired with Ariel. Solange Levy was a difficult young woman, sensitive to slight and quick to anger. When she had arrived at our department to teach the previous September, the irony of her given name had been hard to ignore, but as her personal history became known to us, it was apparent that nothing in Solange's life had given her cause to be sunny. The only child of a mother involved in a series of abusive relationships, Solange learned to take refuge in her studies. She had a gift for mathematics, and by the time she was in high school she'd decided that, in an uncertain world, a discipline that put a premium on reason and elegant proofs could offer her safe haven.

On a snowy December day in 1989, she had been doing her homework and listening to the radio when she heard the news of the massacre at L'École Polytechnique. She was seventeen at the time. The event politicized her and defined her life. She abandoned mathematics and plunged into feminist theory and politics. Ten years later, she was a Ph.D. and a warrior. With her razor intellect, her sleek, muscular body, her Joan of Arc haircut, and her uniform of black T-shirt, black jeans, and ragged Converse high-top runners, Solange seemed more equipped for battle than friendship, but Ariel pierced her armour. The price Ariel's death would exact from her best friend's vision of human existence seemed beyond calculation.

When I opened the door to the Window Room, it was clear that Rosalie Norman's party had reached the sour stage of an event that had gone on too long. The Asti Spumante bottles were empty, the delicate Depression-ware glass plates were cake-smeared, and the pink-throated flowers that had decorated each of our places had begun to wilt. Fully a third of the guests had left, and those who remained were sprawled listlessly in their chairs. Behind her mound of gifts, Rosalie Norman had the fixed smile of the guest of honour at a party that has ceased to be fun. As all eyes turned to me, I remembered my reason for leaving the party. I'd been charged with the task of picking up the bouquet of long-stemmed roses that had been delivered to the Faculty Club bar. The flowers were the final gift. As soon as Rosalie had them in hand, the last photograph would be taken, and we would be free to get back to our real lives.

Livia Brook cut a quick stare my way. "Where are the roses?" In the years since her husband had dumped her, Livia had meditated and soul-journeyed her way into a seemingly shatterproof serenity, but at that moment negative energies seemed to be getting the better of her. She tried to erase her rudeness. "We were beginning to be concerned about you."

Solange gave me a sly sidelong glance. "My theory was that you'd run off with your friend, Kevin Coyle. Not my type, but who could blame you for giving in to temptation?" She leaned back in her chair and raised a toned arm to indicate the decorations. "Such a romantic occasion. I was afraid this event would be *quitaine*." She struggled for the translation. "You know, kitschy – too much – but it was quite lovely. I just wish Ariel had shown up."

I took a step towards her. "Solange . . ."

Her face froze. She had cat's eyes, tawny and green-flecked, and she had a cat's instinct for danger. She knew the worst before I opened my mouth.

"Something's happened to her," she said flatly.

I nodded. "Yes."

Solange moved out of her chair slowly, like someone in a dream state. "She's dead?"

"Her body was found in an archive room in the basement of the library."

"When?" Solange said.

"Not long ago," I said. "Probably within the hour."

Solange covered her face with her hands and turned away, but the other guests had moved to the edge of their chairs. Like clever undergraduates, they were twitching with unasked questions.

I headed them off. "I'll tell you what I know," I said. "But it isn't much."

I gave a quick sketch of events. When I was finished, I turned to Rosalie. "I was grateful that Robert was there," I said. "He was very helpful."

Despite the tears welling in her eyes, Rosalie coloured with pride. "He's a credit to his profession," she said.

"He certainly was today," I agreed. "And it can't have been easy for him to decide how much he could divulge when the case was still unfolding. I guess, at the moment, the only unassailable fact is that the dead woman was Ariel." I looked around the table. "Detective Hallam has asked us all to stick around so the police can ask their questions. It might be best if we just go back and wait in our offices."

Not surprisingly, it was Rosalie, our link with authority, who framed the question that was at the forefront of all our minds. "Do the police know who did it?"

I shook my head. "No," I said, "but I'm sure by now they have some leads."

"It will have been a man." Solange's voice was flat with resignation.

Livia's echo was choric. "A man," she repeated.

For a beat, the only sounds in the room came from the stereo. Carly Simon was singing "The Boy That I Marry." My eyes took in the men in our department. None of them met my gaze. We all knew something ugly was being loosed in this room.

"No one knows who did this, Solange," I said quickly.

She whirled to face the guests at the table. Her eyes blazed. For the first time in my memory, Solange was wearing a dress, a sleek black mini whose hemline skimmed the top of her thighs. When she arrived for lunch, she had pirouetted in it mockingly. "To prove to Ariel I can play the game if I choose to," she had said. The young woman in front of me was through playing games.

Howard Dowhanuik had been sitting closest to Solange. Now he stood and moved to comfort her. His old hawk's face was broken, but his voice was steady. "We're not all the enemy, Solange. Charlie loved Ariel. So did I."

"Bullshit." Solange pronounced the expletive in faux French – *bouleshit*. As these two people whose lives had been transformed by Ariel Warren faced one another, the word hung in the air, sibilant and powerful. Finally, Solange turned away. She reached into her small, black over-the-shoulder bag. For a terrible moment, I thought she was going to pull out a weapon, but all she extracted was a package of Player's and a Bic lighter. She removed a cigarette, then threw the pack down on the table. Her hands were trembling so badly she couldn't make her lighter work.

Wordlessly, Howard took the Bic and lit her cigarette. She dragged on it deeply, then turned and walked towards the window. It had been fifteen years since I'd quit smoking, but at that moment I badly wanted a cigarette. I wasn't the only one. Livia Brook surprised me by taking a Player's from Solange's pack and lighting it. It was as startling as seeing Preston Manning at a Tool concert. Livia's marriage to Kenneth Brook had flamed out in a haze of booze and cigarette smoke, but since they'd split she had become zealous about her health. Everything that entered her body or touched her person had to be organic and unadulterated. Suddenly, it seemed as if the whole world was out of joint.

As the pungent bite of burning tobacco filled the air, I gazed again at the last of Rosalie's guests. When the announcement had been made that Livia was the new head of Political Science, Ed Mariani had whispered to me that she would find running our department as rewarding as herding cats. There was more truth than poetry in the image. We were a group of proud and headstrong individualists, certain we'd worked out the answers to all the questions that mattered. Ariel Warren's death was revealing an unpalatable truth: our assurance was veneer-thin. We were badly in need of direction. Despite the fact that her composure was showing serious fault lines, Livia Brook supplied it.

She walked over to the stereo, flicked it off, and then returned to her place at the table. In her mid-forties, Livia still had something of the undergraduate about her. Her wardrobe ran to corduroy jumpers, tights, and Birkenstocks, and her hair, a mass of shoulder-length curls, now more grey than chestnut, still had a certain Botticelli abundance. She wore little or no makeup. Her great beauty was her skin, which she kept exquisite with Pears soap and hot water. On the wall behind her desk was a sampler done in cross-stitch. "No Surprises," it said, and it summed up both her post-divorce philosophy and her administrative style. Livia did her homework, ran the department with a fair and equitable hand, and, despite her newly acquired penchant for the rhetoric of empowerment and uplift, had the common sense to extinguish brushfires before they flared out of control. It was a valuable attribute in a department as deeply mired in crisis as ours had been when she'd taken over. Now there was another crisis, and apparently Livia had decided that it would be wise to channel our emotions.

"I think a moment of silence so each of us can deal with our feelings privately might be appropriate." Her voice was firm, but as she steadied herself against the table edge, her narrow fingertips trembled. Like grateful sheep, all of us, including Solange, scrambled to our feet, and when Livia bowed her head, we followed her lead.

When a suitable amount of time had elapsed, Livia rescued us from our private thoughts. "Some of you may be uneasy about what you're experiencing right now. Don't judge yourself. Feelings are neither right nor wrong. They simply are, and they deserve validation."

In the months since she'd become department head, Livia had often offered the soothing bromides of the self-help movement as a remedy for overheated passions, but today her delivery of the articles of her faith was flat, like that of an acolyte who had suddenly become an unbeliever. She looked at us with unseeing eyes. When her glance fell on

Rosalie Norman, she appeared to find her focus again. "We have to keep on keeping on. Continuance is the answer," she said. "Rosalie will need some help getting her gifts back to the office."

Grateful for direction on a day that seemed suddenly to have broken from its moorings, people headed for the door. Ed Mariani scooped up an armload of pastel-wrapped presents. As he passed by me, he whispered, "At least we were spared a shower of healing stones from Livia's enchanted ritual bag." He sighed heavily. "Truth be told, I wouldn't mind having a hunk of rose quartz to clutch right now."

"I forget what rose quartz is supposed to do," I said.

"Heal the heart." Ed looked over at Solange. "If I had a piece, I'd share it with her, except I imagine that at this moment she isn't making exceptions for gay men."

"I'll talk to her," I said.

Ed gave me a quick peck on the cheek. "Good luck."

Solange was facing the window again, wreathed in cigarette smoke, which seemed to isolate her private and terrible mourning. I walked over and touched her shoulder.

She turned, and the breath caught in my throat. She was transformed. Her face was ashen and carved with the lines of bitterness that mark those who have seen the worst and know there is nothing better ahead.

"Solange, is there anything I can do to help?"

"It depends." She stubbed out her cigarette on a dessert plate that had been abandoned on the windowsill. "Can you raise the dead, Joanne?"

She ran from the room, and I made no attempt to follow her. When I felt Howard Dowhanuik's arm around my shoulder, I relaxed into it. We walked downstairs in silence. Instead of turning in to the glassed-in walkway that connected College West to the Lab and Classroom buildings, Howard headed for the doors that led outside. "Let's take the long way back to the office," he said. "I need to figure out how I'm going to break this to my son."

"The newsroom at Charlie's station will be getting the story soon. They may have it already," I said. "You don't have much time."

When he turned to face me, Howard's eyes were rheumy. "My grandmother used to say, 'There's this life, the next life, and a turnip patch on the other side.'"

"Not much there to cling to when times get rough," I said.

Howard shrugged. "Have you got anything better?"

As we approached the grassy slope where I'd seen Ariel and her class that morning, I had to admit I didn't. At that moment, it was hard to envision a future that contained anything but pain. The University Day Care Centre was nearby, and the staff had liberated their preschoolers to take advantage of a five-star spring day. Wild with freedom, the children ran and somersaulted down the little hill, a kaleidoscopic, perpetually moving swirl of fluorescent windbreakers and new sneakers. As they called out one another's names in voices bright as May sunshine, I remembered other voices, other children.

Ariel had been a golden child, tow-headed, cobalt-eyed, long-limbed. From the moment she came through the front door for Mieka's party, she had been surrounded by other children. Charlie Dowhanuik had spent much of the party on the edge of the fun, watching intently, his small fingers splayed against his cheek, trying without success to cover the purple birthmark that threatened to engulf his face. When I served the food, he squeezed in next to Ariel. She had reached up, pulled his hand down with her own, and peered at his face closely. "It's not so bad," she said, "but if I get the dime in the cake, I'll give it to you."

When Howard and I passed the closed door of Solange Levy's office and heard weeping, Howard shot me a supplicating look.

"I'll see if there's anything I can do," I said. "You call Charlie."

Solange's door was open a crack. I rapped on it. "Solange, it's Joanne."

"Are you alone?"

On the desk in front of her were her silver bicycle helmet and the lock to her prized Trek WSD, but Solange didn't appear to be going anywhere. A cigarette smouldered between her fingers. She was holding a framed photograph in her hands. As I watched, she ripped the photo out, picked up a snapshot from her desk and slid it carefully into the pewter frame. "I have to protect this," she said. "It's of Ariel at Lake Magog. It was the first day of the New Year, and she was so happy. She'd always been so worried about other people's happiness – so afraid to put her own wishes first." Solange shook her head furiously. "So female and so destructive. But she found her strength on our hike at Mount Assiniboine. There were just the two of us. It was tough. There was a blizzard. There were places where the ascent was straight up the mountain. Once the path under her feet just gave way, but she held on." Solange stared at the photograph. "All her life she'd had fears, but by the time we got to Lake Magog, she knew she'd never go back to being the compliant little girl. She had found her power." Solange's voice broke. "Then some bastard kills her as if she were an animal." For a beat Solange herself seemed torn apart by the violence that ended her friend's life; then she turned to steel. "He won't get away with it."

I followed her as she strode down the hall. There were three people in the main office: Detective Robert Hallam

was watching Rosalie search the drawer of the cabinet where
we kept personnel files, and Livia Brook was hovering
between them like a duenna.

Solange paid them no heed. A counter separated the reception area from the office. When Solange set the photograph
on it, Livia came over immediately. She picked up the
picture, glanced at it quickly, then thrust it at Solange. "It's
too much," she said. "We don't need a reminder of what
we've lost."

"You're wrong." Solange's tone was coldly furious. "We
do need a reminder. We all need to be reminded every
minute of every day that what that monster took from us
was beyond price. Otherwise, there will never be justice."
Solange returned the photograph to the counter, but her
fingers lingered, caressing the curve of the frame. "When I
was young," she said, "I was prepared for confirmation by
a Spanish priest – a fat, useless old man, peddling cruel
patriarchal dogma, but one of his lessons stayed with me.
He told me there was a Spanish proverb I should remember
whenever I had to make a choice in life." Her voice deepened
into a parody of the old priest, and she wagged her finger
theatrically. *"God says, 'Take what you want. Take it, and
pay for it.'"* She turned to face me. "The man who killed
Ariel took the best, Joanne, and if God won't make him pay
for it, I will."

CHAPTER

2

After her diatribe, Solange seemed on the verge of shock. The carapace of the warrior had shattered. She was hugging herself, but as strong as her arms were, they seemed incapable of holding the pieces together, and her tawny green-flecked eyes were unblinking and wary. I reached out to her, but Livia stepped between us and slid her arm around Solange's waist. "She needs to be alone for a while. She has to find the place inside herself that will enable her to accept this."

Robert Hallam raised an eyebrow. "When she finds that place I'll want to talk to her. Meanwhile," he said, turning to Livia, "I'd appreciate a few minutes of your time."

"Of course," Livia said. "Just let me get Solange settled."

Rosalie removed her pale yellow jacket, hung it carefully on the back of her chair, filled a glass at the water cooler, picked up a box of tissues, and followed Livia and Solange into the inner office. Too exhausted to move, I stared at the closed door, hoping against hope that somewhere in Livia's endless store of New Age baloney, there was a mantra that could fix everything. I wasn't optimistic.

Rosalie was back almost immediately, but Livia stayed with Solange for several minutes. By the time she emerged, Robert had his notebook and pencil at the ready, and his foot was tapping. "Let's get to the questions, Dr. Brook," he said. "I haven't got all day, and there are a lot of people to see." I took that as my cue to leave.

When I got back to my office, Howard was waiting for me. He was standing at the window, looking out at the campus. The early-afternoon sun poured in on him, softening his angular features, changing him from a wary old eagle into someone kindly and avuncular. The metamorphosis was more apparent than real. He gazed at me through hooded eyes.

"Is it my imagination or is the number of dumb fucks in the world increasing?"

"I take it your question isn't rhetorical," I said.

"You tell me." Howard ran a gnarled hand over his head. "The young cop they sent to interview me had a pronunciation problem. Every time he said the word 'deceased,' it came out 'diseased.'"

I bit my lip to keep from smiling. "As in 'How well did you know the diseased?'" I said.

"Exactly. Jesus, Jo. That kid must use the word 'deceased' a hundred times a week. You'd think somebody would have told him, wouldn't you? Then, after he left, I tried Charlie's house. No answer, so I called the radio station. They've got the Queen of the Coneheads answering the phones there. She refused to put me through to Charlie directly. Told me it was station policy to screen all calls. I told her my call was important. She said every phone call CVOX gets is important. I told her it was an emergency. She said if I considered myself suicidal, she'd redirect my call to a crisis line; if not, I could leave my name and number like everybody else."

"Did you tell her you were Charlie's father?"

Howard looked abashed. "It didn't occur to me," he said quietly. "Talk about dumb fucks. I'm going to call a cab and go over there."

"Forget the cab," I said. "I'll take you."

"Have the police talked to you yet?"

"Nope, but they know where I live."

Howard frowned. "You don't have to do this."

I picked up my sweater. "True, and you didn't have to stay up with me all night when Ian died or spend hours convincing me the world hadn't come to an end when Mieka dropped out of university or come to the hospital with me when Angus got that concussion playing football . . . Shall I continue?"

He grinned sheepishly. "Let's hit the road."

As soon as I turned the key in the ignition, Howard reached for the radio dial and punched in cvox. It was 2:30 – time for Charlie's show.

Howard turned to face the window on the passenger side. His voice was a gravel whisper. "Do you think he's found out yet?"

"You'll be able to tell when you hear him," I said. "He doesn't hold much back on that show." It was true. I wasn't a fan of open-line radio, and cvox was all talk all the time, but whenever I'd caught "Heroes" I'd been impressed. Charlie's subject was relationships, and he treated his callers' problems with intelligence and a wild, subversive wit. He had taken the show's name from Joseph Campbell's book *The Hero with a Thousand Faces*, and the reference was significant. Many would have dismissed Charlie's callers as malcontents or as charter members of the tribe of the terminally confused. But to Charlie they were heroes engaged in the hero's journey to find answers that would make sense of their lives. His advice to them was a potent mix of eclectic allusion and dark insight that suggested their problems went beyond the classroom or the trailer court, and his audience, comprised largely of the desirable seventeen-to-thirty demographic was huge and loyal.

When the drummer from Dave Matthews Band counted the band into Charlie's theme music, "Ants Marching," Howard stiffened. So did I, but as the music faded and Charlie began his intro, his dark-honey voice sounded as it always did, intense and intimate.

"It's 2:30 on CVOX, Voice Radio, and this is Charlie D, kicking off the first weekend of summer. Hot sun, cold beer, new friends, old loves – a time for revelry. But there are some among us who just can't seem to celebrate the cosmically embedded self. No matter what you do for them, it's never enough. This show is about them, or it's about you if you're one of them.

"Some people,
No matter what you give them
Still want the moon.

"The bread,
The salt,
White meat and dark,
Still hungry.

"The marriage bed
And the cradle,
Still empty arms."

Howard turned to me furiously. "What the hell's he doing?" I raised my hand in a hushing gesture. "Listen."

Charlie's voice was a seeping wound. He was close to the breaking point, but he was also a professional. He didn't falter.

"You give them land,
Their own earth under their feet,
And still they take to the roads.

"And water: dig them the deepest well,
Still it's not deep enough
To drink the moon from.

"This show is about them . . . the ones who, even after you've dug them the deepest well, say it's not deep enough, because it doesn't let them drink the moon . . ."

Howard glared at me. "Well?"

"It's called 'Adam's Complaint.' Denise Levertov wrote it. Charlie uses poetry on his show all the time."

"Maybe to you it's just poetry. But to a cop it's going to sound like a confession. In cases like this, the boyfriend's always a suspect." Howard picked up my cellphone. "Charlie needs a lawyer."

"You're a lawyer," I said.

Howard replaced the phone in the well between our seats. "Do you think he'd let me act for him?"

"Why not?" I said. "You're the best, and you'll come cheap."

CVOX was a concrete and glass box surrounded by larger concrete and glass boxes that sold such commodities as discounted designer fashions, end-of-the-roll carpeting, and furniture that could dazzle your friends for a year before you had to cough up a single dime. The station was indistinguishable from its neighbours, except for the oversized call letters on its roof. The "O" in CVOX was an open, red-lipped mouth with a lascivious Mick Jagger tongue. Spectacular as the sign was, Howard didn't even give it a passing glance. He leaped out of the car before I came to a full stop.

I walked through the double glass doors at the front of the building just as the Queen of the Coneheads was running to block Howard's entrance to the corridor that presumably led to the radio studios. Howard was a big man, six-foot-three and powerfully built, but he was no match for this tiny young woman with three-inch platform shoes and attitude as spiky as her hair.

"No way," she said. "Nobody goes in there unless I say they go in there."

Howard gazed at me beseechingly. He had never found it easy dealing with women.

I walked over and stepped between them. The young woman gave me a quick up and down, decided I was harmless, and relaxed. "This is Charlie Dowhanuik's father," I said. She stared at me uncomprehendingly. I corrected myself. "Charlie D's father," I said.

She nodded sagely. "Right."

"There's been a death," I said. "In the family."

Her small features rearranged themselves into an expression of sympathy. "Bummer," she said. She looked up into Howard's face. "Just give me a second, Mr. D, then I can take you down to the studio." She went back to her desk, called for a back-up gatekeeper, then came over to Howard and took him gently by the arm. "This way," she said. "Incidentally, I'm Esme."

When we were almost at the end of the hall, Esme steered us to the right, down a short corridor, and into a control room. We stood awkwardly while she whispered something to a woman in a black turtleneck, who turned from the array of equipment in front of her, glanced our way, then swivelled her chair to face the glass that separated the control room from the studio. Through the glass I could see Charlie. I had known his mother well, and Charlie was unmistakably her son: black hair, sleepy hazel eyes, aquiline nose, generous mouth. But unlike her son, Marnie Dowhanuik's beauty had been without flaw.

When the woman in the black turtleneck murmured into her microphone, Charlie looked up. He was wearing headphones. She turned to Howard. "You can talk to him now. I'll go to a commercial. Tell him I'm bringing somebody in to finish the show."

In seconds, Howard appeared in Charlie's studio. He sat down in the chair next to his son's, leaned over, swung one of his massive arms around Charlie's slender shoulders and put his mouth to Charlie's ear. For a beat, Charlie listened, then his face crumpled. He had adjusted his headphones so he could hear his father; now he ripped them off and covered his face with his hands.

Viewed through glass, the silent tableau of discovery and grief had the surreal intensity of life inside an aquarium. Instinctively, both the woman in the turtleneck and I looked away. She picked up the phone and summoned someone named Troy to Studio D, then turned to me. "I'm Kendra Gaede," she said. "You're welcome to stay here till they decide how they want to handle this."

"Thanks," I said. "I'd like to be here in case Howard needs me."

He didn't. In a beat, Charlie picked up his headphones and slipped them back on.

"Troy's going to finish for you," Kendra said.

Charlie nodded, then punched a button in front of him. We could hear his voice. "I have to explain why Troy's taking over. Otherwise, the switchboard will be jammed."

"Are you sure you can get through it?" Kendra asked. "Troy can come up with something."

Charlie raised his hand, palm towards us. "The people who listen to this show trust me. I have to be honest with them." Charlie picked up his headphones, and began speaking.

"Over seven hundred years ago, a beautiful woman named Francesca da Rimini told Dante a great truth: 'There is nothing more painful than to remember happy days in times of sorrow.'" The smooth professionalism of his voice shattered against the hard edge of grief, but he soldiered on. "Francesca was one of the damned. I've just discovered that I am, too. The topic for the rest of the show is loss. So if you're lost, today's your day. Troy Prigotzke will be taking over for the rest of the show. Till the next time, this is Charlie D. Be strong. Nothing lasts forever."

His words were brave, but as soon as Troy Prigotzke entered the booth, Charlie slumped. Gentle as a mother Troy took the headphones from Charlie's head and placed them on his own. "Time to go, Buddy," Troy said, and Charlie stood and walked out of the booth; Howard was right behind him.

As Charlie crossed in front of me, I put my hand on his shoulder. "I'm so sorry," I said. I turned to Howard. "Can I give you a lift anywhere?"

Howard shook his head. "Charlie's probably better without too many people around right now. When he decides what he wants to do, we can cab it. I'll call you tonight."

"Do that," I said.

After Charlie and Howard disappeared down the hall that led to the CVOX offices, Esme touched me on the shoulder. "I'll walk you back to reception," she said.

The walls on either side of us were hung with oversized publicity photographs of the on-air personalities of CVOX. The pictures were brightly banal and I passed them without a second glance. But I slowed at Charlie's portrait. He had presented his best profile to the camera, but the lighting was dim and, in a gesture heartbreakingly instinctive and familiar, his right hand was raised to shield his blood-scarred hidden face.

In that instant, I gleaned something of what it was like for Charlie to live in a world full of mirrors and cameras and eyes, and my mind recoiled from this insight into his perpetual suffering. When we reached the main desk, Esme's words wrenched me back to reality.

"I didn't know it was her. I thought when you said there was a death in the family it was like an old uncle or something." She ran a hand through her spiky burgundy hair. "Ariel wasn't much older than me."

"Too young," I said.

She bobbed her head in affirmation. "Way, way too young."

I started towards the door. Esme called after me. "Wait." She walked over to a cupboard behind the desk, took out a shiny black coffee mug and handed it to me. The logo on it was silver except for the wetly red Mick Jagger mouth that hinted at appetites too hip and too dark for talk radio. Cool on cool.

I froze. Esme smacked the palm of her hand against her forehead. "Totally inappropriate, right?" she said. "It's just that I always give these to guests. I'm such a space case."

"Nobody knows what to do in a situation like this," I said. "Giving a person a mug makes as much sense as anything else."

On my way home, I turned on the radio and punched in CBC Radio Two. As I drove across the Albert Street Bridge, the graceful precision of Prokofiev's "Classical" Symphony soothed me. I took a deep breath. With Prokofiev and luck, I might just make it through dinner.

Luck was not on my side. Our new puppy was waiting for me inside the door. He was an eight-week-old Bouvier des Flandres named Willie, my first male dog and my first Bouvier, and so far he had brought credit to neither his gendeɪ nor his breed. He was sweet but not gifted. The day before, my son Angus had come home with the news that it took Bouviers two years to grow a brain. As Willie bounded towards me with the remnants of one of my new sandals hanging out of his mouth, I found myself wondering how he and I could make it through the next twenty-two months.

I took the sandal from him and picked him up. He licked my face wildly. The smell of puppy breath won me over. "Okay," I said. "I was young once myself." I shifted his position, so I could establish eye contact. "But commit this to memory, Willie: during the summer of love, I scaled the heights of ecstasy many times, but I never once chewed a shoe."

I was studying his earnest face to see if my words had penetrated when the phone rang. It was Ed Mariani.

"How's it going?" he asked.

"Okay," I said. "Willie and I were just having a heart-to-heart. He chewed through one of my new sandals."

"Expensive?"

"Top of the line at Wal-Mart."

"Another gold star for one-stop shopping."

"One of these days you'll have to take cold terror by the hand and try it."

He laughed softly. "Jo, I did have a reason for calling. Are you still planning to come over to get the keys to the cottage tonight?"

"I'd forgotten all about it. More coals heaped upon my head."

He laughed. "We'll pass on the coals this time. I just wanted to make sure you still wanted to go out there this weekend."

"Absolutely. Taylor's been rattling on about the lake for the past two weeks. When's a good time for me to come by and pick up the keys?"

"Seven? And, if she doesn't have other plans, why don't you bring Taylor with you? We have a new addition to the family."

"A pet?"

"A nightingale. One of Barry's old clients moved on to the next dimension and left him her bird. Don't laugh. Inheriting a bird is a serious matter, especially if you hate the idea of anything being caged, which Barry and I both do. Anyway, Barry has built Florence the Taj Mahal of aviaries."

"The nightingale is named Florence?"

"We have been spared no indignity," Ed said dryly. "But I promise you Taylor will be dazzled, and if Florence isn't enough, we've laid in a fresh supply of paper umbrellas for Taylor's Shirley Temples."

"You spoil her," I said.

"Not a bit. Your daughter's paintings are going to be worth a fortune some day, and Barry and I want to get in on the ground floor." He sighed heavily. "Jo, I'm glad you're coming over. I really was very fond of Ariel."

"Everybody was," I said.

His correction was gentle. "Not quite everybody."

After I hung up, I was hit by the weight of the day's events. I looked over at my kitchen counter: tins of kidney beans and tomatoes were neatly stacked against the wall. I'd put them there that morning. I'd also chopped a large bowl of onions and celery, and put three pounds of lean ground beef in the fridge to defrost. My plan had been to come home after Rosalie's luncheon and make a pot of chili to take to Katepwa with us the next night. For the first time since New Year's, my whole family was going to be together: my daughter Mieka, her husband, Greg, and my eight-month-old granddaughter, Madeleine, were coming from Saskatoon; my son Peter was driving from Calgary, where he'd just begun work at a veterinarian's clinic; and the rest of us were heading out from Regina as soon as the kids got home from school. Given the unpredictability of possible arrival times, chili had seemed like an inspired idea. It still did. I took the beef out of the refrigerator, threw it in the frying pan, picked up the can opener and started cranking.

By the time the kids got home, the chili was simmering, and I was feeling less fragmented. Angus and Eli, the nephew of Alex Kequahtooway, the man in my life, floated through the house long enough to get Willie on his leash and take him for a run before they drove downtown to get their tuxes fitted for graduation. The week before, Alex had left for Ottawa to teach a month-long class, Minorities and the Justice System, and Eli had moved into Peter's old room to finish off the school year. I was already missing Alex, but the sound of two seventeen-year-olds buzzing about dates and after-grad parties and tuxedos was a potent antidote to lone-liness. Taylor revelled in having Eli around, too. When he arrived, she'd presented him with a drawing of Angus and himself in cap and gown, hanging out of a silvery stretch limo, throwing their mortarboards into the sky. Taylor, wearing a chauffeur's cap, a billowing scarf, and a Cheshire cat grin, was behind the wheel. In art, as in life, Taylor saw herself as the person in the driver's seat.

It was a witty piece, executed deftly. Taylor came by the skill naturally. Her birth mother was the artist Sally Love, and her grandfather was Desmond Love, a man whose name appeared on most art historians' millennial lists of signifi-cant makers of art in Canada. From the moment she could grasp a pencil, Taylor had demonstrated an extraordinary mastery of technique, but her art teacher had pointed me to Taylor's real talent by quoting Marcel Duchamp. "A tech-nique can be learned, but you can't learn to have an original imagination." At seven, Taylor was already impatient with the accessible and fascinated by unexplored territory.

As we headed south on Albert Street towards Ed's, it was apparent my daughter was wired about the weekend ahead. "The minute we get there, I'm going swimming." She darted a glance my way, and headed off the objection she saw coming. "I don't care how cold it is. And after my swim, I'm going to make a little bed on the floor next to mine, so Madeleine can sleep beside *me*. Angus says Saturday night there'll be fireworks and I'm going to hold her so she won't be scared, and Eli says maybe he can build a bonfire and we can have a weenie roast. It's going to be so awesome –" She stopped in mid-flight. "I mean it's going to be really interesting."

I turned to her. "What happened to 'awesome'?" I asked.

"Ms. Cousin says if we use a word too often, it stops meaning anything. She says if we use the word 'awesome' when we talk about an ice cream cone, we won't have a good word to use when we see the pyramids at Giza."

"Ms. Cousin deserves the Governor General's Award," I said. "But you may not have to wait for Cheops to see something awesome. Ed tells me he and Barry have a nightingale."

"A nightingale?" Her eyes were wide. "Just flying around?"

"I don't think so. I think they have an aviary – that's a really big cage."

"I'm glad it's big," she said. "It wouldn't be any good being a bird if you couldn't fly around."

Ed was in the front yard putting in bedding plants. We were a month shy of the longest day, and the light was mellow. He was wearing his uniform of choice: a generously cut shirt that he found so comfortable that he had had it made in a variety of fabrics and a palette of colours. Tonight's was raspberry cotton, and as he approached the car with a flat of deep pink Martha Washington geraniums in his hands, he glowed with well-being.

"Barry's the gardener, but I thought I'd surprise him by putting in the old standbys. He can decide where his prima donnas will thrive."

"Is he out of town?" I asked.

"In New York," Ed said. "At a kitchenware convention. He's doing so well he's thinking of opening two more stores. A prisoner of the work ethic." He bowed deeply to Taylor and crooked his arm in invitation. "But Barry's obsession has dividends for you and me, Ms. Love."

Taylor took his arm. "I've decided to be Taylor Kilbourn, so I can be the same as everybody else in the family. But I'm still going to keep Love for my middle name. What do you think?"

"I like it," he said. He glanced at me questioningly.

"I like it, too," I said. "In fact, I couldn't be more proud."

"In that case, Ms. Kilbourn, will you join me in paying a visit to the world's most expensively housed nightingale?"

I always felt a thrill when I entered Ed and Barry's house. They had designed it themselves to take advantage of natural light, and it was a graceful and welcoming place. We could hear the nightingale's sweet song as soon as we stepped into the living room. It had reason to sing. Its home was a floor-to-ceiling affair of bamboo, glass, and pastel silk screens; the aviary was lovely enough to be a piece of Japanese art. Taylor was enchanted.

I turned to Ed. "When I'm old and addled will Barry build me a space like that? It's magnificent."

"He'd jump at the chance," Ed said. "Barry thrives on challenge. That's why he's been able to stay with me so many years."

"Nobody deserves a hero medal for living with you, Ed."

He blushed. "Rare praise, but deeply appreciated. Now, may I get you ladies a drink?"

"Would it be all right if I looked at my mother's painting?"

Taylor asked. "I can hardly remember her at all any more, but when I look at the paintings she made, I can. I like that, and I like your nightingale, too. You have a lot of stuff that makes me happy."

As I followed Ed upstairs to the kitchen, I thought that Taylor's assessment had been right on the money. I was surrounded by stuff that made me happy, too: a mahogany cabinet that glowed with a collection of mercury glass; a turn-of-the-century daguerreotype of a mother and child; an oval mirror whose bright ceramic border was a celebration of queens, young, old, gorgeous, ugly, real, and mythical. It was, Ed had told me once, a reminder to every queen that, however stunning she believes herself to be, there's always a Snow White waiting in the wings.

Ed took a pitcher filled with something pink and frothy from the refrigerator. He poured Taylor's Shirley Temple into a fluted glass, stabbed a maraschino cherry with the tooth-pick handle of a paper umbrella, and positioned the umbrella carefully against the glass's edge. He turned to me. "Now what's your pleasure?"

I pointed to the frosty pitcher of Shirley Temples. "I wouldn't mind one of those."

Ed frowned in disbelief. "With or without umbrella?"

"With," I said. "It's been a lousy day."

Ed and I took Taylor her drink, then carried our own onto the upstairs deck with its spectacular view of the bird sanctuary and the northwest edge of the university campus. It was almost twilight. Next door, Ed's neighbour was making a last lazy pass across the darkening lawn with his mower, and his kids were playing hide-and-seek in the shadows. In the distance, the haze hanging over Wascana Lake was alive with the sounds of birds deep in the mystery of their epic migration north. Everything was as it had always been; yet everything had changed.

Ed read my thoughts. "Out here it's almost possible to forget, isn't it?" he said softly.

"Have you heard anything more?" I asked.

"Just rumours. I stayed at the office till around four. I thought there might be something I could do. A few students came by to talk. There are some pretty wild stories going the rounds, but apparently the two with the most currency are that Ariel was killed either by an embittered ex-student or by the worker who found her."

"I don't buy the ex-student angle," I said. "Ariel hadn't been teaching that long, and she was pretty intuitive. She would have picked up on a problem before it festered into a grudge. I don't buy the worker theory either. How could someone get up in the morning, shower, shave, dress, and come to work to kill a perfect stranger?"

"It happens," Ed said.

"Not at this university," I said. "Another thing. I've taught here for years, and I've been in that archive room exactly once. There's nothing down there but a bunch of mouldy *Who's Who*s and some bound volumes of old periodicals." I bit my lip in frustration. "As Daffy Duck would say, 'This makes no sense and neither do I.'"

Ed sipped his drink pensively. "Jo, you should probably know there's a third rumour going the rounds. Apparently there's talk that Charlie could be more than the grieving boyfriend."

I put my glass down so hard, the little umbrella toppled out. "Damn it, why don't people *think* before they start spewing garbage like that?"

Ed winced. "I shouldn't have said anything,"

"You didn't *start* the rumour," I said. "And if the story's out there, it's better to know, so Charlie can deal with it. Damn. I was so sure Howard was overreacting, but I guess he was right. This afternoon, we drove out to CVOX because he figured Charlie needed a lawyer."

Ed raised an eyebrow. "A lawyer, not a father . . . ?"

"Charlie had some problems with his father," I said.

"Haven't we all," Ed said tightly.

I turned to him. "All the years we've known each other, I've never heard you even mention your father."

Ed's usually genial face was a mask. "There was nothing to mention. He didn't approve of the choices I made in my life. We quarrelled. He died. Case closed."

"Cases between children and their parents are never closed," I said.

Ed shrugged. "Let's keep the focus on Charlie," he said. "What went wrong between him and his father?"

"Timing," I said. "Charlie was born the night Howard was elected premier. Our daughter Mieka was born the same week. It was wild. We hadn't expected to win the election. Almost all our members were rookies, and they had to learn everything from scratch. The day he was sworn in as attorney general, my husband didn't even know where his office was. Of course, it was a hundred times worse for Howard. He was in charge. Everybody was expected to work fifteen hours a day; then dedication was supposed to kick in. Luckily for us, Mieka was a happy, healthy baby, so she didn't suffer from having an absentee father . . ."

Ed finished the sentence for me. "But Charlie suffered."

"He did," I said. "So did Marnie. When your child is hurting, you're hurting, and a lot of the time Charlie's birthmark made his life a misery. Marnie never coddled him, but she was always there, encouraging him, making him laugh, trying to help him understand why people reacted the way they did."

"And where was his father in all of this?" Ed's tone was wintry.

"Marnie and Howard had a very traditional marriage," I said. "She stayed home with the kids, and he saved the province. A lot of us made the same trade-off." I was surprised at the bitterness in my voice.

Ed's look was unfathomable. "Another untold story?" he asked.

"If it is," I said, "it's one without villains. We all did the best we could. Sometimes it just didn't work out."

"And it didn't work out for Charlie?"

"It didn't work out for any of them," I said. "Charlie always excelled at school. He graduated when he was sixteen. By that time, Marnie and Howard had grown so far apart that when Charlie moved out to go to university, Marnie left, too. She started Ph.D. work at the Centre for Medieval Studies in Toronto. Howard was devastated. He moved east to try to win her back. But the lady was not for wooing. She was a devout Catholic, so divorce was out of the question, but she had no interest in reconciliation. She was having the time of her life."

"Where's Marnie now?"

It was a question I would have given anything to duck. But there was no evading the truth. "In a nursing home," I said. "Her bike was hit by a car when she was on her way to class. Her injuries were incapacitating. She needs total care."

"That won't change?"

"No," I said. "That won't change."

"And Charlie blames his father," Ed said quietly.

I nodded. "He felt that if Howard had been a better husband and father, Marnie wouldn't have left."

"And she wouldn't have been in the wrong place at the wrong time."

"Something like that," I said. "For the first year after the accident, Charlie wouldn't even speak to Howard."

"But they *were* working things out . . ."

"Because of Ariel. According to Howard, she was the one who convinced Charlie to give him another chance."

"Who got another chance?" Taylor was standing in the doorway to the deck. One of her braids had come undone, she had spilled some of her drink on her T-shirt, but as always, she was unfazed.

"Your uncle Howard," I said.

"Ms. Cousin says everyone deserves a second chance," Taylor said. "That's why she didn't send me to the principal's office the time I broke her laptop."

"I never heard about that," I said.

"That's because Ms. Cousin gave me a second chance," Taylor said.

Ed leaped up. "Perhaps it's time for me to get you ladies a refill?"

When Ed headed for the kitchen, Taylor trailed after him. I wandered to the end of the deck to watch the shifting layers of light that are the prelude to a prairie sunset. As Ed had said, out here it *was* almost possible to forget.

The shrill of the cellphone in my bag was an intrusion from another world. Livia Brook's voice was agitated. "Jo, why aren't you here? There are things you and I should talk about before the vigil starts. You've only got about fifteen minutes."

"What vigil?"

"I can't believe you didn't get any of my messages. I e-mailed you and I left word on your voice mail at the office and at home. I've just got your cellphone number from Rosalie. There's a vigil for Ariel Warren tonight in front of the library. It's supposed to start in fifteen minutes."

I looked across the parkway. A line of cars was snaking onto University Drive and knots of students were walking across the grass towards the library. The last thing I wanted to do was join them, but Livia sounded close to tears.

"It's important that we're all at this event. For her. Please, Jo."

I swallowed hard. "Okay," I said. "I'll be there."

I ended the call and dropped the phone back in my bag. When I walked into the kitchen Taylor was perched on a bar stool pouring a bottle of Canada Dry into a blender filled with fruit juices.

"We just have to add the crushed ice," she said.

"I'm afraid it's going to have to be a quick drink, Taylor. We have another stop before we go home." I looked across my daughter's dark head at Ed Mariani. "I had a call from Livia on my cell. There's a vigil for Ariel over at the library."

"Give me two minutes to change, and I'll come with you," Ed said.

Taylor turned to me. "Who's Ariel?"

"A woman I taught with. She and Mieka used to play together when they were little. She died this morning."

"What happened?"

"Someone killed her."

Taylor put the ginger ale bottle down carefully on the counter. "Why?"

"We don't know."

"Is the vigil to find out?"

"No," I said. "Sometimes after a person dies the way Ariel did, people just want to get together to think about the things that make us hurt each other."

Taylor nodded. "Evil," she said.

"Where did you hear about evil?" I asked.

"Spiderman," she said. "Every week, Spiderman has to fight evil. He always wins, but the next week there's always more evil." A frown crimped her forehead. "That's just on cartoons, right?"

"No," I said. "I'm afraid that's the way it is in real life, too."

CHAPTER

3

The distance between Ed's house and the library was an easy five-minute walk; that night it was also a miserable one. Taylor, who usually hurtled headlong into the next adventure, walked quietly between Ed and me, holding our hands tightly. We were not alone. The three of us were part of a sorrowful cortège winding its way up University Drive towards the library. Two young women whom I recognized from the class Ariel had been teaching that morning rushed by, arms linked, faces swollen with grief. I squeezed Taylor's hand, glad to be connected to her and, through her, to Ed.

In good weather, the library quadrangle was filled with students catching a few rays while they read, gossiped, or just zoned out watching plumes of water arc up from the fountain. That night the gathering crowd was tense, and the air pressed down on us, heavy with uncertainty. A portable podium had been set up in front of the doors leading into the library, but no one was standing behind it.

As I peered into the crowd, trying to see who was in charge, Ann Vogel, who had been a student in my Populist Politics class the year before, broke away from the group she was with and headed towards us. I felt my stomach knot. Ann was a sharp-featured brunette in her late thirties who had returned to school to find answers to the Big Questions. Judging from what I had seen of her, the answers she was finding were not to her liking. She was a sour and perpetually aggrieved woman who had involved herself deeply in the life of our department at a time when we had already far exceeded our quota of the sour and aggrieved. Midway through Populist Politics, she had changed her name from Ann to Naama. Assuming the name of the goddess who gave birth to Eve and Adam without the help of any male, even the serpent, may have connected Ann to the source of female power, but it hadn't improved her analytical abilities, and she barely scraped through my class. The other class Ann did poorly in that semester had been Kevin Coyle's International Law. She'd ferreted out the support of two other women whose grades in Kevin's class failed to meet their expectations and set attitudinal-harassment charges in motion.

Had Kevin shown himself to be attuned to the realities of life at a contemporary university, the charges would have sunk without a trace, but he was a crank and an anachronism who still believed academics were put on earth to point out the shortcomings of lesser beings. He had made enough bone-headed public remarks about both sexes to muddy the waters and, bottom-feeder that she was, Ann Vogel had snapped up a veritable feast of comments he had made that could be construed as sexist. Kevin had responded to the charges with his usual pit-bull intransigence, but his defenders had argued that Kevin was a misanthrope, not a misogynist, and the case was about to sputter out from lack of oxygen when a far more serious incident erupted and fanned the flames.

A fourth-year student named Maryse Bergman accused Kevin Coyle of rape. Her tale was unsettling, in part, because the exposition was a familiar one to many who had dealt with people in positions of power. Maryse said that when she had approached Kevin with a request for a letter of recommendation to graduate school, he had suggested a quid pro quo: a glowing reference in return for sexual favours. Here the narrative took an ugly twist. According to Maryse, when she turned Kevin down, he attempted to rape her.

The alleged assault took place late on a Friday afternoon, when most of us had started our weekends, but there *had* been witnesses – not to the attack, but to its aftermath. Maryse, obviously distraught, had run down the hall until she found someone in our department ready to believe and, more significantly, verify her tale. Oddly, Maryse had insisted the police not be called. Later that evening, when Ben Jesse called all of us to alert us to the incident, that behaviour alone had made me suspicious. So had the fact that Maryse travelled in the same circles as Ann Vogel.

By Monday morning, the whispering campaign was spreading and Kevin was seething. According to him, Maryse Bergman had appeared in his office without an appointment. They had talked in general terms about graduate school, then, inexplicably, she had screamed and run from his office. When I asked if he had done anything that could be construed as a sexual overture, he erupted. "As if I would need her," he said. "As if I would need any woman. Or any man for that matter. I don't need anybody. Sex is of no interest to me. I have my work." I had been convinced. Unfortunately for Kevin, I was in the minority.

My public explanation for supporting Kevin was that I believed in due process, but like most justifications, mine concealed as much as it revealed. My motivations were far from altruistic. As someone who had taught university for years, I had watched the chill of political correctness freeze spontaneity, creativity, and intellectual daring. A single lapse of caution could ensnare a teacher in a morass of charges that, even if unjust and unproven, could tar her reputation forever. The possibility that one day it would be my turn to be accused was real. This time I had dodged the bullet, but every time I looked at Kevin Coyle, I knew that there, but for the grace of a missing Y chromosome, went I.

The dénouement of the Maryse Bergman case was surprising, at least to me. The week after her accusation against Kevin, she left town. There didn't appear to be anything sinister about her departure. I saw her in the halls a couple of times, returning books or saying goodbye to friends, then she moved on. The day after she left, a deputation headed by Ann Vogel confronted Ben Jesse accusing him of a cover-up. It was Ben's final battle. After his death, there was a rush to choose an interim department head and make the new appointments. Maryse was forgotten – forgotten, that is, by everyone except Ann Vogel, who kept the rumours on the boil, and by Kevin Coyle, who had to live under the cloud of unproven accusations.

The night of the vigil Ann Vogel wasted no time on pleasantries. "You're supposed to go inside," she said. "The plan is for everyone who is part of the program to come out of the library together."

"I don't understand," I said. "Why would I be part of the program? There are a lot of people who were closer to Ariel than I was."

"For once, I agree with you," Ann Vogel said. "I don't think you should be included either, but Ariel's mother wants you. Dr. Warren says that since you knew Ariel as a child and as a colleague, you could bring a special perspective. It's not a perspective I personally want, but Dr. Warren does, so you'd better get in there."

I turned to Ed. "Could you and Taylor watch out for each other till I'm done?"

Ann Vogel didn't give him a chance to answer. "You'll

have to find alternative child care, Joanne. This observance is for women only."

Taylor regarded Ann with interest. "I noticed that."

A glance around the crowd revealed that Taylor was right. Mao Zedong once said that women hold up half the sky, but at Ariel Warren's vigil it appeared that the sky and everything under it was in female hands. With the exception of Ed, there wasn't a male in sight.

Having discharged her venom, Ann started off. I grabbed her arm. My intent was simply to ask her a question, but my gesture was unintentionally rough, and she peeled off my hand with a look of disdain.

"No need for goon tactics," she said.

"My point exactly," I said. "Who made the decision to exclude men?"

"Some of us feel we can't speak freely if men are present."

"I thought this was supposed to be about Ariel."

"She's emblematic of a larger issue."

"For God's sake, Ann," I said, "listen to yourself."

"Naama," she hissed. "My name is Naama."

"All right, Naama. Now shut up and pay attention. Ariel Warren is not a symbol. She was a warm, gifted young woman, and a lot of us still can't believe she's gone."

Ann took a step towards me. She was so close I could feel her breath on my face.

"Believe it, Joanne. Ariel is dead, and she died for the same reasons a lot of other women die. She lived in a patriarchal society that kills women and children." She laughed shortly. "Why am I wasting my time trying to raise your consciousness? Stick around. You just might learn something."

"I don't think I will stick around," I said.

Ann shrugged. "Suit yourself." She wagged her finger at me. "Now, I'm going to walk away, and this time I don't want to be stopped."

I turned to Ed. "Let's get out of here."

Taylor looked up at me. "What about Ariel?"

Ed and I exchanged glances.

"That's a good question," he said.

"And I was pretty close to giving it a rotten answer," I said. "Damn it, I always let Ann get under my skin. Let's tough it out."

Ed frowned. "This isn't a night for muscle-flexing," he said. "You were right. This *is* supposed to be about Ariel."

I looked down at my daughter. "Do you want to stay?"

But she was concerned about Ed. "Would you be okay going home by yourself?"

"I'd be okay," he said. "Besides, somebody has to drink those Shirley Temples before they lose their oomph."

"*Oomph!*" Taylor scrunched her face at the cartoon word, then for the first time since we'd set out for the vigil, she smiled.

I reached out and touched Ed's cheek. "We'll see you later," I said. "And take it easy on the Shirley Temples. A good man is hard to find."

The vigil for Ariel Warren exists in my memory as a series of images, which revealed truths as familiar to the philosopher as they are to the chiaroscurist. The first was that light is fully appreciated only when it is set against an absence of light; the second was that even the most familiar figures can cast lengthy shadows.

As I watched Ed walk towards the Parkway, I was sick at heart. He was heading west, and while I had balked at the suggestion that Ariel Warren was a symbol, I had seen too many old westerns not to feel a twinge at the image of a decent man disappearing into the sunset. It took an act of will not to follow him.

Livia Brook met me by the fountain. She was wearing a black T-shirt dress and strappy patent-leather flats. Draped around her shoulders was an extravagantly fringed antique satin shawl covered with oversized poppies that appeared to be hand-painted. It was a festive accessory for a mourner, but no one looking into Livia's face could doubt her pain. She had removed the barrettes that usually held her hair in place, and against the cascade of chestnut and grey curls, her face was wan.

"Ariel's mother wants to talk to you before we start," she said.

It was a request I couldn't ignore. Dr. Molly Warren was not a friend, but I liked and respected her. She had been my gynecologist for the past fifteen years, and as far as I was concerned she was just about perfect. She treated my concerns seriously, answered my questions fully, and shepherded me through a difficult menopause with information and brisk good humour. Even when I was sitting on the edge of the table in the examination room, shivering and apprehensive in my blue paper gown, the click of her impossibly high heels coming down the hall reassured me. I knew she wouldn't talk down; I knew she wouldn't scare me needlessly; I knew she'd tell the truth. She had been a rock to me and to many other women I knew. Any of us would have done whatever we could to redress the balance.

A group of women had come together just inside the door. To the right of them, standing in front of the glass case that housed displays from the Classics department, were Molly Warren and Solange Levy. Two facts were immediately apparent: Solange was in deep psychological trouble, and Molly was doing what she could to help. Back in her uniform of black jeans, T-shirt and Converse high-tops, Solange was beyond wired; she was blowing out all the circuits. She was talking non-stop. As she spoke, her hands chopped the air, and her feet danced like a boxer's. Even her black, henna-shined hair seemed charged with manic electricity. Molly

listened with an expression I had seen often: capable, concerned, but with her lips tight, insulating herself against the
weaknesses of the flesh that beset the rest of us.

The moment must have been one of unimaginable horror
for her, but Molly Warren, as she always did, looked as if
she had just stepped off the cover of *Vogue*. If it seemed
cruel to notice her appearance, it was also inevitable. I have
never known a woman to whom personal appearance mattered more. She was not a beauty – Ariel's chiselled good
looks had come from her father – but Molly took meticulous
care of what she had: her skin was deep-cleansed, rehy-
drated, and dewy; her Diane Sawyer haircut subtly layered
and highlighted; her outfits chosen with care and knowledge. Whenever she glided into her Delft-blue outer office
to pick up a file or take a phone call, we patients leaned
towards one another and whispered about her unerring
sense of style.

That night the silk suit she was wearing was soft grey
with a mauve undertone like lilacs in the mist, and her
simple grey Salvatore Ferragamo pumps and bag glowed as
only seven hundred dollars' worth of calfskin can. I imag-
ined her selecting her ensemble in the morning, holding the
bag against the suit, checking the match, not knowing that
by day's end she would be wearing her perfect outfit to a
vigil for her daughter.

I pulled Taylor closer. She leaned across me to peer down
the hall, then up at the huge expanse of glass at the front
of the library. "I've been here a million times," she whispered. "But never at night. It's different." Suddenly, Solange
caught her attention. "What's the matter with that girl
over there?"

"She was best friends with the woman who died."

"And she's acting up?"

"Something like that," I said.

As we watched, Molly opened her bag, took out a prescription bottle, removed a tablet and handed it to Solange. Meek as a child, Solange took the pill and put it under her tongue. Whether it was from exhaustion, medication, or the power of suggestion, she seemed to calm down. She whispered something to Molly, then walked over and joined Ann Vogel and Rae Colby, the director of the Women's Centre.

Molly Warren looked as alone as anyone I had ever seen. She was not a person who invited physical contact, but I had no idea how to approach her except through an embrace. Her body was stiff and unresponsive, but she didn't step away, so I held her, staring uncomprehendingly at the announcement of a lecture on the Eleusinian Mysteries the Hellenic Society was sponsoring and wondering what in the name of God to do next.

Finally, Molly took a step back. Her words surprised me. "I had a battle with myself about coming to this. It seemed wrong to be part of an event at which Ariel's father wasn't welcome."

"Someone told you that?"

"Not in so many words, but Solange hinted that Drew might find the evening uncomfortable. I'm sure her warning was intended as a kindness." Molly made a gesture of dismissal with her hand. "None of that matters now. I'm glad I came. Joanne, have you heard the rhetoric here tonight? It's pretty virulently anti-male."

I shook my head. "We were late."

"Then you haven't heard the rumours that are swirling around."

"No," I said, "but I can imagine they're ugly."

"They are," she said. "And they're irresponsible. Until we have the autopsy results, no one will know whether the crime was sexually motivated. But that's the assumption made by almost everyone who's talked to me. Suddenly all

men are suspect." Molly raised her fingers to her temples
and rubbed in a circular motion. "Joanne, I don't know what
happened to my daughter in that archive room. At the
moment, I lack the courage to imagine it. But there's one
thing I do know. I will not allow Ariel's death to become an
excuse for anybody to push a political agenda."

"Should I talk to the organizers?"

"I already have," she said. "I hoped I'd be able to say a few
words to keep the evening in perspective, but I just can't
seem to form a coherent thought. That's why I asked the
organizing committee to find you. I know I'm putting you
on the spot, but you and Solange are the only friends of
Ariel's from the university that I know. You've seen the state
Solange is in. She's promised she won't do anything to make
matters worse, but she can't be counted on to do much
beyond that."

"You'd like me to say something to keep the focus on
Ariel," I said.

Molly gave me the physician's assessing look. "If I'm
asking too much, tell me."

"You're not asking too much," I said.

She seemed to relax. When her eye rested on Taylor, she
crouched down so that she could talk to her more easily. "I
didn't mean to ignore you," she said. "My name is Molly
Warren, and . . ."

"And Ariel was your girl," Taylor said softly.

Molly's intake of breath was sharp, the reflex of a woman
feeling the probe on an exposed nerve. "Yes," she said. "Ariel
was my girl."

This time when I reached out to comfort her, she waved
me off. "I'm okay," she said. "I just want to freshen up. Is
there a ladies' room around here?"

I pointed. "Down that hall and to the left," I said. "Would
you like me to go with you?"

She shook her head. "All I need is a little time alone and I'll be all right."

As I watched her elegant figure disappear, I thought that it was the first time I'd heard Dr. Molly Warren give a prognosis so far off the mark. I was relieved when Rae Colby joined me.

Rae was a solid, pleasant woman who moved slowly, laughed often, and fought the good fight with a fervour undiminished by thirty years in the women's movement. She was fond of bright colours and chunky ethnic jewellery, but that night she was in ankle-length black, her only jewellery a heavy silver labrys pendant.

She gave me a slow, sad smile. "I've come to ask your daughter a favour, Jo."

"Ask," I said. "Taylor makes up her own mind about most things."

Rae's broad face creased with pleasure. "A woman after my own heart," she said. She turned to Taylor. "Here's the drill. Everyone at the vigil is supposed to have a candle, and I need you to help me hand them out."

"I can do that," Taylor said.

"Good." Rae turned back to me. "The program is pretty informal," she said in her low, musical voice. "I thought maybe we could all just walk out there together." She gestured towards a willowy brunette standing close to the door. "You know Kristy Stevenson."

"We're on the University Development Committee together," I said.

"Then you know how proud she is of the work the library does. We're all sick about Ariel's death, but Kristy has a double burden. The archives are her responsibility. I think she feels a need to be part of the memorial tonight. Anyway, in her non-university life, Kristy has a trio called Womanswork."

"I didn't know she was a singer," I said.

"She paid her way through university playing in a punk rock band. Hard to imagine, isn't it? She's so elegant."

"People are full of surprises," I said.

"Aren't they just? At any rate, the plan is to have Livia speak, then Womanswork sing, and then I thought you could talk. Did you and Dr. Warren agree about what you were going to say?"

"We thought . . . just some personal memories," I said.

Rae's brown eyes misted. "Better you than me," she said. "I don't think I could get through anything personal. Anyway, after you've finished, Naama has a story she wants to tell. Then Solange wants a few moments to talk. I hope she'll be okay. Molly Warren is her doctor, and apparently she gave her some kind of medication to bring her down."

I looked over at Solange. She was gazing at the crowd in the library quadrangle, wholly absorbed in her private reverie. "She seems calm enough," I said.

"Calm is good," Rae said. "There's a lot of emotion out there. We don't need to add to it." She fingered the silver labrys at her neck. "After Solange, I guess Womanswork will do another song, and Livia will announce the candle-lighting. Have I left out anything?"

"It sounds as if everything's taken care of," I said.

When Molly Warren returned, her lipstick was fresh and her jaw was set. "Let's go," she said, and she started for the door. The women in the doorway parted to let her pass; then they followed her outside.

Rae turned to Taylor. "Time to get moving, kiddo," she said. "Those candles aren't going to hand themselves around."

In one of those cosmic ironies that twist the knife of grief, the night into which we stepped burned with beauty. The sun was low in the sky, and the horizon flamed, turning the water of Wascana Lake into molten gold. "Red sky at night, sailor's delight," Rae murmured. The sky might have glowed, but the concrete bulk of the library cast a shadow that plunged the mourners waiting for us into darkness.

Rae picked up a wicker basket of candles and handed it to Taylor. Her hand brushed the top of my daughter's head in a lazy benediction. "It's good to have someone from the next generation with us."

Livia stepped to the microphone. We were long-time colleagues, but that night she surprised me. Even during the agonizing last months of her marriage, Livia had been much in demand by organizations wanting an expert on American politics who wouldn't sabotage their pleasant lunch with dry history or legalisms. The day after her marriage ended, she had asked me to provide moral support at a lunch meeting she'd agreed to address months earlier. She was hungover and heartsick, but she still managed to sparkle her way through her set piece on the relationship between a leader's character and his or her political policies. Wretched as she must have felt, Livia had come alive in front of the crowd. But the night of the vigil, as she adjusted the microphone, her hands were trembling so badly she had difficulty completing the manoeuvre. When she began to speak, she surprised me again. I was expecting another helping of New Age bilge, but she spoke from the heart.

Pulling her shawl around her, as if she were cold to the marrow, she began. "I would give everything I own not to be here tonight," she said simply. "Ariel was my student, my colleague, my friend, my hope." She looked down at the brilliantly coloured shawl as if seeing it for the first time. "Two weeks ago, she gave me this. 'A thank-you,' she said, 'for everything.' It was too much . . ."

I was puzzling over the ambiguity of Livia's sentence when I realized that, although she was still standing in front of the microphone, she'd fallen silent. Ann Vogel was quick to react.

She moved swiftly to the podium, draped her arm protectively around Livia's shoulders, and led her back to the rest of the party. The whole sequence was over in a matter of seconds, but what I saw in the faces of the two women shook me. Livia was expressionless; her eyes had the five-hundred-mile stare of a shock victim. But Ann Vogel was – no other word for it – smirking. Then as quickly as it had appeared, the tableau was gone. Kristy Stevenson and Womanswork came forward quickly and the program continued.

The trio of women who made up Womanswork had a family resemblance: all three wore their dark hair centre-parted and brushed back to frame gentle faces, wide-set blue eyes, and delicately arched brows. They were in tank tops, black slacks, and platforms, and they moved with assurance. Kristy stepped up to the microphone. "We've chosen two songs tonight. Neither of them is ours. I wish they were. I wish I could come out here and tell you that we'd written lyrics that spoke to Ariel's dreams or, even" – Kristy smiled sadly – "just a tune she hummed in the shower. The truth is I didn't know her very well; she was at a fundraiser we did for the Dunlop Gallery a couple of weeks ago, and afterwards she came up and told me she had really connected with a song we did by Beowulf's Daughters. It's called 'The Sparrow Knows.' Here it is."

The voices of Womanswork were strong, and the opening line was a grabber. "*The sparrow knows that the meadhall moments are few.*" As the trio sang, I followed Rae and Taylor's passage through the crowd, warmed by the sense of community that enveloped them. Most women smiled; some reached up to Taylor, thanking her, including her. I had worried about bringing her. Now I was glad I had.

Ann Vogel's tap on my shoulder was the proverbial rude awakening. "You're next," she said. My mind went into free fall. The only anchor I had was the song to which Ariel

Warren had felt a connection, but as I listened to the words, I knew Womanswork was giving me what I needed. When I stepped forward, the sentences formed themselves.

"I don't know which words in 'The Sparrow Knows' Ariel was drawn to," I said. "Maybe all of them. But I know the line that resonated for me. 'Darkness is our womb and destination,/Light, a heartbeat glory, gone too soon.' My memories of Ariel begin and end with sunlight. The first time I saw her she was six years old. My daughter Mieka invited her to her birthday party. Mieka's birthday is October 31 – Halloween – and Ariel came dressed as a sunflower. The yellow petals that circled her face were so bright." I turned to Molly Warren. She smiled, acknowledging the memory. I drew a breath and carried on. "The last time I saw Ariel was this morning. She had taken her class out to that little hill by the Classroom Building."

"I was there!" The voice that came out of the crowd was very young.

"You were lucky," I said. "If you were in that class, you were being taught by someone who knew that all learning is an attempt to pass on the heartbeat glory of light. Tonight it may seem as if the darkness is overwhelming, but that doesn't mean the light isn't there. Ariel heard the call of lightness all her life. Let your memories of her turn back the darkness."

Molly stood up and embraced me as I stepped back from the microphone. "That was just right," she said. "I hope to God it was enough."

As organizer of the vigil, Ann Vogel had appointed herself spokesperson for the students. I had feared she would lob some feminist firebombs, but all she managed was a wet, self-indulgent fizzle about how blighted her own academic future would be without Ariel Warren. Her narcissism was as sickening as Kevin Coyle's, but I was relieved that she hadn't ventured past her obsession with herself. She could have done harm. She didn't, and I was grateful.

As Ann returned to her place beside Livia Brook, I thought we were home free. Solange had given Molly Warren her word that she would behave well, and she was a principled human being. She was in agony, but she would honour her commitment.

As she came to the microphone, she seemed to be in another time and another space. When she began to speak, I wasn't surprised that she returned to what was obviously the best moment of her life. "Last New Year's Ariel and I went to Mount Assiniboine. The air was sharp with the smell of fresh snow and pines. We were very happy: we knew summer would bring wildflowers, and we promised each other we would come back to see them, and that in autumn we'd return to see the larches turn to gold and, in winter, to see the valley fill again with snow." She fell silent. Then she held out her hands in a gesture of helplessness. "I just wanted you to know that Ariel had many plans. I wanted you to know that she died fully alive."

It was a stunning oxymoron. When Solange turned from the microphone and walked back towards us, a sob broke the silence. Rae Colby came out of the crowd, handed Taylor back to me, then Womanswork stepped forward to begin their final song. There were tears in Kristy's voice, but her back was straight, and as she linked hands with the other women of the trio, I could feel their strength.

"This is by the Wyrd Sisters." Kristy said.

The song was "Warrior," the story of a girl who, haunted by her failure to respond to a woman's screams, ultimately transforms herself into a warrior who knows she must fight until *"not another woman dies."* From the moment Solange had told me about her epiphany on the night of the massacre at L'École Polytechnique, I had associated that song with her. As the trio's voices floated high and pure on the still night air, I watched for her reaction. There was none; she had become a woman carved in stone.

When the song ended, Kristy leaned into the microphone. "Never forget Ariel," she whispered, then she lit the candle in her hand and raised it into the darkness. "Never forget any of our fallen sisters. Never forget."

I bent to put a match to Taylor's candle and my own, and when I stood and faced the quadrangle again, the darkness was flickering with scores of tiny flames. Lighted from below, the faces of the mourners seemed alien and frightening. I drew Taylor closer.

Ann Vogel pushed past me towards the microphone. "Never forget," she shouted. The words were Kristy Stevenson's, but Ann turned the gentle elegy into an injunction, harsh with hate. "Never forget," she said, brandishing her lit candle like a club.

As her words echoed over the courtyard, they detonated the rage that lay beneath the grief. The responses exploded in the sweet spring air. "Never forget. Never forget. *Never forget!*"

"No!" Molly Warren's anguish was apparent. She started towards the microphone, but when she put her hand on Ann's arm, Ann turned and locked eyes with Livia.

"Pull her back," Ann hissed. Without hesitation, Livia stepped forward and obeyed.

"Why won't you let me stop her?" Molly asked.

"They need to experience this," Livia said.

"No one needs to *experience* hysteria," Molly said witheringly.

"You don't understand what we're feeling," Livia said.

Molly whirled around. "I was her *mother*," she said, and she had to shout to be heard above the voices calling for vengeance. For a beat, the two women stared at one another, like combatants.

Finally, Molly shook her head. "You're right," she said. "I don't understand what you're feeling, and I don't want to." When her neat figure vanished inside the library, Rae Colby followed her.

Taylor looked up at me. "Is the vigil over?"

"Yes," I said. "The vigil's over." I smoothed her hair. "Taylor, I'm sorry, it was a mistake bringing you tonight."

"It wasn't a mistake," she said. "For a while, it was really nice."

"For a while it was," I agreed. "But not any more. Let's go home."

The library, the Classroom and Lab buildings, and College West were linked by inside walkways. Taylor and I could get back to the Parkway without going through the crowd. The prospect of escaping the ugliness outside was attractive, and as we walked through the cool silent halls, I was grateful my daughter and I had found an easy way out. Like most easy ways out, however, this one came with a price. Just as we were about to turn into the Lab Building, Kevin Coyle appeared.

He was flushed with anger, and one of the lenses in his glasses was missing, so he was glaring at me with one hugely magnified eye and one ordinary eye.

"Your glasses," I said.

"The goddamn lens fell out while I was leaning out of my office window watching those women. It landed somewhere in the grass out there. But I saw enough. This is going to be my case all over again. That same hysteria. Wombs. The Greeks were right."

"Kevin, take a hike. I've had enough."

"*You've* had enough. What about me?"

"Hard as it is to believe," I said, "this isn't about you."

"You're wrong there, Joanne. This is about me. That little council of war just decided that it's about all men. What do you think the nurturers' next move is going to be? I'm not without allies among the students, and one of them came and warned me there are rumours about Ariel and me."

"What kind of rumours?"

"Someone heard an exchange between us and misinterpreted."

"What was the exchange about?"

"It was about my case. I told you before that Ariel had found out something. I was pressing her to tell what she knew. She was reluctant. It must have sounded worse than it was."

"I imagine it did," I said wearily.

"She was on my side, Joanne, and I'm going to go down there and confront those women with the truth before they come up to my office with their tar and feathers."

"Just go home, Kevin. No one's making sense tonight. Everything's too raw. Let it go."

He stepped forward so he could look straight at me. His mismatched eyes were a grotesque sight, but it was a night for the surreal. "If I let it go, it will destroy us all," Kevin said. "I have to be vigilant for you, for me and" – he touched his upper arm – "for her." For the first time, I noticed that he was wearing an old-fashioned black broadcloth mourning band around his upper arm. "Ariel Warren was a good woman, Joanne. So are you. Don't get swept away."

He patted Taylor on the head in a gesture that only someone who had never been around children would make. "Do you play Risk?" he asked.

"My brother does," she said, "but he says I'm too young."

"You're never too young to learn the world conquest game," he said. "When you decide you're ready to learn, have your mother bring you by my office. I always keep a game set up, and partners have been in short supply of late." He drew himself up. "Now if you'll excuse me, I have to go back outside and look for that lens."

Taylor and I watched him stomp off into the night, a rumpled, angry man in search of normal vision.

When we got back to Ed's place, Taylor asked if she could see if Florence was asleep. After she ran inside to check on the nightingale, Ed frowned at me. "I know that porch light isn't flattering, but are you okay?"

"I'm fine, but, as the jocks say, there is a question about how much I have left in my tank."

"Would a nightcap help?"

"I'll take a rain check. Taylor has school tomorrow, and it's already nine-thirty. Way too late."

"How was the vigil?"

"Sad," I said, "and scary – very, very scary."

"Then we'll talk about it another time," he said. "Now, just to prove to you that I can stay on task, here are those keys you came over for." He handed me the keys and an envelope. "Instructions for everything are in here. All the crankiness and idiosyncrasies of the plumbing explained in full. As Livia would say . . ."

"No surprises."

"And," Ed said, "the cappuccino machine is brand new, so it should be problem-free."

"A *cappuccino machine*! Talk about roughing it in the bush. Ed, I hope you know how grateful I am for this."

He waved his hand in dismissal. "No gratitude necessary. Just come back with a sunburn, a smile, and some new photos of that granddaughter of yours."

As soon as I pulled into our driveway, I could hear the pounding rhythms of Tool. Taylor and I walked through the front door into what seemed, after the sombre events of the evening, to be a parallel universe. The house smelled of cooking, and the captain's chest in the hall was heaped with hastily shed jackets and baseball equipment. As I reached over to remove a jockstrap that I didn't recognize from a branch of our jade plant, laughter erupted in the kitchen. Angus and Eli's baseball team had stopped by after practice. I walked into the living room and turned down the volume.

The effect was immediate. My son shot into the living room. He was still wearing his ball uniform; he was sweaty, tousled, and very happy. "We kicked ass, Mum. Whupped them totally."

I held out my arms to him. "Come here and give a needy old woman a kiss."

He scrunched his face. "The day *you're* needy . . ." But he put his arms around me and hugged me hard. "So where have you been, anyway? I thought you were just going over to Mr. Mariani's to get the keys."

"Mission accomplished," I said, fishing the keys out of my purse and tossing them to him.

"Cool," he said. "This whole weekend is going to be cool. Pete coming back, and seeing Mieka and Greg and Maddy. As soon as they get to the lake, I'm taking the baby down to the point."

"Uncle of the year," I said.

My son winced. "Not really."

"Why 'not really'?"

"Because babies are universally acknowledged chick magnets."

"With smart guys like you in the universe, we chicks don't stand a chance, do we?"

"Not a chance. Listen, do you and T want a chili dog? We can scrape the pot and get you a couple of spoonfuls." He gave me a sidelong glance. "What was all that chili for, anyhow?"

Taylor ate her chili dog and went straight to bed. As we talked about the evening, she seemed intrigued rather than disturbed, and I was grateful. She was asleep by the time I

closed her bedroom door. I caught a glimpse of myself in the
hall mirror. No queen would need to search for a poisoned
apple to get rid of me that night. I looked like hell. I went
downstairs, made myself a drink, then walked into the
kitchen where Angus and Eli were cleaning up. They had
the radio on. Eli turned when he heard my step.

"Is it true that a girl was killed up at the university today?"

At seventeen, Eli had the kind of El Greco good looks you
see in Calvin Klein ads. He wore his hair in a single braid in
the traditional way of aboriginal men, and his eyes were dark
and luminous. His radar for pain was extraordinary, perhaps
because he had known so much of it in his short life. Alex
Kequahtooway was raising him, and in my opinion he had
worked a number of small miracles. Eli was doing well at
school, and he was making friends. My son Angus had
helped. He was a generous, extroverted kid who had simply
enlarged his circle of friends to include Eli. It was good news
all the way, except that Eli still seemed obsessed with death
in the way that anorexics are often obsessed with cookbooks
and food preparation.

I sat down at the kitchen table. "That's what I came down
to talk about. The woman who was killed taught in our
department. Her name was Ariel Warren. Mieka and she
were friends when they were little, and she and Charlie
Dowhanuik were a couple."

Angus shot a glance at Eli. "You know who Charlie
Dowhanuik is, don't you? Your idol, Charlie D."

Eli jumped from his chair. "Did Charlie kill her?"

"Why would you think Charlie killed Ariel?" I asked.

Eli's face was miserable. "I listen to his show every day. I
tape his 'Ramblings' when I'm at school. Charlie D is so
cool. He used to talk about his girlfriend all the time." He
looked puzzled. "Except I thought her name was Beatrice.
Anyway, he was always talking about how great Beatrice

was; then a couple of weeks ago, he just stopped. I thought they broke up.

Charlie *had* called his beloved Beatrice. Today's allusion to *The Divine Comedy* had been part of a pattern. Unbidden, an image flashed into my mind. Charlie as a little boy on the edge of the crowd; Ariel taking his hand, rescuing him; Dante, at eight, meeting the seven-year-old Beatrice and knowing "bliss made manifest." Two loves that had lasted a lifetime – or had they? Had something happened to turn Charlie's bliss to suffering?

My son's voice brought me back to reality. "Mum, do you think it would be okay to pack the car tonight, or are you worried about our stuff getting stolen?"

"Go ahead, pack," I said. "I want to get away from here as soon as we can tomorrow evening."

Angus frowned. "Is everything okay?"

I patted his shoulder. "Everything's fine. Make sure you lock the garage door. I couldn't live with myself if someone stole your Tool CDs."

After the boys went off to get their gear, I walked over to the living-room bookcase. It took me a moment to find what I was looking for. I hadn't read *The Divine Comedy* since university, but as soon as I touched the book, I felt a rush of emotion. I had met my husband, Ian, in Classics 300. That period of our lives had glowed with transcendent moments and soaring idealism. Dante had been a good fit for us both, but there had been one passage that Ian had read to me so often he made it my own.

I say that when she appeared from any direction, then, in the hope of her wondrous salutation, there was no enemy left to me; rather there smote into me a flame of charity, which made me forgive every person who had ever injured me; and if at that moment anybody had put a question to me about anything whatsoever, my answer would have been simply "Love" with a countenance clothed in humility.

In the margin, Ian had written a single word: "YES!" By the time he died, my husband would have found the idea that I was the earthly vessel for divine experience as laughable as I would have. Our marriage had been a good one. We had loved and laughed and fought and grown, but somewhere along the line we had revised our definition of love. As I slid *The Divine Comedy* back into its place on the bookshelf, I found myself wondering how Charlie could endure losing the woman who, from the time he was seven years old, he had believed was his shining path to salvation.

CHAPTER

4

The next morning my clock radio blared to life at its regular wake-up time: 5:30. As he heard the synthesizer fanfare that announced the AccuWeather forecast, Willie leaped to attention at his place beside my bed. It might be taking him two years to grow a brain, but my Bouvier had been quick to master the sequence that led to his morning walk.

Climatologist Tara Lavallee was cheerily contrite as she announced that she had to do a complete 180 on her holiday-weekend forecast. A low-pressure zone had stalled over the southern third of the province, bringing with it . . .

I reached over and clicked off the radio. The sky outside my bedroom window was leaden, and rain was drumming monotonously on my window. I didn't need Tara to tell me it was going to be a rotten day.

"Bad news," I said to Willie.

He put his paws on the mattress, shivered with delight, and eyeballed me. I eyeballed him back.

I blinked first. "Okay," I said. "We'll go, but it's going to be a short one."

I dug out my rain pants, windbreaker, and a pair of ancient Reeboks, and Willie and I hit the street at top speed. By the time we reached the bandshell, Willie had absorbed the fact that no matter how hard he pulled at the leash I would still be on the other end, and the rain had grown lighter. There was no reason not to finish our usual run around the lake. There were distractions: for Willie, the new crop of goslings strutting their stuff across our path; for me, memories of the endless day before. I tried to shake them, give myself over to the moment, as Livia would say, but I wasn't able to let go. Every step triggered a memory. By the time we lurched through our front door, my mood was as bleak as the day.

I filled Willie's dish, plugged in the coffee, and stripped off my wet clothes. As I headed for the shower, I glanced at the caller ID on the telephone. Alex Kequahtooway had phoned. I looked at the clock. It would be 8:30 in Ottawa.

In the time it took to dial his cell number, I decided I wouldn't bring up the subject of Ariel Warren. Unless he had talked to one of his colleagues on the Regina police force, it was unlikely Alex would have heard of her death. He had been excited about giving the course on minorities and the justice system to a class of senior civil servants. It was a chance for him to talk to people who could make a difference, and he didn't need to be distracted by problems at home.

When I heard his voice, I almost weakened. "I miss you," I said. "Willie and I just got back from our walk, and I'm standing here naked, wet, and cold. I wish you were here."

"So do I."

"How are you at phone sex?" I said. "Under the circumstances, I'm up for anything."

"So am I," he said evenly. "Unfortunately, I'm in class right now. We take a break in an hour. If you'll leave me a number where you can be reached, I'll get back to you and we can try that new procedure."

The flush started at my toes and ended at my scalp. "Alex, are all those government people sitting there *listening*?"

"That's right."

"I must be pathological."

"Not pathological," he said. "Just healthy. Giving me some energy to rechannel. This is going to be the most inspired class I've taught since I got here."

"Baudelaire said he wrote with his penis."

"The French have some interesting systems," he said mildly. "I'll see what I can do about putting that one into place."

When I stepped out of the shower, the phone was ringing. I picked it up. "Still naked," I said, "but now clean, and with that hemp oil you gave me for Valentine's Day at the ready."

"I'm sorry, I must have the wrong number." The voice of the woman on the other end of the line was familiar.

"You don't have the wrong number, Livia. I should apologize. I was expecting someone else."

"I'm glad you have love in your life," she said.

Her tone was guileless, but I felt a pang. There was no love in Livia's life, at least not the kind that involved hemp-oil massages. Late one night when we were walking to the parking lot together, Livia had confided that since her marriage ended she had been celibate and that celibacy brought her peace. I had scrambled unsuccessfully for a sensible response, but driving home I realized that if my husband had dumped me as publicly and as brutally as Kenneth Brook had dumped Livia, I might have considered celibacy, too. He had chosen his wife's birthday party to do his dirty deed and, after three years, the memory of that evening still made me want to bury my head in the sand.

From the outset, the party had been out of control: the drinks were too strong, and the toasts too frequent; the meal was served so late that people simply rearranged the food on their plates, poured themselves another double, and lurched towards the next indiscretion. When Kenneth Brook tapped his glass, boomed that he wanted our attention, and draped an arm over Livia's shoulder, the room fell silent. It seemed that, despite their tempestuous relationship, Kenneth was about to pay tribute to his wife. But Kenneth had other fish to fry. As he announced that he had managed to both inspire and impregnate one of his graduate students, he could barely keep the smile off his face. When he added that, as a man of honour, he had no alternative but to marry his child's mother, I think he honestly expected we would burst into applause, but we weren't that drunk. Stunned sober, people mumbled their goodbyes and left. Livia wandered off to another room. Kenneth disappeared out the front door, presumably in search of a more receptive audience. Alone with the carnage of the aborted party and none too sober myself, I decided to put the food away. Like many decisions that night, mine wasn't wise.

When I opened the kitchen door, I saw that Livia had taken refuge there. She was leaning against the counter, singing "Happy Birthday" and trying to light the candles on her store-bought birthday cake. She was very drunk. As she swayed towards the forest of candles, match after match flared, then burned out between her fingers. She hadn't managed to ignite a single candle, but the blue icing roses on her cake were almost buried beneath a mulch of charred matches.

"Let me help you with that," I said.

When she turned to face me, I saw that she was crying. Her gaze had the watery despair of a drowning woman. "It's my party," she said, then she lit a fresh match and returned to her Sisyphean task.

I didn't see Livia Brook again till the following September. Classes were over, and she spent spring and summer on the

West Coast drifting through the misty regions of New Age thought. When the fall term began, Livia reappeared, tanned, thin, and carrying some sort of ritual bag adorned with bells and filled with gemstones guaranteed to heal the heart, ward off evil, and focus the mind. I had never been a proponent of enchanted bags, but Livia's seemed to have power. For the first time since I had known her, she was sober, focused, and purposeful.

During her marriage to Kenneth Brook, Livia's life had centred on her husband. Beyond teaching her classes and picking up her paycheque, she had shown little interest in the day-to-day business of the university, but suddenly she was inviting colleagues for tea and soliciting their opinions about where our department was headed. Invariably, these tête-a-têtes moved from the abstract to the personal. As they poured out their career ambitions and disappointments, Livia's colleagues were warmed by what Ed Mariani referred to as her "rampant empathy." There was talk that when Ben Jesse's tenure was over, a woman as perceptive as Livia would make a fine department head.

When the Kevin Coyle case erupted, the rampant empathy that had caused Ed and me to raise our eyebrows saved our department. Ben Jesse asked Livia to meet regularly with the women who had accused Kevin until the charges against him were given a fair hearing. Ben's confidence that open communication would contain the women's anger proved ill-founded, but the women trusted Livia, and when Ben died we all knew that Livia was our best hope for achieving reconciliation. Every member of our department supported her proposal that we make a special effort to recruit female candidates to fill the two vacancies created by Ben's death and an early retirement.

Landing Solange, who was brilliant, had been a coup for our small university; however, Livia had been forced to argue Ariel's case vigorously. Ariel's paper credentials were acceptable rather than extraordinary, and she had interviewed poorly. The hiring committee found her warm and likeable, but equivocal about academic life. Livia, who had met Ariel the summer before at a women's retreat on Saltspring Island, maintained that Ariel was simply suffering from post-dissertation ennui, and that by the time September rolled around she would be itching to get into a classroom. And Livia had a clincher. Unlike Solange, Ariel was a prairie girl who loved her birthplace. Our university wouldn't be a stepping stone for her; it would, Livia assured us, be "forever."

Livia had been right about Ariel – at least in part. The students had loved her, and she had been a glowing presence in our department. That morning when I heard Livia's voice I felt the debt of her gift, the weight of her loss.

"What's up?" I asked.

"It's about Ariel's class," she said. "There are still three weeks to go, and you're the logical one to take over."

"Livia . . ."

She cut me off. "I know you planned to do some writing this spring, but plans change. I've learned that."

"So have I," I said. "Ian's death taught me that nothing is certain. But Livia, I'm not getting any younger, and I haven't exactly got a dazzling list of publications."

"You still have the summer," Livia said quietly. "Ariel doesn't. Jo, she was so committed to this class."

I could feel my pendulum being drawn into Livia's rhythm. "Okay," I said. "As soon as we get back from the lake, I'll come up to the university and grab a syllabus and a class list."

"Come this morning," Livia said. "Then you'll have the weekend to get prepared. Rosalie will have everything ready for you."

I did not accept the yoke gladly, but as I drove to the university, I knew I had no right to complain. As Livia had pointed out, I did have the summer; besides, Alex had called, and for a novice he gave great telephone.

Ariel's picture was still on the counter in the Political Science office. In front of it was a bud vase holding a single, perfect ivory rose. When I called hello, Rosalie looked up from her computer. She had done something new to her salt-and-pepper hair. For as long as I could remember, she had worn it tightly curled in the style my daughter Mieka called a Kurly Kate do. Now, the curl was relaxed into soft waves, and the colour was a uniform and becoming silver. "Nice look," I said.

Rosalie reached up eagerly to touch her freshly feathered bangs. "The bridal book says not to try a new style the day of the wedding, so I thought I'd practise." Her voice was as tentative as that of a girl preparing for her first date.

I tried not to smile. Until she met Detective Robert Hallam, Rosalie had approached life with the flexibility of a sergeant major. She knew exactly how life should be lived, and she was not forgiving of those of us who didn't measure up. Love had come late to Rosalie. She was in her late fifties, and Robert was her first romance. When they met, he had been as intransigent and judgemental as she, and their mutual transformation had been a joy to watch.

"If I were you, I'd stop practising," I said. "You're not going to improve on that look. Now, come on. Fill me in. How are the wedding plans coming along?"

Her brow furrowed. "Pretty well, I think, except Robert's been assigned to Ariel's case, so he's going to be putting in some long hours. He warned me last night that I'm going to have to be making some decisions for both of us." She reached forward to save the work on her machine. "Joanne, did you go to the vigil for Ariel last night?"

"Yes."

"I should have," Rosalie said. "But I was still so upset, and I know it sounds selfish, but I want to enjoy this time before my wedding."

"That's not selfish," I said. "You were better off at home. The evening got pretty unpleasant towards the end."

"Robert had reports from some of the officers there. They said the situation was explosive."

"I didn't notice any police," I said.

"They were female detectives, in plainclothes," she said. Her voice lacked spirit. It was obvious her mind was somewhere else. She adjusted the diamond solitaire on her left hand. "Joanne, do you have a minute to talk?"

"Of course." I pulled up a chair, so we could talk face to face. "Is there something I can help with?"

She laughed nervously. "It's this business of being engaged to a policeman. I thought, since you and Inspector Kequahtooway are a couple, you might be able to help."

"If I can."

"I never know how much I should ask Robert about his work. I don't want him to think I'm nosy; on the other hand, I *do* want him to know I'm interested."

"Maybe it's best just to follow Robert's lead. A lot of the time, police officers live in a grim world. If Alex is any indication, sometimes they need to talk about anything *except* the case; other times they seem to need to talk it through."

Rosalie looked thoughtful. "Last night, Robert must have needed to talk it through. I've never seen him so upset. Ariel's case is really getting under his skin."

"I guess until they have a suspect . . ."

"But they do have a suspect . . . at least they've brought someone in for intense questioning."

"Who is it?"

"His name is Kyle Morrissey. He's the young man who found Ariel's body. His company sent him to work on some problem with the air conditioning in the sub-basement. He says he just took a wrong turn and ended up in the archive room." She glanced around quickly to make sure we were alone. "Joanne, the police have had dealings with him before. Apparently, he has a violent temper."

"So, why is Robert uneasy?" I said.

Rosalie's face registered her distress. "He's not certain they have the right man."

"Why?"

"Instinct. Robert says that crimes like these typically involve rape. This one didn't."

I could feel the pinprick stirrings of anxiety. "So there was no evidence of forced sex?"

"None. She was just . . . slumped onto a table facing the front door. She was stabbed in the back. Robert said death was instantaneous." Initially, Rosalie's words had been halting; now they began to tumble out. "Robert said Ariel died from a single wound, surgically clean – doesn't that sound terrible? And she didn't struggle. There was nothing to indicate that Kyle Morrissey had tried to force himself on her. In fact, he called for help as soon as he found the body."

"How did he get in? I thought those rooms were always kept locked."

"They are – at least the doors the public uses are. But there's a back door that workmen use. It opens up from the crawl space that has all the heating equipment and plumbing for the building."

I leaned towards her. "Rosalie, maybe you shouldn't say anything about this to anyone else."

She looked stricken. "You mean I might compromise the case?"

"I guess, until the case is solved, the fewer people who know about the details the better."

"I haven't told anyone but you," she said.

"Good." Her eyes still sought reassurance. I did my best. "Rosalie, it's okay. When you told me, you knew it wouldn't go any further."

"Because you're in a relationship with a police officer, too."

"Right."

The cloud lifted. "It's like a sisterhood, isn't it?" she said.

"That's what it is," I said, "a sisterhood, so if you want to talk about this to anyone, you can talk to me."

"What can she talk to you about?" Neither of us had heard Livia come into the office. Her hands clutched the poppy-painted silk scarf draped around her shoulders, and the shadows under her deep-set eyes were so dark she looked as if she'd been beaten. I remembered her hopes for Ariel and felt a pang in case I had made things hard for her on the phone.

I turned to her. "We're just ironing out the details about the class."

Rosalie rose with a start. "I've made up a file with copies of the syllabus and the class list. Ariel kept her grades on our shared drive on the computer, so I've printed them out for Joanne."

"Sounds like everything's in order," I said, standing.

"Not quite." Rosalie frowned. "I called the bookstore. Ariel was using *Political Perspectives* as her text in that class, but the bookstore is out of it, and by the time they can get it in, the class will be over." She took a key from her desk drawer. "Joanne, would you mind going to Ariel's office and getting her copy of the text? I should have done it, but I just couldn't bring myself to open that door."

I took the key. "There's no reason you should," I said. "I'll be back in a minute."

I tried to be matter-of-fact, but the truth was I dreaded going to Ariel's office. I'd been in it only a handful of times, but it was as characteristic of her as her thumbprint. She had surrounded herself with a cheerful clutter of books and journals, and a gallery of soft-sculpture figures of family and friends that she'd made from scraps of odd and lovely material. She was a person who loved process. A few weeks earlier, she'd called me in to show me how she'd placed a low table in front of her window and begun to grow a flat of tomato plants from seeds.

The office had celebrated the many pleasures of her life, but when I turned the key in the lock, I walked into a room that was oddly impersonal. Ariel's desk was clear; the books on her bookshelves were neatly arranged according to subject and author, but the folk art and the photographs were gone. So were the table she'd placed under the window and the tomato plants that sprouted to life on it. I checked the section of books devoted to introductory politics: *Political Perspectives* was not there. I glanced through the other texts: *Political Perspectives* was still among the missing.

I walked back to the main office. "Rosalie, did someone take away Ariel's things?"

"Not that I know of. Is something missing?"

"Everything that was personal."

Rosalie followed me down the hall and peeked around the corner. Her face became troubled. "It wasn't like this last Monday. I had to take some photocopying in, and it looked the way it always did. The police were in here last night, but I can't imagine they'd remove anything."

"They wouldn't," I said. Then I closed the door, locked it, and handed Rosalie the key. "Maybe Livia will know something about it."

But when we got back to the main office, there wasn't a soul in sight.

I started for the stairs. Then, haunted by the absence of
Ariel in that room that had once teemed with her life, I
doubled back and rapped on a door that was seldom rapped
on any more.

It had been two years since I'd been in Kevin Coyle's
office. His frequent assaults on mine made reciprocal visits
unnecessary, but a quick glance around the room assured me
that all was as it had always been. His floor-to-ceiling bookshelves were jammed with thick books made from cheap
paper. Their covers were dense with Cyrillic lettering and
maps splattered in blood. The politics of Eastern Europe had
a painful history of exsanguination. The brown overstuffed
reading chair was still in its place by the window, and the
illegal hotplate upon which Kevin made coffee and toasted
sandwiches was still in plain view. But that day, as always,
the most prominent feature of Kevin's office was the four
games of Risk he had set up on the dining-room table with
the sawed-off legs that dominated the room.

In the good days, students, mostly male but some female,
would spend hours in Kevin's office, playing Risk, talking
politics, eating toasted sandwiches and drinking Kevin's exe-
crable coffee. It had been a long time since students had ventured through that door, but Kevin had left everything at the
ready – waiting for the Restoration.

"You're like Miss Havisham," I said.

"You think I don't know whom you're talking about," he
grunted, "but I do. Miss Havisham was that loony old broad
in *Great Expectations* who got jilted at the altar and kept
everything just as it had been on the day of her wedding.
You'll note I'm not wearing a wedding gown and there's no
mouldering wedding cake in sight. You'll also note that I'm
not insane. On the contrary, I'm a sane man in an insane
world. May I offer you a cup of coffee?"

"Did you make it within the last two days?"

"Within the hour," he said. "I'm turning over a new leaf."

"Then I'll take a chance. Kevin, I need some help."

He brought me the coffee in an orange and brown striped mug whose earth tones were as faded as the earth-friendly activism of the seventies. The coffee was surprisingly good, and I told him so.

"I've learned the secret," he said mysteriously.

"Kevin, I'd love to sit here and talk coffee with you, but I need some information. As the one department member who's here day and night, do you have any idea who cleared out Ariel's office?"

He couldn't suppress the triumph in his eyes. "She and I did."

"When?"

"A week ago Tuesday. It was around eight-thirty at night. I was here, working on my appeal, and I heard noises coming from down the hall. I went over to investigate. I was listening at the door when I heard a crash. I didn't wait to be invited in. Ariel was on the floor. She'd been standing on her chair getting down the books from the top shelf of her bookcase when she slipped. She was all right, just shaken up a bit. She told me she'd been packing up her things, which was a fairly obvious statement since there were boxes all over the place. I asked if she needed some help getting the boxes downstairs to her car. She said she did." He lowered his voice. "I have a private dolly on loan from the library."

"That's obliging of them," I said.

"It would be if they knew I had it," he agreed. "At any rate, it took us two trips to get everything into her truck, but we made it. Of course, I was curious about what she was up to, so when we loaded the last box on, I asked her, in a jocular way, whether it was moving day. She said no, she was just simplifying because she didn't know what lay ahead."

"Did she seem frightened?"

"Not frightened, just tense and resolute. Before she got in her car, she kissed me." Remembering, Kevin touched his cheek. "Then she said, 'People were wrong about you. That's the next battle, and I'm not looking forward to it.'" Kevin's face darkened. "Until that moment, it was a wonderful evening, but I pushed it too far. That's a flaw of mine. Have you noticed?" He glared at me, waiting for a response.

I let him glare. Finally, hating silence, he continued. "That's when Ariel and I had the exchange that Ann Vogel and her friends are getting such mileage from."

"What exactly was the exchange?"

"It was obvious Ariel had learned something, so I pressed her to tell what she knew. She said she couldn't until she'd talked to someone else first. Of course, I was certain the person she had to speak to was a member of the odious group of women. So I said, 'Stay away from those harpies or you'll be sorry.' All I meant was that she'd lose the ground she'd gained, but I must have shouted because apparently I was overheard. Unfortunately, no one overheard her response."

"Which was . . . ?"

"Which was, 'I already am sorry.'"

"Did you tell the police this?"

"Of course. They wrote it down very carefully. I'm sure the report has already been consigned to the shredder. Isn't that how the authorities process all statements from middle-class white men over fifty?"

"Can it, Kevin. Let's keep the focus on Ariel. Did she tell you anything more about why she was clearing out her office?"

"Just that she was separating what she needed from what she didn't need."

"That was it?"

"That was it."

I finished my coffee and stood up. "I'm glad you were there," I said.

He shrugged. "I'm a human being, Joanne. That brings certain obligations."

As I walked down the corridor to my office, I had to admit I was spooked. Why had Ariel cleaned out her office four weeks before her class was over, and what had she meant by "the next battle"? Something else was troubling. Despite his promise to call me, I hadn't heard from Howard Dowhanuik. That mystery, at least, appeared to have a solution within my reach, but when I got back to my office and dialled Howard's apartment, there was no answer. I checked my machine at home. There were two messages: the first was from Marie Cousin thanking me in advance for being a parent-helper the next week when Taylor's class visited the Legislature; the second was from Howard telling me he was worried about Charlie, and he'd be in touch.

The day stretched ahead. I could do what a sensible woman would do: shop for groceries, pack, get ready for the long weekend; or I could see if Charlie would talk to me. Ed Mariani had told me once that the first lesson a journalist learns is that everyone wants to tell their story. Something in my bones told me that a man as obsessed as Charlie had been would want to tell his. Luckily, I had a credible excuse for paying him a visit. If I was going to teach Ariel's class on Tuesday, I'd need her copy of the text. I went back to the main office and flipped through Rosalie's Rolodex.

Ariel's address was a surprise: 2778 Manitoba Street was downtown, in a neighbourhood in which, depending on your bent, you could get cured by a Chinese herbalist, saved at a Romanian Catholic Church, or beaten to a pulp if you chose to hang around after dark. The city's core was an unlikely choice for two young people with good incomes

and privileged backgrounds, and as I drove past businesses
that promised to cash cheques, no questions asked, and
second-hand furniture stores with year-round sidewalk sales,
I began to wonder if I had ever known Ariel at all.

The house she and Charlie had shared was a thirties bungalow with a fresh coat of paint the colour of Devonshire cream,
dark green louvred shutters, lace curtains, and wicker hanging
baskets filled with scarlet double impatiens. Nestled between
a pawnshop with barred windows and an adult video store,
the perky innocence of number 2778 came as a sweet shock,
like discovering Donna Reed in a Quentin Tarantino movie.

Charlie and Ariel had made two concessions to the realities of their neighbourhood. The front lawn was protected
by a chain-link fence and, as I stepped onto the porch, the
dog that began barking in the backyard sounded like it meant
business. After five minutes, the dog was still barking, no one
had come to the door, and my idea about ambushing Charlie
into supplying some answers seemed hare-brained rather
than inspired. As I headed back to my car, I tried to step carefully around the water pooling on the walk, but despite
my efforts, my feet got wet. By the time I reached the car, my
temper was frayed. It was a toss-up whom I was angrier at:
myself for thinking I could play Nancy Drew, or Charlie for
leaving his dog out in a downpour.

The penny dropped. It had been raining constantly since
5:30 that morning. I hadn't been close to Charlie for years,
but if the Jesuits are right about the boy being the father of
the man, I couldn't imagine the Charlie I knew growing into
a man who would leave his dog out in the rain. I retraced my
steps and walked by the side of the house and peered over
the gate into the backyard. A man in a khaki slicker, whose
hood hid his face from view, was trying to feed paper into a
smouldering hibachi. The dog, a Rottweiler, was beside him.

"Why don't you wait for the rain to stop, Charlie?" I said.

But when he turned, the man facing me wasn't Charlie. With his strong features, wire-rimmed glasses, and slick, swept-back hair, he had the look of a man who was accustomed to dominating the situation: a lawyer or an actor. He didn't greet me, and his silence seemed like a professional tool.

"I'm looking for Charlie Dowhanuik," I said.

The man remained silent. His expression wasn't hostile, but it wasn't welcoming.

"I'm a friend of the family."

He shrugged. "What's Charlie's mother's name?"

"Marnie," I said. "Marnie Sullivan Dowhanuik."

"Where does she live?"

"Good Shepherd Villa, in Toronto."

He walked towards me, and unlocked the gate. The Rottweiler stayed at his side. As I came through the gate, I held my hand out, palm up, to the dog. He sniffed it eagerly; then he let me scratch his head. The man watched with interest. "You passed the name test and you passed the Fritz test," he said. "That's good enough for me. My name is Liam Hill, and I'm sorry for being suspicious, but it's been that kind of day."

"Joanne Kilbourn," I said. "Have you had to deal with a ghoul patrol?"

"The stream has been steady," he agreed. "I guess it's human nature, but when you know the people involved, it's hard to see tragedy as a spectator sport."

"So you're a friend of Charlie's."

"And of Ariel's," he said. "Look, we're getting soaked. Do you want to continue this inside the house?"

"Sure." I gestured towards a sheet of yellow legal paper smoking wetly in the hibachi. There was handwriting on it. "That's not going to work, you know."

He stiffened. I saw immediately that he had given my words a significance I hadn't intended. I didn't want to alienate him. At the moment he was the only link I had. "It's too wet now," I said. "Why don't you try later?"

I could see him relax. "Let's go inside."

Fritz loped happily ahead, and I followed. We walked across the deck into the kitchen, an attractive room with hardwood flooring, old fashioned glass-faced cupboards, an ancient slope-shouldered Admiral refrigerator, a huge gas stove, and a picture window that looked onto the garden. Flush against the window was a butcher-block table. On the table, Ariel's tomato plants languished, dry and yellowing. Unexpectedly, my eyes filled.

Liam Hill didn't notice. He had his back to me, hanging his slicker over the back of a chair. When he turned, I saw that he was wearing a navy sweatshirt with white lettering.

"St. Michael's College," I said. "I went to Vic, but my first serious boyfriend was at St. Mike's. His name was Bob Birgeneau, and he told me that he knew I was a nice girl, but that other boys wouldn't know I was a nice girl if I kept wearing slacks to class." I smiled. "Sorry," I said. "Too much information."

"Not too much information," Liam Hill said. "Just an interesting sociological nugget. Shall we sit down?" He pointed towards a built-in breakfast nook just off the kitchen. Like the refrigerator, it was a period piece, a restaurant-style booth with wine leatherette banquettes facing one another across a Formica-topped, chrome-edged table. "Incidentally, we're a little more enlightened about dress codes at St. Mike's now."

I slid into my place, and Liam Hill slid into his across from me.

"I feel like I should be ordering a cherry Coke and fries." I said.

He smiled. "Whatever happened to cherry Cokes?" Then he leaned towards me. "I probably should have said this off the top. I'm not going to talk about Charlie."

"Fair enough," I said. "Actually, I was hoping to talk to Charlie myself. I thought he might need a friend."

"How well do you know him?" Liam Hill asked.

"Not well at all any more. He and my kids knew each other when they were growing up. My connection is really with his parents, which, of course, now pretty well means Howard."

"You and Howard Dowhanuik are close."

"He's my oldest friend."

"For Charlie's friends, that's not necessarily a recommendation."

I could feel my temper rise. "There are two sides to every story, Mr. Hill."

Actually, it's Father Hill," he said, "and you're right. I do only know Charlie's side of the story."

"Charlie was never very charitable about his father," I said.

"Perhaps his father hadn't earned charity."

"That's an odd comment coming from you," I said. "Has your order started charging for *caritas*, Father Hill?

He winced. "I'm sorry, Mrs. Kilbourn. This hasn't been anyone's finest hour."

"Then don't prolong it," I said. "Tell me when Charlie will be back, and I'll be on my way."

Father Hill's face gave away nothing, but the pulse in his neck fluttered as he weighed his decision. Finally, the scales tipped in my favour. "Charlie won't be back for a while. He went to Toronto to see Marnie."

I was incredulous. "To see Marnie? Is she better?"

"There's been no change in her condition. Charlie just wanted to be with his mother. Your friend, Howard, went with him."

Liam Hill's words were innocent, but something in his
tone got under my skin.

"Howard doesn't need me to defend him," I said, "but, for
the record, you're wrong about him. He's a good man, and
he made a real difference in the lives of a lot of people here."

"And his wife and son paid the price," Liam Hill said
quietly.

"You knew Marnie before the accident?"

He shook his head. "No, she was already at Good Shepherd
when I met her. But Charlie told me she was brilliant. He said
there was nothing she couldn't have been, if she hadn't had to
sacrifice everything –"

I cut him off. "Marnie Dowhanuik didn't sacrifice everything."

Father Hill shifted his gaze. "We all have our own perception of reality," he said mildly.

"Don't humour me," I said. My voice was loud and angry.
When I spoke again I tried to take the volume down a notch.
"This isn't a perception. This is the truth. For many years,
Marnie and I were as close as sisters. Father Hill, she wasn't
a victim. She was smart and funny and . . . she was *Marnie* –
driving stubborn voters to the polls, handing out placards at
rallies, cooking turkeys for all those potluck suppers. And
her cabbage rolls . . ." I smiled at the memory. "She could
make a pan full of sensational cabbage rolls in the time it
took me to find the recipe. I remember once we'd been at a
constituency dinner in the basement of Little Flower
Church. At the end of the evening, when she and I came
out to the parking lot, she was carrying this big roasting
pan filled with leftovers. Howard was surrounded by men
hanging on his every word. Marnie waded through all those
fawning guys and handed him the roaster. 'Howie,' she said,
'I made these cabbage rolls, I delivered them to the church
hall, I reheated them, I served them, I washed the plates they

were eaten off, I paid the party ten bucks for the ones that were left; the least you can do is carry them back to the damn car.'"

Father Hill laughed softly. "Nice story," he said.

"There's more to it," I said. "You can imagine how those men were gaping. After all, Howard was the premier, and Marnie was just the missus, but she had this great smile, and she gave those guys the full wattage. Then she delivered the *coup de grâce*. 'Another thing,' she said. 'That speech you're all creaming your jeans about – I wrote it.'"

Liam Hill raised an eyebrow. "She sounds like quite a woman."

"She was," I said. "Maybe Charlie never realized that. Kids' perceptions of their parents' lives aren't always accurate. Father Hill, I wouldn't accept Charlie's word as gospel on this. He had his own burdens, and they may have distorted his view. But don't diminish Marnie. The fact that her bike was hit by a car was a tragedy, but her life wasn't." I slung my bag over my shoulder. "Now, I *did* have a purpose in coming here. I'm taking over the class Ariel was teaching, and I'm going to need her textbook. It's called *Political Perspectives*. It's a quality paperback with a blue and red cover. Could you check her desk for it?"

"No problem," he said, but there was something half-hearted about his agreement, and I wasn't surprised when he returned empty-handed.

"No problem, but also no luck," he said.

"Thanks for trying," I said.

I pulled up the zipper on my jacket, then glanced at the tomato plants on the table. "Ariel babied those plants from seeds," I said. "I hate to see them dying. Would you mind if I found a place outside to put them so they could get some of this rain?"

"I'll give you a hand," he said.

We were silent as we carried the tiny peat pots outside. We found a place on the deck where they could get plenty of rain, but where, if the wind came up, they'd be protected. As we set the last one in place, Fritz, who was still inside, began barking.

"Sounds like you have company," I said. "There's no need for me to trail mud through the house. I can leave by the gate at the side."

"Okay," he said. "I'm glad you came, Mrs. Kilbourn. It's always useful to have another perspective." He offered me his hand. "It's good you thought about the tomato plants."

When the back door closed behind him, I sprinted to the hibachi. The fire had sputtered out. I grabbed the charred piece of legal paper, folded it once, and dropped it in my purse.

As I let myself through the side gate, I saw why Fritz had been barking. Two police cars had pulled up in front of the adult video shop next door. The cruisers were empty, so the officers had apparently already gone inside. I was gawking as I walked to my car and, before I slid into my seat, I took a final glance. In an uncurtained window at the front of the second storey, an old woman was watching me. When our eyes met, she lifted her arm very slowly and waved at me. I waved back.

As soon as I was in the car, I took the piece of charred paper from my bag. The acrid smell of smoke hit my nostrils. The handwriting was sprawling and fanciful, not Ariel's small, neat script. Only one sentence was visible, but the words cut to the bone. "Nothing will ever separate us again." Then there was a single initial: "C."

CHAPTER

5

As soon as I got home, I went to the family room and took down *The Divine Comedy* again. I was obeying an impulse I would have had difficulty explaining, but when the book fell open at Dante's description of the Vestibule of Hell, where the Futile run perpetually after a whirling standard, I didn't hesitate. I slid the burnt fragment of Charlie's letter between the pages and replaced the book on the shelf. I might not have been the coldest beer in the fridge, but I recognized symbolism when I saw it.

My son's room was private territory, and I didn't enter it without cause. That afternoon, I had cause. I needed to tap into my office mail, and Angus's computer was the only one in the house with a modem. After I turned on his computer, I glanced up at the bulletin board above his desk. He called it his Zonkboard, and from the time he was ten, it had been a montage bristling with evidence of his deep but shifting passions: skateboarding, the Blue Jays, endangered species, water polo, the Referendum, hiking, Buddy Rich, the women of Lilith Fair. That afternoon, wallet-sized photos of members of the graduating class of Sheldon Williams C.I.

were thumbtacked between articles about the perfidy of the
New Right and the excellence of John Ralston Saul and
Drew Barrymore. The Zonk Factoid of the Day was a newspaper clipping: "The Inuit of Greenland believe that a person
possesses six or seven souls that take the form of tiny people
scattered throughout the body." It was, I thought as I turned
back to the computer, an oddly comforting possibility.

I typed a message announcing that on the following
Tuesday I would begin teaching Ariel Warren's Political
Science 101 and asking anyone who had a copy of the text
Political Perspectives to lend it to me until the end of classes.
It was only after I hit send that I realized I'd cast my net too
wide. Instead of limiting my request to our department, I'd
entered the universal address for faculty and staff at the
entire university. I discarded the idea of a follow-up message.
In spring and summer, there were so many people who never
opened e-mail that I would have been clogging the system.

I was rereading my original note when Angus came in. He
leaned over and peered at the screen. "I thought you had the
summer off."

"So did I," I said.

He gave me an awkward pat. "Well, you still have the long
weekend, so let's rock. Taylor's downstairs saying goodbye
to her cats. If we don't make our move soon, she's going to
fall apart."

I sighed with exasperation. "I've been through this with
her a dozen times," I said. "Sylvie O'Keefe is going to feed
Benny and Bruce, and Jess is going to come over to play with
them. It's only three days, Angus."

He shrugged. "Tell that to T."

It was raining hard by the time we turned off onto the road
to Katepwa. On the highway, we had listened to the drive-
home show's homage to the pleasures of barbecue and

summer love. A fiery romance wasn't on my weekend agenda, but the talk of sizzling meat was a reminder that within the next couple of hours I was going to be surrounded by a cottage full of hungry people. The dining room at the Katepwa Hotel served fine food at moderate prices, and it shared a kitchen with the Katepwa Pub, which served equally fine food that was cheap and available for take-out. As I slowed in front of the hotel, the boys and Taylor strained for a look at the lake. The rain was so heavy we could barely make out the beach, and as soon as I opened the car door I could hear the pounding of whitecaps against the shore.

Jackets pulled over our heads, we raced to the pub. Judging from the crowd inside, it was apparent that others caught in the downpour had felt the pull of a clean well-lighted place. The Katepwa Pub was jumping. Taylor drifted towards a group crowded around a big-screen TV that was showing a Jodie Foster movie; the boys headed for the shuffleboard table. The centre of gravity was shifting.

"Everybody back here with me," I said. "You're all under-age, and we're here to get food."

Angus perked up. "What are we getting?"

"The special," I said. "I don't want to hang around while they cook dinner for seven people from scratch."

"I wonder what the special is?" Angus asked.

"Chili," Eli said. "It's written on the chalkboard over there."

"But we had chili dogs after ball last night," Angus groaned.

"Sometimes the universe unfolds as it should," I said.

Angus frowned. "What's that supposed to mean?"

I gave him a short jab in the shoulder. "It means there was a cosmic decision that, despite your best efforts, our family was destined to eat chili tonight."

The road to Ed and Barry's was winding and muddy. Twice, we were within a hair's breadth of sliding off the road, and twice, Eli, who had been entrusted with holding the hot food, manfully swallowed his yelp of pain when he got splashed. By the time we got to the cottage, the rain had stopped, but I was still edgy. Two of my children still had to drive that road, and one of them was with her husband and my only grandchild.

Ed and Barry had waterfront property. The cottage was new, built five years earlier, but they had designed it to be timeless, and it had a rambling, wicker-and-wisteria grace, a closed-in porch overlooking the lake, two full bathrooms, and a Jacuzzi. In short, it was perfect, or it would be once everybody had arrived safely. As soon as we parked, Taylor and the boys flew out of the car. Willie was right behind them.

"Can we just look at the lake?" Angus said.

"After you've carried everything in from the car, you can look at the lake all weekend," I said.

There were only two bags I insisted on handling myself; both were paper, and both bore the logo of the Saskatchewan Liquor Board. By the time I walked through the front door with them, the car was cleaned out, and the boys and Taylor and Willie were racing past me on their way to the beach.

When I touched a match to the already-laid fire in the fieldstone fireplace in the living room, it roared to satisfying life. I carried on to the kitchen, placed my paper bags carefully on the table, found the kind of Dutch oven I dreamed of owning before I died, dumped the chili in, and turned on the burner. Dinner was under way. Some nights, I just had all the moves. As a reward, I poured myself two fingers of Glenfiddich and wandered out to the porch, so I could have a good view of Willie and the kids chasing each other along the shoreline. When Willie loped onto the dock, I knew there was nothing between his ears that would allow him to make the correction necessary to avoid disaster. His cannonball into the lake when he came to the end of the dock seemed as inexorable as a law of physics. So was the fact that as he splashed to shore, Taylor, Angus, and Eli waded out to greet him. It was a grey day, but I could see their laughter, and warmed by the whisky, my nerves began to unknot. Fifteen minutes later, Peter's ancient Jeep rolled in, followed closely by the sensible Volvo station wagon that had replaced Mieka and Greg's bright yellow Volkswagen Bug the week after Madeleine was born. Suddenly, the odds that I would make it through the weekend had turned in my favour.

The first moments of the reunion of my two oldest children were shot through with the currents of love and competitiveness that had always flowed between them. They were eighteen months apart, and their feelings for each other still had the primal intensity of the nursery. It didn't surprise me that, after the initial round of hugs and greetings, they ended up together, arms draped loosely around one another's waists, connected again. Physically, they were very different. Peter was tall, reed thin, pale, and serious, the inheritor of my late husband's black Irish genes; Mieka was dark blond, hazel-eyed, with skin that tanned easily and pleasing curves that would become roundness after forty, and Rubenesque after fifty. Seeing them side by side again, I felt the familiar rush of pleasure.

My son-in-law looked at them with amusement. "The road company Donny and Marie." He leaned down and brushed my cheek with a kiss. "Good to see you, Jo."

"Good to see you, too." I said. I took my granddaughter from his arms. "And it's wonderful to see you." As she gazed at me, Madeleine dimpled with the look her mother described as "crazed with delight."

"Look at that smile," I said. "I knew she'd remember me."

Greg shook his head. "Hate to break it to you, Jo, but the old geezer who pulled us out of the mud at the turnoff showed Maddy his gums and got the same response. That little lady's smiles go everywhere."

"You'd better start reading 'My Last Duchess' to her," I said. "Promiscuous smiling can get a woman in a heap of trouble."

Mieka's mind wasn't on Robert Browning. She narrowed her eyes at the beach. "What are the kids doing down there?"

"Resisting temptation," I said. "I told them it was too cold to swim, and you'll notice that they are obeying the letter of the law – wading only up to their kneecaps."

Peter turned to his sister. "Race you down there," he said. "And since you're still packing those new mum pounds, I'll spot you thirty seconds."

After they took off, Greg shrugged and picked up a suitcase. "Must make you proud of your parenting skills when you look at those two, Jo. Come on inside and I'll buy you a drink."

"I'm way ahead of you." I said.

I led him through the living room, pointed out the liquorboard bags, and took Madeleine out to the porch. There was a rocker in the corner by the window and I commandeered it. I rested my chin on top of my granddaughter's head and pointed.

"Look down there at the lake," I said. "Your mum's pushing your uncle Pete into the water."

Greg came in carrying a bottle of Great West beer. He snapped the cap, leaned forward, and peered out the window. "It's great to see Mieka happy again," he said.

"Is something wrong?"

"Not with us," he said quickly. "But Ariel's death has hit Mieka hard. The minute we heard about it on the provincial news, I wanted to call you, but Mieka said this was something she had to talk to you about face to face. She and Ariel have been pretty tight the last couple of months."

On the beach, Eli, soaked to the skin, waved wildly. I waved back, then turned to Greg. "I had no idea they'd even kept in touch."

"They hadn't, but when Maddy was born, Mieka found Ariel's address on the university e-mail and sent her an announcement. Then they picked up where they left off."

He touched the bottom of his Great West to his daughter's bare stomach, and she gave him a look that would have curdled milk.

"There goes Father of the Year," I said.

"I'll win her back," he said. "She can't resist my version of 'Louie, Louie.'"

"Who can?" I tucked Madeleine's shirt inside her shorts. "Greg, I'm glad Ariel and Mieka connected again."

"Me too," he said. "It seemed to mean a lot to both of them, especially after Ariel got pregnant."

"After Ariel *got pregnant*?"

Greg flushed. "Maybe that wasn't supposed to be general knowledge."

"Everything about Ariel's life will be general knowledge now," I said grimly.

"It's going to be a zoo, isn't it?" Greg said.

Instinctively, I drew my granddaughter closer. "Yes," I said, "it's going to be a zoo."

Dinner that first night at the lake was close to perfect. Semi-penitent about their forbidden swim, the kids threw themselves into dinner preparations. Taylor laid out the plates and cutlery, the boys cut up fresh vegetables, Peter made garlic bread, Greg poured the milk and opened the wine, and Mieka sugared the berries and whipped the cream for strawberry shortcake.

Finally, we gathered at the round oak table and, enclosed by the circle of light cast by the overhead lamp, we ate and laughed and ate some more. When Angus proposed a vote on the question of whether this chili was the best I had ever made, the ayes triumphed. By the time Willie was licking the last of the whipped cream off the strawberry-shortcake plate, Madeleine's eyes had grown heavy. At Taylor's insistence, we took Madeleine down to the bedroom she and I were sharing. Mieka positioned her daughter in the centre of the king-size bed, and Taylor crawled in beside her; then Mieka and I sat on the edge of the bed and took turns making up stories about the patches on the quilt that covered them until they were both asleep.

For a moment, Mieka and I stood looking down at the girls. "Taylor's dream has come true," I said. "All week, she's been talking about having Madeleine bunk in with her."

Mieka's expression was impish. "Do you want to make *my* dream come true?"

"If I can."

She lowered her voice. "Let me put up Maddy's crib in here, so I can spend a night alone with her father."

"It would be my pleasure," I said.

We walked outside together to get the crib. Mieka opened the back gate on their Volvo wagon, then peered up at the sky. "Looks like it might clear off."

I moved closer to her. "I feel very blessed tonight."

My daughter's face was uncharacteristically grave. "So do I."

For a moment we were silent, then I said, "Greg told me that Ariel was pregnant."

My daughter's eyes widened. "You didn't know?"

"No," I said. "But I'm glad she felt close enough to you to tell you."

"And it was just a fluke we'd become friends again," she said sadly. "I was ringing the bells after Maddy was born to make sure that everyone I'd ever known heard the good news."

"Your dad and I did the same thing when you were born. Unfortunately, that was before e-mail. When I saw our long-distance bill the next month, I cried for an hour."

Mieka laughed softly. "Poor Mum. Anyway, most people just e-mailed back, but Ariel sent a beautiful box of books: *Madeline*, of course, but also *Goodnight Moon* and *The Runaway Bunny* and *The Very Hungry Caterpillar*. She also sent Maddy a note. It was so poignant. Ariel said that these had been her favourite books when she was a little girl. She said she hoped Maddy would forgive her for reading them before she sent them, but she wanted to get back to a time when she was happy. Of course, as soon as I read the note, I called her. I was all raging hormones – Earth Mother, certain I could fix everything. Mum, Ariel was so different than I thought she would be."

"How did you think she would be?"

My daughter shrugged. "Dismissive?"

"Why would she be dismissive?"

My daughter rolled her eyes. "Mum, Ariel had a Ph.D. before she was twenty-seven, and as you remember only too well, I dropped out of university halfway through my second year."

"Does that bother you?"

"Most of the time, no, but Ariel was always so perfect." Mieka pulled the portable crib out of the car and slammed down the gate. "Do you want to hear a nasty little admission? When I heard Ariel had a job in your department, I was jealous."

"Jealous?"

"I had this image of you and her chatting away about world affairs and going to lectures together. You know, like the daughter you always wanted."

I touched her arm. "Mieka, you're the daughter I always wanted."

Unexpectedly, her eyes filled with tears. "Oh, I know that most of the time, but sometimes I wonder if . . ."

"If what?"

"If nothing. I must be PMS-ing. Anyway, that first time I phoned her, Ariel didn't talk much about herself at all, but she had a lot of questions about me. She wanted to know if I'd felt more connected to life since I'd had Maddy. And she wanted to know – and this is truly bizarre – how you reacted when I dropped out of school."

"Why would she care about that?"

"I don't know . . . She never mentioned it again. After that we mostly e-mailed each other. She had a bunch of theoretical questions about pregnancy – just girlfriend stuff – and then she phoned at Easter and made the big announcement. Two weekends ago, she came up to Saskatoon with an ultrasound photo of her baby. She'd brought Madeleine a gift – a German teddy bear. Ariel said the bear's name was Serendipity, and she hoped it would always remind Maddy to pay attention to lucky interventions in her life."

My daughter was fighting tears. So was I.

"This just keeps getting worse," I said. "When Howard and I drove out to tell Charlie yesterday, I didn't realize that he'd lost Ariel *and* their baby."

Mieka didn't respond, but even in the sepia light of early evening, I could read the truth in her face.

"Charlie wasn't the father," I said.

The shake of her head was almost indiscernible. "No," she said. "The baby wasn't Charlie's."

"Whose then?"

"I don't know. But Mum, somehow I had the sense that the father was someone who just *contributed*. Ariel was so determined to have a child."

"To take her back to the time when she was happy?"

Mieka bit her lip and nodded affirmation.

My daughter and I put up the portable crib beside the big bed and tucked the girls in. When we came back to the living room, there were muted cheers.

"Finally!" Angus groaned. "Listen up, you two, Greg has found something he swears is totally cool."

I stopped in my tracks. "If it's a board game, I'm going to go back there and crawl in next to Maddy."

"Not a board game," said Greg. "A game of exploration in which we test the limits of the human psyche to endure suspense." His accent became plummy, with each vowel lovingly elongated. "We invite you to a weekend with the Master of the Macabre, Mr. Alfred Hitchcock. It appears our hosts here at Katepwa own the complete Hitchcock *oeuvre*."

"I'm up for anything that doesn't have a Teletubby in it," said Mieka.

"I thought," said my son-in-law, "that we would begin with that a paean to the virtues of voyeurism, *Rear Window*."

"Never heard of it," said Angus.

"I've never even heard of Alfred Hitchcock," said Eli.

"Well, hold on to your popcorn," said Greg, "because you're in for an experience that will explode your kernels."

In the first minutes after Greg slid *Rear Window* into the VCR, I had the sinking feeling that, like many of us who had been glorious in the fifties, the movie had aged badly. The sets were undeniably cheesy, Grace Kelly's uptown accent grated, and Eli and Angus wondered loudly about Jimmy Stewart's sanity in ignoring a woman who, despite her pearls and addiction to cocktail dresses, was clearly a hottie. But it wasn't long before we were all seduced by the possibility of murder in the apartment across the way. By the time Jimmy had snagged the murderer and Grace had snagged Jimmy, everyone in the room was a Hitchcock convert. As the closing credits rolled, Angus said, "That really *was* cool. When we get home, I'm going to get some serious binoculars."

"Over my dead body," I said, and everyone groaned.

I awoke the next morning to my granddaughter's hungry howls. As I padded into Mieka and Greg's room with her, I noticed the glow of what looked suspiciously like dawn outside the windows. I crossed my fingers. If we were lucky, climatologist Tara Lavallee was going to have to do another 180 on her holiday-weekend forecast. Fifteen minutes later, when I took a noticeably heavier and happier Madeleine from her mother's arms and headed for the kitchen, sunshine was pouring through the skylight. The gods were smiling. It was going to be a banner day.

Over breakfast, we floated possibilities. After agonizing between the pull of two highly desirable options, Taylor went with Greg and the boys to fish, and Mieka, Madeleine, and I drove to Lebret to a teashop that was famous for its rhubarb pie and local crafts. When we met back at the cottage for lunch, everyone except Greg had caught their limit, and Mieka had spent a week's profits from her business on hand-woven willow picnic baskets and placemats the colour of marigolds. That night we had a fish-fry, sucked in our breath with amazement at the fireworks, then came back inside to watch Eva Marie Saint and Cary Grant dangle from Mount Rushmore in *North by Northwest*. Eli and Angus decided they were up for a double feature and watched *Psycho* till two. Madeleine slept through the night again, and the next morning Madeleine's mother came to the breakfast table with the Mona Lisa smile of a woman savouring the pleasures of being well and truly loved.

Sunday was a blue and golden beach day, and we soaked up every blue and golden moment. At suppertime, Eli supervised a wiener roast at the outdoor fireplace, and that night we watched *Vertigo*.

On the other Hitchcock nights, my kids and I had second-guessed everything from hairstyles to characters' motivations, but from the first frames of *Vertigo* we were rapt, wholly absorbed by this tale of a broken man clinging to the belief that he could be saved by a woman and of the woman who was the tragic object of his obsession. Even Angus was silent as the final credits rolled, stunned by the desolation of *Vertigo*'s final image.

When Eli flicked the lights back on, Peter surprised me by asking if I wanted to go outside for some fresh air.

I grabbed a sweater, and we headed for the beach. As we walked out on the dock, I mulled over a dozen possible revelations, but Peter's words surprised me. "How certain are they that Kyle Morrissey killed Ariel?"

I stopped and turned to face him. "Where did that come from?"

"I'd just like to know if the police are sure they have the right guy." His tone was falsely casual. "I thought someone at NationTV might have given you some inside info."

"We pretaped last week's show, and I haven't talked to anyone at the station since Ariel was killed. Pete, you're not a 'Hard Copy' kind of guy. What's all this about?"

For a moment, the only sounds were the slap of water against the pilings under the dock and the bark of a dog somewhere along the shore.

"It's about Charlie Dowhanuik," Peter said finally. "Ever since I heard about Ariel, I haven't been able to get him out of my mind. We were never tight when we were in school. I always liked him, but he was so wild it was scary."

"That wildness worried his mother, too," I said. "She told me once that Charlie didn't have friends, he had fans.

Marnie thought other kids hung with Charlie just to see what he was going to do next."

Peter laughed. "Yeah, he did bring new meaning to the term 'living on the edge.' And most of the time it was a lot of fun to be around him. But sometimes he was just too intense." His eyes met mine. "Mum, he was always too intense about Ariel."

"And that's what's worrying you now?"

"He was crazy about her – crazy in both senses. Any bone-head would understand him loving her. Even in high school, Ariel was absolutely stellar, but Charlie was fanatical about her. I remember one time I ran into him at the mall. We were just shooting the breeze when Ariel walked by holding hands with a guy. It wasn't a big deal – just the usual girl-boy thing – but Charlie got this look like somebody had kicked him in the stomach. Then he said, 'Sometimes I think it would be easier if I was dead . . . or if she was.'"

I felt a chill, but I tried to sound reassuring. "Pete, every-thing in high school is hyper-intense. People grow up."

My son raked his hand through his hair. "I know, and I know Charlie sounds as if he really has it together. I listen to his show whenever I'm back in Regina. He seems like the coolest guy on the block, but . . ." Peter chopped the air with his hand. "But nothing," he said. "I'm suffering from Hitchcock overload. You're right. High school isn't real life. And Charlie got his happy ending. He and Ariel were a couple. He would have done anything for her."

In the lake's dark waters, the moon's reflection was a vortex. The final lines of the poem Charlie had recited on-air the day of Ariel's death pressed upon my consciousness with such urgency that I spoke them aloud: "Dig them the deepest well,/Still it's not deep enough/To drink the moon from."

Peter frowned. "What's that?"

"Just a line from a poem."

Pete grinned ruefully. "If I've driven you to poetry, it's time to change the subject. What do you think about going back to the house and cracking open a cool one?"

"I think it's a terrific idea," I said. "This is the old Queen's birthday, and it should go out with a bang not a whimper."

Our family logged an album-full of Kodak moments before we went our separate ways at the end of the holiday weekend, but Monday night, as I crawled into my own bed in the city, the image that haunted me was one that existed only in my imagination. It was of Charlie Dowhanuik, heartsick and angry, watching the girl he loved walk away with another boy. When I finally drifted off to sleep, I was still puzzling over two linked and unsettling questions: How much did Charlie know about Ariel's pregnancy, and when did he know it?

I awakened the next morning to the sound of the phone ringing. When I picked up the receiver and heard Howard Dowhanuik's *basso profundo*, I began to wonder about telepathy. As always, Howard wasted no time on niceties. "That priest who's staying at Charlie's house called. He says you've been checking up on us."

"It's a good thing I took the initiative," I said. "Otherwise I never would have discovered that you and Charlie were in Toronto."

"I gather from the frosty reception I'm getting now that you're pissed off because I didn't consult you."

"I'm not pissed off," I said. "Just confused. Howard, what are you and Charlie doing visiting Marnie?"

When he answered, the bravura was gone. "My son wanted his mother."

"Is Marnie capable of . . . ?"

He cut me off. "Marnie's capable of nothing. She has to be fed. She wears a diaper. When she laughs, she shits herself."

I had known him for twenty seven years, and I thought I knew the full range of his anger: faked indignation at an opponent's attack; icy fury when a jab hit home; withering disdain for those he believed had betrayed him. But the wrath in his voice as he described his wife's condition came from a place I didn't recognize – it was rage at the very nature of existence.

It sucked the sense out of me, and my response was as empty of meaning as one of Livia Brook's New Age banalities. "But Charlie's finding something he needs there."

"Apparently," Howard said, dryly. He had never been easy with talk of emotion. He coughed to cover the awkwardness. "Jo, I didn't call to get into all that touchy-feely crap. I need you to do a little asking around at NationTV."

"For what?"

"Charlie wants to know more about this guy the police have picked up in connection with Ariel's murder."

"He can probably get most of what I know from checking the Internet," I said. "I'm sure the media here are working overtime to keep the curious informed."

"There's always stuff that isn't made public. You know that."

Remembering his pain about Marnie, I tried to keep the asperity out of my voice. "Howard, you must have a dozen cronies in the Crown Prosecutor's Office who can give you inside information."

"I don't want them to know I'm asking."

"This isn't a good idea," I said. "Nothing I find out about Kyle Morrissey is going to bring Charlie any comfort."

"Damn it, Jo. Don't give me a hard time. Just do it." Then Howard added a word he didn't often use with me. "Please."

"Okay," I said. "I'll ask around. What's your number there?"

"I'll call you."

The phone went dead. I stared at the blank display screen, aware that once again I'd been handed a task I could neither embrace or refuse. As I snapped on Willie's leash, I remembered how, on dismal mornings after Rose, my old golden retriever, died, I had clung to the thought that, come spring, my new dog and I would amble around the lake, taking time to smell the flowers and whatever else of interest came our way.

I looked into Willie's anxious eyes. "Time to hit the street, bud, but those flowers are going to have to wait."

When I arrived at the Political Science office, I noticed two things: the vase beside Ariel's picture was filled with daffodils, and Rosalie Norman was already at her desk. She was reading, but as soon as she heard my step she slapped her book shut. "Caught me," she said.

"Something steamy?" I asked.

"I wish," she said gloomily. She held up the book so I could see the cover. It was an ancient edition of *The Joy of Cooking*.

"I don't think reading Irma and Marion Rombauer is an indictable offence," I said. "Are you planning a special meal for Robert?"

"If only it were that easy," she said. "Joanne, I'm going to have to confess this to someone, sometime." She closed her eyes, and the words tumbled out. "I've never learned how to cook. I don't even know how to boil an egg."

"How did you get by all these years?"

"Mother. She was a born cook, and since she passed away, I've just had my main meal at noon here at the university, and warmed up a bowl of soup for supper." Rosalie handed me *The Joy of Cooking*. "Mother swore by this, but it was published in 1951. Do you think it's still okay?"

I looked at the page Rosalie had marked. The heading was "Sweetbreads, Brains, Kidneys, Liver, Heart, Tongue, Oxtails, etc.," and Irma and Marion Rombauer recommended their use for girls who knew there was no substitute for a juicy steak or a glistening roast but whose slenderized pocket-books made them feel "as broke as the ten commandments."

"Well?" Her voice was anxious.

"The prose is a little dated," I said, "but the recipes look good. What kind of meal does Robert like?"

"Anything that starts with a slab of meat and ends with whipped cream."

I handed the cookbook back to her. "Let the Rombauers be your guides," I said. "You couldn't make a better choice. Now, I'd better move along. This is my first day with Ariel's class."

Rosalie winced, but she squared her shoulders, obviously determined to soldier on. "Good news there, at least," she said. "There was a copy of *Political Perspectives* propped outside the office door when I arrived this morning. It's in your mailbox."

When I checked the front page, I saw that the name and office number were Ariel Warren's. I turned back to Rosalie. "No note?"

"Not if there isn't one inside."

I leafed through the book. It was heavily annotated, but there was nothing explaining where it had come from. I told Rosalie I'd see her later and headed for the office of the one person who might be able to shed light on the mystery, but when I rapped on Kevin Coyle's door there was no answer. It was the first time in two years that he hadn't been there when I'd stopped by. As I headed for Ariel's class with the folder containing her class list and syllabus in my hand, I was uneasy. The world was out of joint, and when I walked into Ariel's classroom, nothing I saw suggested an imminent return to harmony.

In a configuration that was as rare as it was disturbing, all the women were sitting on one side of the room, all the men on the other. The room was layered with emotions: tension, confusion, and grief. There was nothing to gain by adding my own feelings to the mix.

I kept my approach coolly academic. I introduced myself, explained that I'd be teaching the rest of the course, then wrote my name, office and phone numbers, and e-mail address on the board. When I turned to face the students again, they were bent over their notebooks, writing. We were back on track, and I wasn't about to take any chances.

"I understand from your syllabus that your mid-term is this Thursday. Here's what you'll need to know." An hour and ten minutes later, I had given them a lecture that was comprehensive and deadly boring. It was what an Australian academic I knew referred to derisively as "a chalk and talk class," but it had done the job. Immersed in a familiar ritual, the students relaxed. As the class ended and they began throwing their notebooks and texts into their backpacks, the tension knotting my shoulders eased. Ariel's Political Science 101 class and I were on our way.

Relieved, I turned to clean the boards and discovered that I'd exhaled too soon. Solange Levy was waiting in the hall outside the door. She was wearing a black T-shirt, jeans, and her trademark Converse high-tops. Her henna-burnished hair was slicked back from her face. It had been only three days since Ariel's death, but Solange, whose marathon bike rides had kept her strikingly fit, already had the gaunt, smouldering-eyed look of heroin chic once prized by fashion photographers.

"It's okay to come in?" She brushed past me without waiting for an answer. "I have an announcement about Ariel." The room fell silent. Solange raised a slender arm towards the side of the room where the men had been seated. "Go, if you wish," she said. Her action was both stunningly rude and uncharacteristic. Solange's deeply felt feminism had never affected her rapport with male students. The men's faces hardened, but none of them left.

For a beat, Solange stared at them, then she gave them a curious half-smile. "I've set up a Web page for Ariel on the university's site. There's a guest book for anyone who wishes to share her memories of our friend." She took a step towards the women's side of the class, then chalked the page's URL on the blackboard. "If you have thoughts about the manner of Ariel's death, don't feel constrained about expressing them." She reached into her purse and pulled out a plastic bag; it was filled with the kind of round metal lapel pins I was familiar with from political campaigns. Without explanation, Solange began distributing them to the women. When one of the men held out his hand, she hesitated, shrugged, and gave him one. The other men in the class approached her, and she gave them pins, too.

Finally, it was my turn. The design on the pin was striking: a stylized line drawing of a sunflower on a black background. Across the upper arc of the circle the words "Never Forget" were inscribed in flowing script. When I put the pin on, the sharp metal point pricked my finger. I watched numbly as a delicate tracery of blood flowed from the stem of the sunflower onto the white silk of my new summer blouse.

CHAPTER

6

When I got back to my office, Kevin Coyle was sitting behind my desk, staring at my computer.

"You should lock your door," he said. "Vermin are afoot."

"So it would seem," I said. I dropped my books on the top of the filing cabinet and sat down in the chair opposite him. It was the chair reserved for students, and a person of sensibility would have taken the hint. Kevin didn't. He had replaced the missing lens in his Coke-bottle horn-rims. The Dali-esque look was gone, but his magnified gaze was still unsettling.

"There's new madness," he said. Then, spotting the pin on my blouse, he leaned across the desk and peered at it. As he absorbed the pin's message, his face grew grim. "More trouble for me," he muttered. "And I suppose you've heard those women have got themselves some kind of propaganda space on the machine." He thumped my monitor to identify the source of his latest crisis, then handed me a slip of paper with a Web-site address. "Here's where they are, but I need you to show me how to find them."

"Kevin, have you ever even *turned on* a computer?"

"Why would I?" he barked.

I stared at him. "Because as of five years ago, all the members of this department were supposed to be computer literate; because Rosalie was handling stuff for you that you should have been handling for yourself years ago; because we all have to submit our grades electronically now; and if you win your appeal, you're going to have to . . ."

He scowled at me. "All right," he said. "I'm ready to learn. As the Buddhists say, 'Leap and the net will appear.'"

"And I'm the net," I said.

He nodded. "I'll bring you coffee. You can find the propaganda while I'm gone."

I moved to my own chair, turned on the computer, and waited.

When Kevin came back, he handed me the orange and brown striped mug and examined the screen. "The information isn't there."

"Kevin, if *I* bring up the Web site for you, there's no leap."

He dragged the student chair over so it was beside mine. "Okay," he said. "Teach me."

For someone who had spent years railing against computers as the handiwork of the devil, Kevin Coyle proved to be a surprisingly quick student.

He made a few false starts, but within minutes the Web site appeared. It was striking: a black screen with a yellow dot glowing in the lower left corner. As I watched, the dot etched a graceful sunflower. It was an image I had introduced myself, yet I felt a stab of anger at this fresh proof that my private memory had suddenly become public property. The sunflower vanished, and Ariel's name flowed across the screen, followed by the dates of her birth and death. There were some photos and, in the guest book, a dozen e-mailed memories. All grew out of the nine brief months Ariel had taught at the university. Solange had not cast her net wide, and even a quick glance revealed that the Web site had the sweetly elegaic flavour of a high-school yearbook.

I turned to Kevin. "Perfectly innocuous," I said. "Looks like you lost your status as the last of the Luddites for nothing."

Kevin stabbed at the computer screen with his forefinger. "What are those?"

"Just links to other sites that may be of interest to people who cared about Ariel."

"How's that one connected to her?" he asked, pointing to a site with the address "redridinghood."

"Easy enough to find out," I said. I clicked on the word "redridinghood," and swivelled my chair to face him. "Even a child can do it," I said.

He was staring at the monitor, transfixed. "That's not for children," he said. I followed his gaze. The picture filling the screen was of a woman: her gender was the only fact a viewer could know for sure. Violence had obliterated her other distinguishing characteristics. The hair surrounding her face was a rusty mat of dried blood. It was impossible to tell if, in life, she had been a blonde, brunette, or redhead. Whether she had been pretty or plain was anyone's guess. Someone had pounded her face into the livid pulpiness of a rotted eggplant. Her naked body had been hacked at, her breasts severed, her genitals slashed.

I scrolled down the page to see if there was explanatory text.

The quotation that appeared on my screen was evocative:

"... the better to eat you with my dear"
This site is devoted to all the Red Riding Hoods – to all the women who have been devoured by the wolves that walk among us.

I shuddered.

"Someone just walked over your grave," Kevin said absently. He took the mouse and clicked on "NEXT." There was page after page, each with a photo of the murdered woman; each had been taken from a different angle, but they were all equally blood-drenched and appalling. The worst picture was the last because, as the caption indicated, it had been taken just hours before the woman died. The photo recorded what must have been a pleasant moment for her: a good-looking young man wearing an Armani suit, a Santa Claus hat, and the punchy look of the slightly drunk was raising a glass to her.

Red Riding Hood #1 wasn't looking at him; she was gazing at the camera with a steadiness that suggested a woman who wasn't easily deflected by party tricks. Her short black hair had been brushed back sleekly from her heart-shaped face, and a silvery T-shirt glittered through the opening of her smart black jacket. The outfit was festive yet professional, exactly the kind of outfit *Marie Claire* or *Cosmopolitan* or *Flare* would suggest a successful woman should wear to a holiday gathering at the end of a business day. By anyone's criteria, Red Riding Hood #1 was a success. A newly minted MBA from Queen's University, her curriculum vitae was so impressive that, the caption said, she had created the job she wanted with a venerable Bay Street brokerage firm and had landed it after one interview. The photograph had been taken at her company's traditional supper gathering on the last working day before the Christmas break. After the firm's partners sang "God Rest Ye, Merry Gentlemen," the carol which, for seven decades, had been the signal that the company Christmas party was at an end, the good-looking young man in the Santa cap followed Red Riding Hood #1 home to her shining new condo in the Annex, and raped and murdered her.

Another click took us to Red Riding Hood #2, a real-estate agent with a client who had said he was keen on finding a property that could be a real hideaway. Red Riding Hood #3 was a shift worker in a plant that made pasta; Red Riding Hood #4 was a kindergarten teacher; Red Riding Hood #5 had a husband who couldn't live without her. In all, there were a dozen grim little folk tales, each with its own stomach-churning, mind-numbing illustration.

The last click took us to a familiar passage. It was the moral Charles Perrault had appended to his version of Little Red Riding Hood three hundred years earlier:

From this story one learns that children,
Especially young girls,
Pretty, well-bred, and genteel,
Are wrong to listen to just anyone,
And it's not at all strange,
If a wolf ends up eating them.
I say a wolf, but not all wolves
Are exactly the same.
Some are perfectly charming,
Not loud, brutal or angry,
But tame, pleasant, and gentle,
Following young ladies
Right into their homes, into their chambers,
But watch out if you haven't learned that tame wolves
Are the most dangerous of all.

When I read our children the story, I'd always stopped before I came to Perrault's moral. I hadn't wanted my daughter to grow up believing that men were the enemy; I hadn't wanted my sons to grow up seeing themselves as predators to be feared. I thought about my granddaughter, a girl whose smiles went everywhere, and wondered whether the world into which Madeleine had been born would allow for such a benign omission.

I braced myself for a blast of blowtorch rhetoric from Kevin, but it didn't come. He was as shaken as I was. "Unspeakable," he said. His hugely magnified eyes were anxious. "But this horror show is only going to make things worse. Not just for me," he added quickly, "for all of us."

I pushed my chair away from the desk and stood up.

"Are you bailing out on me?" Kevin asked.

"No," I said. "We'll sink or swim together on this one. I'm going to ask Solange to remove the link to 'Red Riding Hood' from her Web site."

The door to Solange's office was open. She had visitors: Livia Brook was there, her poppy shawl loosely knotted over a white turtleneck, and – bad luck for me – Ann Vogel was there, too. Six months earlier, Ann had claimed a new identity as Naama. Now it appeared she had metamorphosed again. As Naama, she had been a woman who flowed: shoulder-length hair that streamed behind her, diaphanous, ankle-length skirts and loosely cut, filmy blouses that floated as she walked through the halls. Now her hair was henna-burnished and buzzed into a Joan of Arc cut, and she was wearing jeans, a T-shirt, and Converse high-tops. The attempt to ape Solange was an act of such teenage hero worship, I was embarrassed for both women, but Ann was beyond shame.

When she spotted me, her irises became pinpoints of loathing. "This is a private meeting," she said.

"Then I won't intrude," I said. I smiled at Livia and walked over to Solange. "When you're free," I said, "I'd like to talk to you about your Web site."

Solange nodded assent, but Ann Vogel wasn't about to give anyone a graceful compromise. "The women in our group have no secrets from one another," she said tightly, "but, of course, you wouldn't understand about sisterhood."

"I'm all for sorority," I said. "I'm just not a big fan of hate groups. Incidentally, Ann, if I were you, I'd let the buzz cut grow out. I'm not sure the paramilitary look works for you."

"You really are a bitch, Joanne." She enunciated each word separately, Bette Davis style.

Solange raised a finger to silence her. "Joanne is not our enemy," she said. She turned towards me; the bruised-eye pain of her gaze made it difficult not to look away. "You have a concern about the Web site?" she said. The words seemed pulled from her, as if even articulating a sentence caused her anguish. I thought of the French phrase *Elle vit à reculons*. She lives reluctantly.

It would have been unconscionable to add to her grief. "What *you've* done is perfect, Solange," I said. "The tributes to Ariel strike exactly the right note. It's the hot link to the 'Red Riding Hood' site that troubles me."

Ann was clearly furious. "Why should we listen to you? You've already sided against us once."

I tried to isolate her. "I've never had a quarrel with anyone but you," I said. "You used Kevin Coyle to forward your own agenda, and I don't want to see you doing the same thing with Ariel's death."

Solange's eyes grew wide. "Ariel's death must not be used," she said.

I could feel the momentum shifting to me, and I pressed ahead. "No," I agreed, "it mustn't. The night of the vigil, Molly Warren told me that what she feared more than anything was having Ariel's death politicized. This tragedy is deeply personal for all of us."

Ann's eyes glinted. I had linked the words "political" and "personal"; for a fanatical feminist the bait was as irresistible as catnip to a Siamese.

I hurried on before she could pounce. "I know the catechism," I said. "I know that the personal is political, but the whole purpose of the Web page is to let the people who cared about Ariel share their memories and their sense of loss. Later, we can think about larger implications, but the focus now should be on Ariel. Besides, linking her page to the 'Red Riding Hood' site is placing Ariel's death in a political context that might not even be accurate. Kyle Morrissey hasn't been charged with her murder. From what I've heard he may never be."

"What do you mean?" Livia said.

"I mean the case is weak," I said. "It's possible that Ariel was killed by someone else. For all we know the murderer is a woman."

Ann took a step towards me. Her fists were clenched, and she was shaking with rage. "Get out," she said.

We were on the edge of real ugliness, but Livia stepped between us. She was pale, but in control. "Joanne, we'll reconsider the 'Red Riding Hood' hot link. I'll make certain that we give your suggestion a fair hearing."

"But I can't stick around to argue my own case."

Livia took my arm and led me out into the hall. When she spoke her voice was low and intimate. "Given the history you share with some of the women who created the Web site, perhaps it would be best to let them discuss it privately. Joanne, you know this department is all I have now. Trust me to do the right thing." She leaned forward and kissed my cheek.

Whether it was the poignant reference to our shared past, the familiar smell of Pears soap, or the brush of cool silk I felt when her poppy shawl touched my arm, I was drawn into her orbit. "All right," I said, "I'll trust you."

Kevin was still hunched over my computer when I got back. When he heard my step, he started. "Well . . . ?"

"They're going to discuss it," I said.

"What do you think our chances are?"

I cringed at being included in Kevin's possessive pronoun, but I smiled at him. "Livia says we have to trust her. And I do."

He scowled. "Well, I don't. Why would I trust a woman who has wanted my head on a plate for two years?" He shrugged. "You've just given me all the justification I need for spending some of my dwindling savings on surveillance."

"You're going to *hire* somebody?"

"Good God, no. I'm going to buy a computer. I'll find it easier to trust those handmaidens of the victim culture if I can keep an eye on them." He started for the door, but when he came to the threshold he turned. "Thank you for being my net."

"You didn't need a net, just a push."

He grinned, revealing more silver fillings than I'd seen in twenty years. A man with ancient dental work, a lens held on by masking tape, a limitless supply of white, short-sleeved polyester shirts, and an uncertain future. My heart went out to him.

"Be careful, Kevin."

"In the computer store?"

"Everywhere," I said.

Alone in my office, I was edgy. I picked up the phone and dialled.

When I heard Ed Mariani's blithe greeting, I felt as if I'd re-established contact with the world as I knew it.

"Can I buy you lunch?" I asked.

"Only if you promise to bring along the latest photos of Madeleine at the lake."

"I haven't even taken the film in yet," I said.

"And you call yourself a grandmother," he said. "But I'll still eat lunch with you. Does noon at the Faculty Club suit?"

"Noon is fine," I said, "but let's go off-campus. I've had enough of this place."

"That sounds ominous."

"It is. Ed, have you seen that Web page Solange has created for Ariel?"

"I didn't even know it existed. I haven't been at the university since last week."

"Count your blessings," I said. "But I'd be grateful if you'd check it out and another site it's linked to: 'Red Riding Hood.'"

"'Red Riding Hood' – that's intriguing. You do know, don't you, that both Luciano Pavarotti and Charles Dickens are on record as saying they identified strongly with that little girl. I'm past the age for tripping through the woods with a picnic basket, but if it pleases you, I'll be more than happy to give the site a whirl. Now about lunch . . . have you got time for Druthers?"

"I do if you do," I said.

"I have all the time in the world," he said.

The comment was more than a pleasantry. The amount of time that elapsed between the placing of an order and the arrival of food at Druthers was legendary. So were the short fuses of the restaurant's father-and-son chefs. More than one patron's meal had ended abruptly when the father, hurling curses, exited through the restaurant's front door, and the son, also hurling curses, exited through the back door. But the menu was inventive, the food invariably excellent, and the atmosphere, when father and son were in accord, sublime.

That spring afternoon, as I walked through the front door of the old converted house in the Cathedral district, it appeared that Ed and I were in luck. James and James Junior, father and son, greeted me with smiles and ushered me to the cool peace of the Button Room, my favourite of the restaurant's three small dining rooms. The Button Room took its name from its walls, which were hung with framed shadow boxes filled with antique buttons of incredible variety: military buttons of shiny brass bearing the insignia of once-proud units; mourning buttons of jet or of hair taken from the head of the newly deceased and woven into stiff discs; tiny buttons of mother-of-pearl or satin that the fingers of eager bridegrooms had fumbled undone as they claimed their trembling brides. The linen at Druthers was always snowy, and the flowers, exotic. Today a single fuchsia orchid blazed in our bud vase.

Ed rose when he saw me. "I've ordered martinis," he said. "After seeing that Web site, I thought that we needed more than a Shirley Temple."

James Junior brought the martinis, ice blue with two olives apiece, handed us the menus and announced the specials: wild mushroom pâté; grilled tomato gazpacho, sweetbreads Druthers, mixed greens; coffee chocolate-chunk cookies.

I didn't even open the menu. First, the Rombauers and now Druthers. It was obvious that sweetbreads were in the air, and I never bucked synchronicity. Ed followed my lead.

After James Junior withdrew with our orders, Ed raised his glass. "To sanity," he said. "Although it appears to be fast disappearing from our troubled world. That 'Red Riding Hood' site is heartbreaking, Jo. To think of Ariel being one of that long, sad line . . ."

For a moment, we were both silent. Wrapped in our private thoughts, we sipped our martinis. They were excellent but ineffectual. The liquor burned, but it didn't wipe out the memory of that long, sad line of girls and women, and of Ariel among them.

Finally, Ed broke the silence.

"I have some news," he said. "Kyle Morrissey wasn't a stranger to Ariel. Val Massey called me this morning. He's working for the *Leader Post*, and he's been assigned to Ariel's story."

Val Massey was an old student of ours. "How's he doing?" I asked.

Ed smiled. "Dazzlingly. Bob Woodward in the making. At any rate, when he found out Kyle Morrissey had lived next door to Ariel . . ."

"Wait a minute," I said. "There's nothing next door to Charlie and Ariel's place but an X-rated video store."

Ed nodded. "EXXXOTICA. That's where Kyle lives, or at least lived until December when he ran into a little trouble with the police."

"The assault charge that went away," I said.

Ed raised an eyebrow. "And who's *your* source?"

"Rosalie's betrothed," I said. "And Detective Robert Hallam says this case doesn't feel right to him."

"That's pretty much Val's take, too," Ed said. "He's spent some time with Kyle's aunt, Ronnie. Apparently, there's something a little weird there, but Val says Ronnie is quite an advocate for her boy, and she's managed to convince Val that Kyle's only feelings towards Ariel were ones of gratitude."

"Gratitude for what?"

"Until December, Kyle worked at EXXXOTICA. It's the family business. Anyway, after Kyle's narrow escape, his aunt Ronnie decided that the kind of clientele who came in to rent triple-X movies, might not be creating an ideal milieu for her nephew, and that it might be wise to get Kyle out of harm's way."

"Good decision," I said.

"According to Val, it was," Ed agreed. "Kyle liked the job he found with the air-conditioning company. Incidentally, he had listed Ariel as one of his references. Apparently, she helped him find the place he moved into too. It's in those student apartments over on Kramer Boulevard."

I took a deep breath. "Ed, did Val mention the possibility

that Ariel's interest in Kyle might have been more than that of a friend?"

Ed stiffened. "I take it you have a reason for asking that question."

"I do," I said. "Mieka and I had a heart-to-heart at the lake. Ariel was pregnant when she died, and the father of her baby wasn't Charlie Dowhanuik."

"You're not suggesting that Kyle Morrissey . . . ?"

"I'm not suggesting anything," I said. "All I know is that Mieka believes that Ariel wasn't romantically involved with the father of her baby."

"An accident?" Ed said.

I shook my head. "A helping friend. And that opens the field to a number of possibilities. I wondered if Kyle Morrissey was one of them. I saw his photo in the paper. He's a good-looking man."

Ed gave me a small smile. "A bodybuilder, dark and beautiful, but not my type, and not Ariel's. According to Val, when it came to brains Kyle Morrissey was paddling in the shallow end of the gene pool."

"Not swift?"

"Not swift," Ed said. "And not 'helping friend' material. Ariel was a compassionate woman. If she thought Kyle Morrissey had been roughed up by the system, she would have done what she could to help him start over. That might have included helping him find a job and an apartment; it would *not* have included asking him to father her child." Ed ran his finger over the frilled edge of the catelaya bloom. "I'm no expert on these matters, but what I don't understand is why Ariel had to seek out anybody. She had it all: beauty, brains, grace. If she wanted to have a baby, why didn't she just wait for the right man and get one the old-fashioned way?"

"I think she felt she was running out of time," I said.

Ed frowned. "She was twenty-seven. You can't be talking about biological time."

"No," I said. "I think Ariel felt she might be running out of time to live the life she wanted."

"And Charlie Dowhanuik wasn't part of that life?"

"Apparently not."

At that moment, James Junior arrived with the wild mushroom pâté, and out of deference to the wizardry in the kitchen, Ed and I moved to lighter topics: the weekend at the lake, a wood sculpture Ed and Barry were having installed on their deck, Madeleine's perfection. But despite our banter, the martinis, a half-litre of Pinot Noir, and sweetbreads so succulent even the Rombauers couldn't have improved upon them, Ed's question hung in the air between us, a shadow at the feast.

When we left Druthers, Ed looked up at the high blue sky. "Given the morning we've put in, I suggest we both take an afternoon off," he said. "I'm going to make myself a pot of camomile, stretch out in the hammock, and get back to *À la recherche du temps perdu*."

"Do you know I've never managed to get past the first chapter of that book?"

"I've never made it past page three," Ed said cheerfully, "but on the first truly sweet day of May, I always try. It's my summer ritual. And how are you going to extract the joy from this glorious day?"

"Checking out someone else's remembrance of things past," I said. "I'm going to try to get Kyle Morrissey's aunt to talk to me."

The only parking space I could find was in front of the used-furniture mart. There was a special on inflatable furniture –

just in time for summer. I passed it up and continued down the street towards the video store.

The old lady was at her perch at the open window upstairs, and as soon as she saw me, she called out. "Nobody's home at the dead girl's house," she said, "but I know things you'll want to hear."

"What kinds of things?"

"Come up and find out," she said.

"I'll be right there," I said.

Not an errant weed or faded bloom marred the perky, girl-next-door charm of Ariel and Charlie's bungalow on Manitoba Street. As a house-minder, Father Hill's price was obviously beyond rubies. The lawn in front of EXXXOTICA could have used his ministrations. The dusty shoots that made their way through its hard-packed dirt were ready for extreme unction, but the woman down on her knees in front of the porn video store wasn't praying. She had a razor blade between her fingers and she was scraping at her front window. Someone had papered it with photocopies of the image I had seen on Ariel's Web page: the black background, the stylized sunflower, and the words "Never Forget."

The woman craned her neck to give me the once over. She was my age, with a mane of waist-length sun-streaked hair, a narrow face, close-set green eyes, the leathery tan of a rodeo rider, and an unusually large Adam's apple. She was wearing jeans, a very brief white halter top, and a look of abject disgust. She tapped at the glass with the razor blade. "As if I ever could forget," she said in a voice that could have been either an alto or a baritone. "Look at the mess they made of my window."

I thought the words had been rhetorical, but she was being literal. She waved the razor blade in a gesture of frustration. "I said, *look at my window*. My grandmother recognized you. She watches your show every Saturday night. Look at my window, so you can tell your audience what you saw."

"Ms. . . ."

"It's Ronnie. Ronnie Morrissey. My grandmother's name is Bebe, and she's a big fan of your show."

"Then she knows we don't do investigative journalism. We just talk about politics. I'm not even a reporter. I teach at the university."

"But *you're on TV.*" She paused to let the words sink in. In the real world, the distinction I had made was irrelevant. "You know people who can help us get the truth out. My nephew didn't kill anybody. He couldn't kill anybody." She made a fist with one hand and punched the palm of the other. Her nails were nicely shaped and painted a shimmering mauve, but not even her careful manicure could disguise the fact that Ronnie Morrissey's hands were meathooks. "Do you have kids?" she asked.

"Four," I said.

"I was never blessed," she said, "but I raised Kyle like he was my own. I know what he's capable of doing, good or bad. If the cops called me and said Kyle got into a fight with someone who called him a dirty name or if they said he'd knocked back a half-dozen beers and relieved himself in the middle of Albert Street, I wouldn't be happy, but I'd believe them. I don't believe this, not for a single, solitary minute." She knitted her brow. "Any of your kids boys?"

"Two," I said. "One of them's twenty-four; the other's seventeen."

"Then you know how it is," she said huskily. "Now do me a favour and check out what they did to my window."

Ronnie hadn't made much headway with her cleanup. The area she had cleared was the size of a TV screen in a motel room, and there were still bits of black paper clinging to the glass, but I leaned forward obediently. Inside was a display of xxx movies with titles like *Extreme Cat Fights*, *Operation Penetration*, and *Come Gargling Sluts*. Framed by the sombre black of Ariel's poster with its by-now familiar plea, the movie titles had a certain film noir eloquence.

"Quite the mess, eh?" Ronnie looked at her razor blade thoughtfully. "And they've done this to his apartment and to the locker at the place where he works. Where he *worked*," she corrected herself. "They put him on unpaid leave. An innocent man, but that doesn't mean a darn thing any more. The police are still hassling him, too. Kyle doesn't react well to pressure, so last night we packed up his stuff and moved him back here. It's a darn shame – he was so proud of being independent. Look, Ms. Kilbourn, I'd better get back to my scraping. Bebe will fill you in, but you get it straight." She cupped her hands around her mouth and shouted up at the old woman in the window. "I'm sending her up, Bebe."

"I'm ready for her," Bebe shouted back.

As Ronnie led me down the three steps that took us into EXXXOTICA, I wondered whether I was ready for Bebe. Convex security mirrors had been installed in the area around the cash register, and as Ronnie and I passed them, I caught sight of our reflections: two distorted funhouse women entering a distorted funhouse world. I'd been in some desolate places in my life, but my shoulders slumped under the weight of the store's dingy misery. The room was long and narrow, and the light that made it past the handbills the Friends of Ariel had pasted on the front window was murky.

To reach the door that led to the living quarters, we had to navigate our way through racks of videos which offered the voyeur a smorgasbord of sexual delights: man with woman, man with several women, women together, men together, men with young girls, men with young boys. For the adventurer, there were dominatrixes with whips and dungeons,

animals who were more than men's best friends, and oppor
tunities galore to revel in the joys of leather, chains, masks,
uniforms, adult-sized baby clothes, and golden cascades.

Ronnie paid the videos no heed, but I did, and the fact that
the people who rented them lived in my city, shovelled snow
from their sidewalks, walked past me in the park, and stood
beside me in the checkout counter at the grocery store gave
me pause. It was *bizarro mondo* out there, which might have
explained the complex system of locks that had been
installed on the door that separated the store from the
house's living quarters. Magician-like, Ronnie pulled a ring
of keys from inside her halter top and opened the locks. The
world on the other side of the door was reassuringly normal:
a small entranceway with a floor of terra cotta Mexican tiles,
a telephone table, and wallpaper with a vaguely Navajo
pattern in sand, mango, and turquoise.

"Up the stairs and straight ahead, you can't miss it,"
Ronnie said, then she abandoned me.

Later, I came to realize that the walls of Bebe's room were
painted a soft dove grey, but my first impression was of
retina-searing pink. Bebe, as it turned out, was not simply a
watchful neighbour. She was an entrepreneur, and her business was reclaiming and refurbishing Barbie dolls. It was
impossible to calculate at a glance the number of Barbies in
her sunny front room, but it must have been in the hun-
dreds. Hair braided into perky cornrows, teased into airy
beehives, swept into chic chignons, or twirled into ringlets,
Bebe's battalions of Barbies were marshalled on every flat
surface, poised to tackle the many roles of women at the
beginning of the new millennium. But whether they were
headed for the bike path, the ball, the board meeting, or the
birthing room, all of Bebe's Barbies were sallying forth in
outfits crocheted from the same durable nylon yarn in the
same eye-popping shade of bubble-gum pink.

Bebe was pretty sassy herself. She was wearing sequinned tennis shoes, white slacks, and a white sweatshirt with the legend "I Drove the Alaska Highway." Her hair was dandelion fluff, she had a dab of cerise rouge on the wizened apple of each cheek, and her eyes were the blue of a distant sky. She was very, very old.

"I'm ninety-five," she said. "Might as well get the question marks out of the way so you can pay attention to what I'm saying."

"Good policy," I said, wishing Ronnie shared her grandmother's candour.

Bebe indicated the chair opposite her. "Take a load off your feet," she said. "Though it's not as much of a load as I'd have thought seeing you on TV. I've heard it said the camera adds ten pounds. That must be true."

As she watched me take the seat she had assigned me, her eyes never left my face, but the crochet hook in her hands kept flying. "I recognized you the other day. That's why I waved. I wanted you to go on TV and tell the country that Kyle is innocent, but you didn't come in. You should have. That show you did Saturday night was as soft as boiled turnips. 'What Would Queen Victoria Think of Today's Canada?' Queen Victoria wouldn't give a damn, and neither did you. I was watching your face, Joanne Kilbourn. You knew that show was mush."

"We pretaped it, so we could get away for the holiday weekend," I said meekly.

Her crochet hook sped on, leaving behind it the gently undulating flares of the skirt for an evening gown. "I told Ronnie that's what you done," she said. "So can we expect more of the same on this week's show?"

"There is no show this week," I said. "We're through for the season."

"Then how can you tell the country that Kyle is innocent?"

"Is he?" I asked.

Her old chin jutted out defiantly. "As innocent as you are."

I leaned towards her. "Then tell me what I need to know," I said.

"Kyle didn't kill Ariel Warren," she said. "They were friends. He brought her up here to meet me. It took me five seconds to cipher out the relationship." She lowered her voice. "Kyle's not much in the brains department, but he's got enough brains to know that Ariel Warren was out of his league."

"He could have found that frustrating," I said.

"Coulda, woulda, shoulda," she snapped. "Useless words." The crochet hook flashed angrily. "The point is he didn't. Didn't find it frustrating. Didn't kill her. Case closed."

It was time to try another tack. I leaned forward and peered out Bebe's window. "You have a good view of the street up here," I said.

"I see everything," she said flatly. "And I've got the scrapbooks to prove it. Look at this." She pulled a scrapbook from a pile beside her and handed it to me. "Open it for a surprise," she said.

The book was filled with newspaper clippings of people who would have considered themselves movers and shakers in our small city. Beside each picture was a list of xxx movie titles.

"I read the *Leader Post*, cover to cover, every day." Bebe explained. "When I spot a photo of one of our customers, I cut it out. Then at night I get out the rental book and I write down what they rented. You never know when something like that might come in handy."

I closed the scrapbook and looked at her steadily.

She read my gaze. "But we're not here to talk about that, are we? Today is about Kyle. As usual the cops have got their blinders on. There's a lot likelier possibilities than our boy but, of course, nobody's ever accused the cops of being able to take in the big picture." Her mouth snapped shut, defying me to disagree.

"I need more than your opinion, Bebe," I said.

"I've got more than my opinion. I could see every move she made. And the one she lived with, too," she added triumphantly.

"Charlie."

The hook stopped, and the old blue eyes looked at me with real interest. "Charlie," she repeated. "So that's his name. I never did know it. He kept to himself – not that you'd blame him with that face. The only time he went out was in the afternoons – I guess that's when he worked."

I took a deep breath. It was time to ask the question that had been nagging at me from the moment I saw the dying tomato plants on the kitchen table of the house next door. "Bebe, when was the last time you saw Ariel?"

She didn't hesitate. "Two weeks ago Tuesday," she said, rosy with the excitement of a person who had a humdinger of a story to tell. "About this time of day. Usually, you can set your clock by that guy with the face, but that day he came home early. He went inside. He wasn't there long, then she came out, and Charlie was chasing after her. He was kind of crying and yelling at the same time."

"Could you hear what he said?"

Her old head bobbed vigorously. "I had to lean out the window to pick it up clearly, but I heard every word, and I wished I hadn't. I don't like to see a man act like a whiny kid, and that's how he acted." She raised her voice in a falsetto. "'Don't leave me. I'll do anything. I'll be anything. Just stay.'" Bebe made a moue of disgust, and resumed her normal tone. "You would have thought he'd have more pride," she said, "especially with another man there, listening to every word."

I was baffled. "Where did the other man come from?"

"He was in the house with Ariel when that Charlie came home early." She stopped crocheting, pursed her lips thoughtfully, and raised the little party dress in the air. "Needs another flounce, don't you think?"

"A dress can't have too many flounces," I said.

Bebe narrowed her eyes at me. "You think I don't know you're making fun, but I do."

"I'm sorry," I said.

"No, you're not. You're worried if you get my dander up, I won't finish my story, but I will. It's too good a story *not* to finish. Now," she said, "what I surmise is this – Charlie walked in and caught Ariel and her new boyfriend doing what comes naturally."

"Having sex," I said.

She rolled her eyes and tweaked her thumb and forefinger over her lips in a buttoning gesture.

"All right," I said. "You don't have to be explicit. Had you ever seen the man before?"

"Just that once, but I'll never forget him." Her eyes sparked with lust. "A magnificent-looking man – like an African prince."

"He was black?"

"As the ace of spades," she said. "And if the police had any brains at all, they'd be out looking for him and for that one with the birthmark and they'd be leaving Kyle alone." She jerked her crochet hook free of the brilliantly pink yarn. The little dress was complete, and the interview was over. I picked up my purse and stood up.

Bebe waggled her finger at me. "Make sure you pass along what I told you to someone who can get it on the air."

"I appreciate your seeing me," I said.

Her expression grew shrewd. "Do you want to show your appreciation?"

I opened my bag. "I don't have much cash with me. Could I write you a cheque?"

"I don't want your money. I want Barbies." She pointed to a large wicker basket beside her chair. It was half filled with dolls, naked but with hair newly washed and fingers tipped with fresh pink nail polish. "You get these from garage sales. Of course, they're not like this when I get them. They're a mess, but I clean them up, and make their little outfits. I'll pay you two bucks a doll – no more, or my profits get eaten up. Be sure to check their feet. That's where the puppies chew, and I can't sell a doll if the toes are chewed off.

"I'm not very good at garage sales. I never seem to find the bargains."

"Even a blind pig gets an acorn once in a while," she said. "Give it a try."

"All right," I said. "I'll give it a try."

She picked up a fresh skein of yarn. "Now tell me again what you're going to do."

"I'm going to hit the garage sales and look for Barbies. I won't pay more than two bucks apiece, and I'll check their feet to make sure they're not chewed."

Bebe Morrissey stared at me in disbelief. "Jesus Christ and all the saints of heaven," she said. "How did you ever get a job teaching at a university? What you're going to do, Joanne Kilbourn, is go to your friends at NationTV and tell them to start sniffing around the African prince and the guy with the birthmark. And you're going to tell them to leave our Kyle alone."

CHAPTER

7

We own the last swimming pool in our neighbourhood. Savvy people, sick of summers plagued by sluggish pumps, cracked tiles, clogged filters, and four-figure bills for chemicals, have had their pools filled in. More than once, as I've opened the envelope from Valhalla Pool Service, I've considered them wise, but Taylor loves to swim. She is not a natural mermaid. Her body is small and dense, but she fights gravity and churns through the water with such antic joy that every spring we pull off the pool cover and begin again. And because she is too young to swim alone, more often than not I struggle into my shapeless old suit and join her.

That Tuesday afternoon, there was no altruism in my decision to take the plunge. By the time I got back from visiting EXXXOTICA, my head was reeling from the aftershocks of a martini and wine at lunch and a day's worth of information that had wrapped itself around my brain and wouldn't let go. A big-time headache was on its way, and I was counting on hydrotherapy to banish it.

Ed Mariani had been wise to dig out his Proust. It *was* a sweet spring day. The lemony afternoon sun was warm, and the air was heavy with the scent of lilacs. It was a day to swim and, apparently, a day to bask. Willie followed us down to the pool and, as soon as he'd settled in at poolside, Taylor's cats, Bruce and Benny, streaked out of the house and took their places across the pool where they could catch a few rays and keep an eye on him.

After fifteen minutes, the water began to do its magic. With every lap, the tension loosened its grip on my temples; by the time Taylor, tired of paddling alone, began to swim beside me so we could chat, I was ready to keep up my end of the conversation.

"There's a meeting tomorrow for the parent-volunteers before we go on our field trip to the Legislature," she said.

"T, when our kids were little, I just about lived at the Legislature. I don't think I need to be oriented."

She duck-dived and swam a few strokes underwater, conveniently out of earshot. When she surfaced, she was ready. "There may be stuff you don't know."

"Try me."

She dipped under and came up, showering drops. "What's the building made out of?"

"Italian marble."

She bobbed back under, and came up with a new question. "How many Members of the Legislative Assembly are there?"

"Fifty-eight."

Now it was a game. This time she swam underwater to the end of the pool. "What does the Speaker do?" she asked breathlessly.

"Keeps things moving along; keeps the members in line."

"Okay," she said. "I guess you know enough." As suddenly as if a cloud had passed over it, the joy went out of her face. "Have the police caught the man who killed Ariel?" she asked.

"Not yet," I said.

"But they *are* going to catch him." The water beading her eyelashes made her look like a frightened naiad.

"Taylor, what's making you so scared?"

"I don't know," she said. "I just remembered how that woman at the vigil said men had to be stopped or they'd kill us all."

"I don't remember anyone saying that."

Taylor swiped her nose with the back of her hand. "You weren't there. You were talking into the microphone. It was that lady with the flowers on her shawl . . ."

"Livia Brook."

She nodded. "Livia said it to the woman you don't like – the one who told us that men couldn't come to the vigil."

She shivered; whether it was from the power of the memory or the chill of the water I couldn't tell. I put my arm around her shoulder. "Time to get out," I said. "But Taylor, I don't want you to worry about this any more. Everyone was upset the other night. People said things they didn't mean. No one's going to hurt you."

"Or you." Her tone was urgent. "Or Madeleine or Mieka."

"No one is going to hurt any of us," I said. "There isn't an enemy out there."

"Good." She tried a small smile. "Can I stay in the pool a little bit longer?"

"Nope, your lips are turning blue, and you know the rule."

"When lips are blue, the swim is through," she said morosely.

"You've got it," I said. "Now, I'll race you to the house."

We grabbed our towels and started to sprint towards the deck. We were halfway across the lawn when Angus and Eli strutted out the back door. It was obvious at a glance that Taylor and I were getting a dress rehearsal of the grad outfits:

blindingly white dress shirts, subdued but deadly ties, sports jackets and slacks that still dangled price tags, real shoes.

The boys struck *GQ* poses. "So do you think Brad Pitt should pack it in?" My son's words were confident, even cocky, but his eyes were anxious.

"Brad's lucky he lives in a two-income household," I said. "You guys are dynamite." It was no exaggeration. Angus's resemblance to his father was so striking I could feel my throat close, and Eli looked both handsome and uncharacteristically assured. Alex's nephew had not had an easy life, but as I looked at him that afternoon it was almost possible to believe that all the valedictory-speech clichés about new dreams and new lives might prove to be true.

The moment was too precious to lose. "Let me get the camera," I said.

They groaned, but they pulled out their combs.

As soon as I had the boys posed in front of the prettiest of our lilac bushes, Taylor dropped her towel, and squeezed in between them. "This is so much fun," she said.

By the time we'd snapped photos of every permutation and combination of the boys, Taylor, Willie, and the cats, we had used up a whole roll of film, and it *had* been fun. Too much fun to keep to ourselves. On our way back inside, I touched Eli's arm.

"Let's call your uncle," I said. "Tell him what we've been up to. He should be a part of all this."

Alex picked up on the first ring. "No civil servants listening in," he said when he heard my voice. "You can be as brazen as you like."

"Brazen will have to wait," I said. "Right now, I'm standing with a shivering seven-year-old and two young men in extremely expensive new sports jackets. We've just taken some world-class pictures, and we thought you might want to hear about them."

"I wish I was there," he said.

"So do I. But having Taylor describe the scene will be almost as good."

Taylor had a deft hand with narrative, and she described the photo session in meticulous detail; she also told Alex about Florence Nightingale and about how she, herself, got to sleep with Madeleine all three nights when we were at the lake. When Angus finally wrested the phone from her, she ran upstairs to get changed. The boys gave Alex separate but equal play-by-plays of their team's last three ball games. When Eli gave the phone back to me, he was grinning. "My uncle says he's proud of me."

"He has every reason to be," I said. "Now, you guys vamoose. It's my turn."

Alex seemed relaxed and happy. "The boys sound good," he said.

"They are good."

"Anything new with you?"

"I'm one of the parents going on the tour of the Legislature with Taylor's class on Friday. There's an orientation meeting tomorrow which I'm skipping."

"Tell Taylor that if she needs back-up to keep you on the straight and narrow, she can call on me."

"Taylor is unavailable," I said. "She finally decided to get out of her bathing suit. She was turning blue and her teeth were chattering, but till the end she maintained she wasn't the slightest bit cold."

"Stubborn like you."

"Inner-directed like me," I said.

He laughed. "I miss you. Ottawa's beautiful, but this isn't exactly my scene. Too many chiefs and not enough Indians. It's good to close my eyes and imagine you and the kids at home enjoying the spring." Suddenly, his tone became grave. "From what Bob Hallam tells me, though, it's not all blossoms and birdsong there. I take it there's a reason you haven't mentioned the Ariel Warren case."

"It wasn't because I didn't want to," I said. "But every time I weakened, I remembered all the work you'd put into that course you're giving. And Alex, you know as well as I do that there really isn't anything you can do from there but listen."

"Actually, Jo, I can do better than that. I can give you some advice to pass along to Howard Dowhanuik. Robert Hallam is very anxious to talk to Charlie. Unfortunately, both Charlie and his father seem to have pulled a disappearing act. As close as you and Howard are, I'm guessing you can reach him with a message. Tell him to bring Charlie back to Regina. There are a lot of questions that need answers, and Bob Hallam will go easier on Charlie if he's co-operative."

"I'll tell him," I said. "Alex, I miss you."

"Think how great it's going to be when we're together again."

"Do you remember what Napoleon wrote to Josephine?"

"We didn't do much French history at Standing Buffalo."

"Then it's time to complete your education. Napoleon said, 'I'm coming home in three days. Don't wash.'"

"So you'd like a three-day warning."

"I'll settle for three minutes," I said. "Time enough to warm the hemp oil."

When I hung up, I tried calling Good Shepherd Villa in Toronto. The woman I talked to told me Howard and Charlie left after Marnie had her supper, but she promised she'd have Howard call me. The mention of supper reminded me that I hadn't done anything about ours. I rummaged through the cupboard till I found a box of fusilli and put on a pot of water to boil. The kids liked pasta salad and I had some ham left over from the weekend.

Just as I dumped in the fusilli, Eli walked into the kitchen. He'd changed out of his sports jacket and slacks into the summer uniform of shorts and sandals. As he came over to the stove, I saw that his mood had changed, too. His exuberance had been replaced by a kind of tense watchfulness.

"I was just talking to your uncle," I said. "He's getting anxious to come home."

"It'll be good having him back." Eli's tone was flat.

"Something on your mind?" I said.

"Charlie D isn't doing his show today. He didn't finish it on Thursday and he didn't do it Friday or yesterday either. I got a buddy of mine to tape the show when we were at the lake. This guy named Troy is doing 'Heroes' now."

"And you're worried," I said.

"It's not just some stupid fan thing," Eli said defensively. "Charlie D has really helped me. Last fall, when I'd just started going to Dan Kasperski, I felt like such a loser. Not many kids are so messed up they have to see a shrink."

"Lots of kids are," I said. "And lots of adults."

Eli went to the drawer, took out a big metal spoon, came back and stirred the fusilli. As we talked, he kept his gaze on the boiling water. "I know that now," he said. "But it's because of Charlie D. I found 'Heroes' by accident. I was looking for some hard rock and all of a sudden there was Charlie D talking about how the first law of Buddhism is that life is suffering." He turned to me. "Can you imagine how great it felt to find out that I wasn't a freak? That it was the same for everybody?"

"I can imagine; in fact, I can remember."

His obsidian eyes widened. "You felt that way, too?"

"I felt that way, too."

"Maybe that's why you're so nice now."

"Thanks," I said.

"It's true. And it's because of what Charlie D says. Once

you know that everybody's suffering, you can get past your own skin, and that's when the fun begins."

"He's right," I said.

"It worked for me." Eli's voice rose with excitement. "As soon as I realized that everybody had garbage to deal with, things started getting better. When I told Dan, he said that a lot of his patients never missed 'Heroes.' Dan said life's a wild and wacky ride, and we all need a lot of guides to get us through. Then he said I could do a lot worse than to travel with Charlie D for a while."

"That's a pretty high recommendation," I said. "I don't know many psychiatrists, but I think Dan Kasperski is brilliant."

"So is Charlie D," Eli said. "Even my Popular Culture teacher, Ms. Cyr, thinks so. For the last couple of months, she's been letting our class listen to 'Ramblings.' That's the part at the beginning of the show where Charlie talks about the topic of the day. We've had some good discussions about what Charlie's said." Eli stirred the pasta mechanically. "He was so sharp and so funny, but lately he's gotten really bitter. One of the kids said Charlie sounded like he was going through a major meltdown."

"Did it sound that way to you?"

"Yeah." Eli made a gesture of helplessness. "You didn't have to be a shrink to know Charlie was in serious trouble. I can't describe it, but I've got some of the tapes. Ms. Cyr is letting me do my major project on Charlie's show."

"Could I listen to the tapes?"

"Sure. I'll get you some from the last couple of weeks and some from before so you can hear the difference."

"Good. And Eli, I can put your mind at rest about one thing. Nothing's happened to Charlie. He just had to get away for a while. He and his dad went to visit Charlie's mum in Toronto."

Eli's shoulders slumped with relief. "I was afraid he might have tried to kill himself."

"Did he sound that bad?"

"Yeah," Eli said. "At the end, he did."

By the time I'd drained the pasta and mixed the dressing, Eli was back with a carrying case. "The 'Ramblings' are all in order," Eli said, "and they're all dated. Listen to them. You'll see what I mean."

I didn't open the tape case until Taylor had had her bath and we'd read two chapters of *Charlotte's Web*. I wanted to give Charlie D my full and undivided attention, and that would have been impossible with Taylor bouncing around. After she and I had said our final good nights, I went downstairs, made myself a stiff gin and tonic, and carried it and the tapes up to my bedroom.

In a house where anarchy and noise are the order of the day, my bedroom is an island. It's an airy room with ecru walls, flowering plants, and stacks of books and magazines that I intend to read some day. The two stars of my room are the mahogany four-poster that had been in Ian's family for two generations and the deep, pillow-strewn window seat that was my treat to myself when we renovated the house. From the window seat, I can look out onto our backyard and the creek beyond it. It's a view that always brings me comfort, and as I slid the first of the tapes into my stereo, and Charlie's dark-honey voice filled the room, I knew that, in the hour ahead, I would need to draw comfort from every source I could find.

Charlie didn't interpose a filter between himself and his audience. The stream of consciousness I heard seemed to flow uninterrupted from a deep and private place within him. As I sat in my pretty room, with my children just a touch or a phone call away, the image of this lonely blood-scarred man, isolated by the glass of the control booth, offering up his lonely acts of communion with strangers, broke my heart.

None of the "Ramblings" was longer than three minutes. In all, there were perhaps thirty-six minutes of tape. Not much, but enough to know that when Eli said Charlie was in the middle of a meltdown, he was right on the money. The formula of "Ramblings" was a simple one: Charlie chose a quote, then played verbal riffs on it.

The early "Ramblings" were a lot of fun. Most of Charlie's sources wouldn't have made the cut for *Bartlett's Familiar Quotations*, but they were great jumping-off points for his particular brand of edgy wisdom. He played some wicked variations on Kris Kristofferson's observation that "You should never sleep with anybody crazier than you," and he went the distance with Roughriders' quarterback Steve Sarkisian's musings on mindset: "You can't get too high or too low. You have to keep chucking."

But in the two weeks after Ariel left, Charlie began to draw from a well that grew progressively deeper and darker. The emotions driving the riffs described an arc familiar to anyone who had ever been dumped: disbelief, confusion, anger, bitterness. But on the show he did the day before Ariel died, Charlie had found himself in a place the lucky among us will never know.

On that show, Charlie took as his text a poem by a man named Peter Davison. The poem was called "The Last Word," and in it Davison used the metaphor of an executioner standing axe in hand over his kneeling victim to describe the pain of a lover who wants to become an ex-lover. The image goaded Charlie into a diatribe whose words froze the marrow.

"Hey, all you executioners out there, cringing in horror at having to watch the edge of the axe nick through flesh and creak into the block, do you want to change places? Do you want to be the one who hears the axe singing through the air towards the small bones in the back of the neck? No more crocodile tears, executioner. In a minute, you can wash up and go home to a bed warmed by a new lover. No new loves or new beds for the one on the other end of the axe. He's finished, sentenced to purgatory, doomed to an eternity of remembering the scent of your perfume as you leaned close to make sure the blow was fatal."

I reached over and flicked off the stereo. I was numb, stunned by the nakedness of Charlie's revelations. Little wonder that Robert Hallam had been anxious to speak to him. I put the tapes in the case and walked down to Eli's room. He was at his desk, reading, but the set of his shoulders told me he'd been waiting for me. He jumped up when he heard my step. "What do you think?"

I tried to lighten the mood. "Charlie seems to have forgotten what Steve Sarkisian says about not getting too high or too low."

Eli rewarded me with a small smile that vanished as soon as it came. "You can see why I was relieved when you said they were zeroing in on somebody else for his girlfriend's murder," he said.

"He's lucky to have you on his side," I said.

Eli met my eyes. "I was the lucky one," he said. "Charlie saved my life."

As I walked downstairs to let Willie out for his last run of the night, I couldn't shake the dread that had enveloped me when I listened to the tape of Charlie's "Ramblings" the night before Ariel was murdered. But whatever his demons, Charlie had been Eli's saviour; I had to hope that by now he had found a measure of peace.

I was standing on the deck watching Willie chase a moth, when the phone rang. The voice on the other end made me wonder about the power of telepathy.

Howard's rumbling bass was falsely casual. "So did you find out anything?"

"I found out plenty," I said, "starting with the fact that Charlie and Ariel knew Kyle Morrissey. Until Christmas, Kyle was their neighbour, which makes it highly unlikely that you needed *me* to find out about him. Damn it, Howard, if you had told me you wanted me to check the water for alligators, I would have done it gladly, but I don't like being lied to."

Howard's exasperation was apparent. "Put yourself in my place, Jo. What was I supposed to do, ask my oldest friend in the world to find out whether there was evidence suggesting my son killed the woman he loved? Use your head."

"I did use my head. I followed the leads I had. I asked the right questions. And right now, I wish I could just push the delete key and send everything I've learned into the ether."

"It's that bad?"

"It may be," I said. "And Howard, anything I have, the police will have soon – if they don't have it already."

"What have you got?"

There was no way to spare him. "Ariel was pregnant when she died," I said.

There was silence, then Howard spoke two words, filled with grief and wonder. "A grandchild."

"No," I said. "Charlie wasn't the father."

"How the hell did you find that out?"

"Ariel told Mieka."

"What else?"

"Ariel and Charlie weren't together when she died. She'd left him two weeks earlier. The old lady next door saw Ariel leave the house with another man. Apparently, Charlie followed them out of the house and begged Ariel to come back."

"Shit."

"There's more," I said. "Alex's nephew, Eli, is a big fan of Charlie's. He tapes 'Heroes' every day. He wanted me to listen to some of the shows Charlie's done lately."

"And . . . ?"

"They're devastating. You have to get Charlie to come back to Regina. I was talking to Alex tonight: he says Detective Hallam has a lot of questions, and it would be better for Charlie if he came back voluntarily to answer them."

"It's not that simple. Charlie's really fucked up, Jo. He blames himself for Ariel's death."

"Does he have reason to blame himself?"

In a move I'd seen often during the political days, Howard deflected the question. "I've had my arguments with the Church, Jo, but the Pope is right about one thing. Hell *is* a state of mind. From the moment Charlie found out that Ariel was dead, he's been in hell, and he's taken me on a few little side trips with him."

"What do you mean?"

"You're not going to like this," he said grimly. "After his show was over that day you and I went to CVOX, Charlie asked me to take him down to the morgue to see Ariel."

"And you *did*?"

"I know it was crazy, but Charlie said he had to see her. I tried to talk him out of it, but he wasn't hearing me." Howard's voice grew low with embarrassment and pity. "He said he had to hold her in his arms one last time."

"Oh, Howard, no."

"I pulled some strings. Got him in. It was a big mistake, Jo. He wouldn't leave her. I had to get an orderly to help me drag him away. When we left the room he was still reaching out to her. . . ."

An image flashed in my mind, but it wasn't of Charlie being wrenched from his beloved under the pitiless lights of a hospital morgue; it was of the lithograph that had hung in my grandfather's study. Beneath the picture of Orpheus and Eurydice were the words "Stretching out their arms to embrace each other, they grasped only the air." When I was a child, those words had seemed to me the absolute incarnation of loss. Fifty years later, they still did.

"Jo, are you there?" Howard's nervousness was apparent.

"Yes," I said. "But I still think you should have stopped Charlie from leaving town."

"Christ, Jo. You're not usually obtuse. His girlfriend's been murdered, and everything my son says makes him sound guilty. When we were at the morgue, he kept apologizing to Ariel, saying it was his fault she was dead. I was watching the orderly's face. He was about ten seconds away from calling the cops. All I could think of was getting Charlie someplace where nobody could hear him. When he said he wanted to see Marnie, I jumped at the chance."

"How is he now?"

"When he's with Marnie, he's fine. We haven't told her about Ariel, so when Charlie talks to her, it's as if Ariel's just waiting at home for him. Charlie talks about their house and that Rottweiler they have. It's almost like he escapes when he talks to his mother. Marnie's in a world where reality's a little shaky, and that's where he wants to be."

"He may want to be there, Howard, but he can't stay there. You have to bring him back."

The silence between us was eloquent. "I know," he said finally. "I'll take care of it. Meanwhile, I need another favour."

"What?"

"Talk to Marnie. Charlie's friend Liam Hill called yesterday. He told her that story you'd passed along about that night at Little Flower when she shoved the cabbage rolls at me. Marnie loved it. I've been trying to think of some more political stories, but I can't remember any that she's in."

"I guess that says something right there, doesn't it?" I said tightly.

"Jo, if you want to tear a strip off me, you'll have to wait for another day. At the moment, there's not much left to tear. Have you got any stories with Marnie in them?"

"Sure," I said. "Put her on."

At first, the sound on the other end of the line was like a gargle. I shrunk from imagining the person from whom it came. When I'd visited her in the hospital in Toronto the weekend after her accident, Marnie had looked so much like the Marnie I had always known that I was certain she'd break free of all the tubes, rip off her ridiculous surgical turban, and we'd escape to the nearest bar and talk about our three favourite topics: kids, politics, and what we were going to do with the rest of our lives. But when I'd looked into her eyes, it was clear that the surgical headdress wasn't a temporary accessory to be abandoned when real life returned. Like the wimple or the purdah, Marnie's sterile turban was emblematic of the fact that the life of the woman behind it had changed forever.

I had sat by Marnie's bedside, held her hand, and chatted. There was never any response. When Sunday came and I kissed Marnie's forehead, left the pain and the stench of antiseptic behind me and boarded the bus that took me to the airport, I felt the lung-bursting exhilaration of a prisoner headed for freedom. It was not a memory I was proud of, but it was the truth, and that night as I heard Marnie's voice on the other end of the line, guilt washed over me. I hadn't called her and, except for a card on her birthday, I hadn't written. Sins of omission. But I was being given a chance at redemption.

"Howard tells me you guys have been telling war stories," I said. "I was just thinking of a couple myself. Remember that time you and I were campaigning down in Thunder Creek, and we went to that trailer on Highway 2?"

"Gloves." Marnie's slurred enunciation stretched the single word painfully, but her delight was obvious.

"Right," I said. "That woman who answered the door naked as a jaybird except for her yellow rubber gloves. They came up to her elbows, but it was the only part of her that was covered, and there we were trying to find a safe place to look and you said . . ."

"Bad time." Marnie's voice had been music, but now her cadences were distorted like an old record played at the wrong speed.

"Right. You said, 'We'll come back. We've obviously come at a bad time.' And she said, 'What makes you think it's a bad time?'"

Marnie made a sound – a laugh that morphed into a sob. "Voted."

"Right," I said. "She voted for us. She even said she'd take a lawn sign."

For the next five minutes I told stories. Marnie punctuated the familiar anecdotes with gurgled words and laughter, and I tried to banish the memory of Howard's terrible statement of fact. "When she laughs, she shits herself."

Finally, I couldn't take it any longer. "It was great talking to you, Marnie," I said. "I'll call again."

"Soon," she said. She laughed her new growling laugh. "Good times," she said.

"Yeah," I said. "They *were* good times."

When Howard came on the phone again, I was fighting tears.

"Howard, I am so sorry," I said. "For everything."

"Look, Jo, we're up to our ass in Catholic guilt at this end. We don't need any of that watered-down Protestant crap."

"Okay," I said. "What can I do?"

"Help me save Marnie's son."

"Howard . . ."

"I know, I know," he said wearily. "Just do what you can."

I hung up the phone and walked downstairs to the family room. Bebe Morrissey wasn't the only scrapbook keeper in our city. It had been many years since I had clipped out articles and carefully pasted them on the soft cheap pages because I believed that what Howard and my husband and the rest of us were doing was so important we'd want to remember it forever.

I had to riffle through a lot of yellowing scrapbooks before I found what I was looking for. There was no shortage of photographs of Howard and Ian and the others giving speeches, wowing audiences, building the province. But that night my interest was not in the men.

Finally, I found a photograph of Marnie Dowhanuik and me that had been taken on a long-ago election night. Fresh-faced and exultant, we were handing around coffee and sandwiches at campaign headquarters. The caption under the photograph read, "They also serve . . ."

I ripped the page from the book, wrote "Screw them all!" on the bottom, put it in an envelope, and addressed it to Marnie at Good Shepherd. It was a start but it wasn't enough. Marnie deserved more.

I picked up the phone and dialled Mieka's number in Saskatoon. It was time to find out more about the man who had fathered Ariel's child.

I could hear Madeleine crying in the background when Mieka picked up the phone.

"Troubles?" I asked.

"Temper. Maddy went to all the trouble of crawling over to the CD player, now Greg won't let her push the buttons."

"Tell him to distract her with his world-famous rendition of 'Louie, Louie.'"

Mieka laughed and relayed the message. I could hear Greg singing, then silence from Madeleine.

"Good call, Mum," my daughter said admiringly.

"It's the singer, not the song," I said.

"You sound a little down," said my daughter. "Something wrong?"

"No, everything's okay."

"Just okay?"

"I keep thinking of Ariel. So many people loved her."

"You're thinking of Charlie."

"Yeah," I said. "I'm thinking about Charlie and, Mieka, I'm thinking about the other man in Ariel's life. Did she ever give you a hint about who the father of her baby was?"

For a beat there was silence, then Mieka said, "I promised her I wouldn't say anything, but I guess there's no harm now. I don't know the man's name, but I do know that he was an academic."

"At our university?"

"Yes. And Mum, that's all I know. Ariel was very discreet. Now, I have to boogie. Greg's run out of verses of 'Louie Louie,' and Madeleine looks like she's ready to howl."

As my daughter and I said our good nights, my nerves were taut. I was certain I knew the identity of the father of Ariel's baby. The fact that the man was an academic wasn't exactly a clincher, and Bebe Morrissey's description of Ariel's companion on the day she left Charlie had rung no bells for me. But finding an African prince who was teaching at our prairie university wasn't exactly like looking for a needle in a haystack. In fact, as Willie and I turned out the lights and trudged up to bed, I was sure that, by noon the next day, the father of Ariel's baby and I would have talked face to face.

CHAPTER

8

Fraser Jackson had been a member of our Theatre department for five years. I had never thought of him as an African prince, but I had played with the thought that he might be the doppelgänger of Yaphet Kotto, the actor who portrayed the Black Sicilian Lieutenant Al Giardello on "Homicide: Life on the Streets." Both men were in their mid-forties, heavy-set and physically powerful, with strong features and smiles that came infrequently but were worth waiting for. Both spoke with the reverence for language that reflected classical training.

The two men were alike in another, more profound, way. Both possessed the intensity of those whose tumultuous inner lives are kept in check only through rigorous self-discipline. More than one woman I knew had been intrigued by the possibility of discovering what lay behind the interior walls Fraser Jackson had erected around his essential self, but Ariel Warren had, seemingly, been drawn to him first for professional reasons.

One windy fall afternoon I'd run into her on the academic green. She was wearing a fluffy red turtleneck and bluejeans, and she'd taken off her sandals so she could walk barefoot through the leaves. Her long blond hair was corn-silk fine, and when she stopped to talk to me the wind lifted it into a nimbus that shimmered in the yellow autumn light.

"Look at this," she said. In her hand was a small leaf whose centre vein bisected its surface into two distinct planes of colour: scarlet on one side, gold on the other. "Perfect symmetry," Ariel said softly.

"Miracles all around us," I said.

"Especially in September," Ariel agreed. "Joanne, I just spent two hours watching Fraser Jackson with his Advanced Performance class. He's letting me audit."

"That's a fair commitment of time on your part," I said.

Ariel put her hand up in a halt gesture. "I know, I know. I should be churning out papers and ingratiating myself with my new colleagues, but this feels so right. Fraser is amazing, and so much of what he does is pure instinct. He has this innate sense of what's going on inside a student, and he's so gentle with them."

"Sounds like a great teacher," I said.

"He's a pretty decent human being, too." Ariel twirled the perfect leaf between her fingers. "Today, after everyone wandered off after class, he asked me if I wanted to work on a piece – just for fun. Of course, I pointed out that I was auditing and it wouldn't be fair for me to add to his workload. He said, 'Just let me hear your voice. There must be a poem you liked enough to remember.'"

"So what did you choose?"

A flush started on Ariel's neck and spread upward to her face.

"Not something salacious," I said.

"Worse," she said. "The Hippocratic oath. Talk about bizarre, but when your mother is a doctor . . ."

"You don't have to explain," I said. "My father was a doctor. I remember looking it up, too."

"I'll bet you didn't memorize it," Ariel said. "And I'll bet you never stood in front of the mirror watching yourself swear by Apollo and Aesculapius and Hygeia and Panacea and all the gods and goddesses that you'd 'prescribe regimen for the good of your patients according to your ability and judgement and never do harm to anyone.' "

"Most of my serious mirror time was devoted to trying to look like Sandra Dee."

Ariel looked baffled.

"Sandra Dee was the Cameron Diaz of the fifties," I said.

Ariel grinned. "Gotcha! Anyway, I think I was trying to be hip and ironic when I dredged up poor old Hippocrates today, but Fraser listened very seriously, and suddenly I was very serious, too. Then the strangest thing happened. When I got to the line 'I will preserve the purity of my life and my art,' I couldn't speak. Fraser reached out and took my hand, and I finished. Then he asked me what I thought had happened. I was so embarrassed I told him the truth . . ."

"Which was?"

Ariel gave the perfect leaf a final twirl and handed it to me with an enigmatic smile. "That I need to find out what happened to that girl in the mirror who believed in the purity of life and art."

She never spoke to me about Fraser Jackson again. I had never seen them together on campus. I hadn't even associated them in my mind till I'd spoken to Mieka. Yet I was certain that he was the man to whom Ariel had turned when she sought a father for her child.

As I walked back from Political Science 101 class on Wednesday morning, I was wholly absorbed with the problem of how to get Fraser Jackson to open up to me. My arms were full of essays, and when I reached to open the door to the main office, they shifted, and the copy of *Political Perspectives* that had appeared so fortuitously minutes before my first meeting with Ariel's class, slid to the floor. I bent to pick it up and knew I had my opening.

Rosalie was at her computer. She was wearing a sweater set the colour of violets, and she was beaming. "Guess what?" she said. "I cooked an entire meal for Robert, and he loved it."

"Congratulations," I said. "What did you make?"

"All his favourites." As she recited the menu, she ticked the items off on her blunt-edged fingers: "Roast beef with suet pudding, fried potatoes, onion rings, broccoli in cheese sauce, rolls and butter, and gravy, of course."

"Of course," I said. "And for dessert?"

"Chocolate eclairs," she said. "But I cheated. I bought them frozen at Safeway." A tiny frown crimped her forehead. "Am I wrong, or are you looking a little disapproving?"

"Not disapproving," I said. "It's just . . . Rosalie, how old is Robert?"

"Sixty-one," she said.

"If you want him to see sixty-two, you might want to cut back a little on the cholesterol."

She took my meaning. "A new cookbook?"

"Maybe just a more judicious selection from the old one."

Rosalie whipped out the Rombauers from under her desk. "I'll get right on it," she said.

"Before you do, I have a question. Yesterday, when Ariel's book turned up on our doorstep, you said there was no note."

"That's because there wasn't one."

"I know, but I forgot to ask you if the book was in any kind of wrapping."

"It wasn't wrapped up," she said. "Just stuck in an inter-office envelope. But your name wasn't on it, and there was no sender's name. I checked."

"Is the envelope still around?"

"I haven't sent anything out." She walked over to the shelf under our mailboxes and removed a stack of large brown envelopes. "I'll go through these if you'll tell me what to look for."

I glanced at the envelope on top. "No need," I said. "We hit the jackpot, first time out." I pointed to the last address.

"The Theatre department," she said. "I don't get it."

"I think we've found our secret Santa," I said.

I dropped off my books, and headed off in search of Fraser Jackson. His office was in our campus's shiniest new bauble, the University Centre, a building with a soaring glass entrance, floor tiles arranged to represent an abstracted aerial view of our province's southern landscape, a painting of a huge woman, defiantly and confidently naked, an upscale food court, two theatres, a clutch of offices that tended to student affairs, and the departments of Music and Theatre.

When I stopped in front of Fraser Jackson's door, a student passing by told me that Professor Jackson was in the Shu-Box, the nickname that had inevitably attached itself to the theatre donated by philanthropists Morris and Jacqui Schumiatcher.

It took a moment for my eyes to adjust to the darkness of the theatre, but I felt my way to a chair at the back, settled in, and watched as a student massacred one of the loveliest passages in *The Tempest*. Jeff Neeley, the young man onstage, was the quarterback of our football team, and he recited Caliban's speech at breakneck speed, as if he had to unload the words before he was sacked.

When Jeff finished, Fraser rose from his seat in the front row and walked over to him. Jeff's body tightened, but Fraser's voice was disarmingly soft.

"You're finding it hard to connect to this." It was a statement of fact, not a question. "You know that moment that comes when you first wake up and what you're waking up to is a hundred times worse than what you're leaving behind?"

Jeff knitted his brow, then the light bulb went on. "Yeah," he said. "Like when I wake up the morning after we've lost a game. The worst was last year against the Huskies. All I could throw were interceptions. Then in the final play I got clocked and fractured my femur. They shot me full of Demerol. I was dreaming that I'd run into the end zone for a touchdown and we'd won; then I woke up." He shook his head in wonder at a world that had such moments in it. "I would have given my left nut to have drifted off again."

Fraser's nod was empathetic. He was wearing Nikes, jogging shorts, and a sweatshirt. His body was hard-muscled and athletic; it was easy to believe he understood the power of Jeff's dream. When he put his hand on Jeff's shoulder and locked eyes with him, the fact that he'd made a connection was apparent. "I knew you had an instinct for what this scene's about," Fraser said. "Now use what you just told me, and let's hear it again – from the top."

Jeff squared his shoulders and began: "Be not afeard; the isle is full of noises. . . ." By the time he got to "The clouds methought would open, and show riches/Ready to drop upon me that, when I waked/I cried to dream again," he had me. He wasn't Kenneth Branaugh, but he wasn't bad.

Jeff glanced towards Fraser expectantly.

"Not there yet," Fraser said. "But definitely within field-goal range. Keep working on it."

As Jeff sprinted past me towards the doors that would release him into the world of sunlight and scrimmages, his relief was palpable, but I knew my ordeal was just beginning.

Fraser Jackson was slumped in a seat in the front row with a script, but as soon as he spotted me, he smiled and stood up. "Did you catch the performance?"

"I did."

"There's still a perception among the jocks that Theatre is an easy credit. I'm doing my best to get the word out that it's not."

"If the entire Rams team transfers into Poli Sci, I'll know who to thank," I said.

His laughter was deep and reassuringly warm. "What can I do for you, Joanne?"

"You've already done it," I said. "I came to thank you for sending me Ariel's copy of *Political Perspectives*."

He exhaled heavily. "How did you know it came from me?"

"You used an inter-office envelope. Your department was the last addressee, and I knew you and Ariel were close."

His eyes were wary. "I wouldn't have made much of a spy," he said finally.

It was now or never. "Maybe not," I said, "but Ariel believed you'd be a good father."

Pain knifed his face, but he was an actor who had learned strategies for containing emotion. He shifted his gaze from me to the empty pool of light on the darkened stage. "She told you?"

"It must have been a terrible loss for you," I said.

"It was," he said huskily. "It's been hard not being able to talk about it."

"Do you want to talk about it now?"

In the half-light of the theatre, Fraser Jackson's profile had the power that made me understand why Bebe had called him an African prince. "Can I trust you?" he said.

"I don't know," I said.

"A conflict of interests," he said, "because of your friendship with Charlie Dowhanuik's father?"

"Yes."

"I need to talk," he said, "so I'll have to take my chances.

Would you mind if we went outside? I could use a cigarette."

On our way through the lobby we passed a display of origami and a young woman crying at a public telephone. The origami was clever, and the young woman's tearful iteration, "I gave you five fucking months of my life," was plaintive, but Fraser was oblivious.

As soon as we passed through the doors, he lit up and dragged deeply. When he walked over to an arrangement of large rocks that the students had designated an unofficial smoking area, I followed. Fraser chose a slab of marble large enough for us to sit on side by side. He finished his cigarette, and pulled another from the pack. He shook his head in disgust. "I don't need this. Grabbing the nearest prop is a trick incompetent actors use when they're trying to think, of their next line. They believe it distracts the audience."

"You have an audience of one," I said. "And I'm not going anywhere."

His eyes met mine. "Okay," he said. "No tricks." Unexpectedly, he smiled. "Did you ever hear that song 'I Feel Ten Feet High and Bulletproof'?"

I nodded.

"From the moment Ariel told me she wanted me to be the father of her child, that's the way I felt."

"But you must have been surprised."

"Any man would have been." He looked at me thoughtfully. "Of course, you are too polite to say your next line."

"Which is . . . ?"

"Which is that I must have been more surprised than most men would have been because I'm black." He spread out his hands in front of him as if to check the reality of his statement. "Not tan or café au lait or pleasingly brown, but black – black as sin or pitch or Toby's proverbial ass. What's more, my features are distinctly non-Caucasian. I'm sure these sobering facts would have given you pause, Joanne."

"Yes," I said. "If I'd been looking for a father for my child, I would have considered the donor's background."

"Rightly so," he said. "A woman would be a fool to leave such matters to chance. I'm sure you remember the old limerick students in genetics class used to help them remember Mendel's Law.

"There was a young lady named Sarkey,
And she fell in love with a darkey,
The result of her sins,
Was quadruplets, not twins,
One black and one white and two khaki."

There was no anger in Fraser Jackson's voice; he was travelling a path he'd been down a thousand times. Nonetheless, I found myself flinching at the old poem and eager to distance myself from its casual racism. "Fraser, if we were talking about love here, genetics would be irrelevant. I could understand Ariel falling in love with you. I could understand any woman falling in love with you. But Ariel's decision wasn't about love, was it?"

He shook his head and put the unlit cigarette back in the pack. "No," he said. "What she wanted from me wasn't love. She came to my office one Friday afternoon last February and asked if I was up for a walk. It was a crazy idea. It had been snowing all day, and the temperature was dropping. By the time we got down to the boardwalk by the bird sanctuary, the wind had come up and the snow was swirling. We were hanging on to one another's arms and laughing like eight-year-olds. The university and the Parkway were five minutes away, but we couldn't see a thing except one another. Ariel said it was like being inside a snow-globe. Then all of a sudden, she just stopped laughing and asked me.

"She told me I was her first choice, but if I said no, she'd find someone else. She said there would never be any oblig-ation, financial or emotional, to her or to the baby, and that the only 'condition' she had was that she wanted her baby's conception to be a natural one – no visits to the lab for sperm donations; no sexual encounters dictated by basal thermometer temperatures. She wanted us to make love on a regular basis until she became pregnant."

"And you agreed."

"I was honoured."

"But she stayed with Charlie all the time you and she were . . ."

"That wasn't the plan," he said tightly.

"Then why did it happen that way?"

"Charlie," he said, and it was hard to imagine how a single word could be infused with such contempt. "Your friend Howard's son is a consummate games player."

"In what way?"

Fraser shook his head. "He made her the centre of his life. For a woman like Ariel, that was a heavy obligation. Whenever she tried to leave, there were threats."

"He threatened her . . ."

"That would have made her choice easy. No, Joanne, he threatened to kill himself. She couldn't leave."

"But she did leave. Two weeks before she died, she moved out . . ."

"It was after she saw the ultrasound photograph of the baby. Seeing our child made us both realize there were larger obligations."

"Did Charlie know about the baby?"

"Watching a woman as closely as he watched Ariel – I don't see how he couldn't have."

"Fraser, did it ever occur to you that one reason Ariel chose you to father her baby might have been to prevent Charlie from convincing himself the baby was his."

"I'm not a stupid man, Joanne. The thought occurred to me. I also realized that Ariel wanted to make her decision irrevocable. That didn't make me love our child any less."

He stood and took out his cigarette pack, but instead of lighting up, he arced the package through the air so that it landed in a garbage bin ten metres away. "At least I can do this for them," he said.

I watched him walk away a big man who, for a few magical, ardent weeks, had been ten feet tall and bulletproof. But even as Fraser Jackson had gloried in his good fortune, there had been a silver bullet waiting. As I rose to walk back to my office, my limbs were heavy, made leaden by the weight of evidence that seemed to link Charlie Dowhanuik to the sequence of events that had resulted in the deaths of Ariel and her baby. Whether or not to convey what I'd learned to Howard Dowhanuik was no longer an option, but it wasn't going to be easy to tell my old friend what I had learned about his son. I needed time and quiet; what I got was Kevin Coyle in full manic mode.

As he approached me from the hall outside his office, his eyes glittered huge and intense through his thick glasses, and his grin, a dentist's nightmare of ancient silver fillings, was fearsome.

"You look like you've been mainlining locusts and honey," I said.

"A Biblical allusion," he sneered, "and as such, increasingly irrelevant. Who needs God now that we have the Internet? Come have coffee, and I'll show you my new toy."

I followed Kevin into his office. He poured our coffee – mine into the orange and brown striped mug that was apparently now reserved permanently for me. He gestured to the low tables that had once held his prized games of Risk. The board games were gone now, replaced by a high-end computer system with all the bells and whistles.

I sipped my coffee. "Impressive," I said.

"The coffee or the Complete Home Office?" he asked.

"Both." I raised my cup to him. "Kevin, I have to hand it to you. When you commit, you commit."

He caressed his seventeen-inch monitor. "The whole world appears on this screen," he said solemnly. "Anything I want to learn about, buy, own, peruse, discuss – it's all here for me."

"Eden," I said.

"Another Biblical allusion," he said, "but this one is acceptable because the metaphor works. My machine can conjure up Eden, but it also brings serpents." He dropped to the floor, knelt before his computer, and logged on to the Internet. Then he called up the Web page devoted to Ariel and clicked from it to "Red Riding Hood." "They haven't taken it off. Worse yet, the Friends of Ariel have undergone a metamorphosis. They are now the Friends of Red Riding Hood, a name change which allows them to focus on fresh atrocities."

I looked over his shoulder at the monitor. The role of Red Riding Hood #1 had been taken over by another hideously mutilated woman. I tried to keep my voice even. "When it comes to abuse, there are always fresh atrocities."

He peered up at me. "But aren't we supposed to be remembering Ariel Warren?"

I thought of the young woman who had been so moved by the shining idealism of a single line in the Hippocratic oath. "They're just using her," I said. "I'm going to make Livia put a stop to it."

Rosalie wasn't in her customary place in the outer office, but Livia's door was open, a sure indication that she was inside. She wasn't alone. As I walked towards the door, I could hear raised voices. When I stopped to listen, I discovered that the topic under discussion was me.

Ann Vogel's voice was harsh. "Joanne Kilbourn is not one of us. You remember who she sided with in my attitudinal-harassment case."

"I wasn't here," Solange said calmly, "so I *don't* remember. It wasn't my battle, and it wasn't Ariel's. Until the vigil, I never had any feelings one way or the other about Joanne. She's certainly easy to dismiss: middle-aged, middle-class, middlebrow . . . middle-everything. But that night she said exactly the right thing. Perhaps there's more to her than we thought. I'm beginning to think she might be right about allowing Ariel to become just another morality tale on 'Red Riding Hood.'"

"Which, of course, implies that I'm wrong." Ann was beyond fury. "What has Joanne Kilbourn ever done for you? Did she get you a job? No. We did. Livia and me. I was the student representative on the committee that hired you. There were male candidates who had much better paper qualifications than either you or Ariel, but we made sure the department hired women this time."

Solange's response was icy. "We were qualified."

"Being qualified is never enough for a woman. You know that. What Livia and I did wasn't pretty, but it was necessary."

"Naama, stop." Livia's voice was a little light on New Age empathy. In fact, she sounded downright threatening. "You've said enough."

"We've all said enough." Solange sounded weary. "Let's leave this for another time."

When Solange emerged from Livia's office, Ann Vogel was right behind her. She grabbed Solange's arm and spun her back before either of them had a chance to see me.

"I reinvented myself for you," Ann said. "I . . ."

Solange cut her short. "This isn't high school. No one asked you to become someone else. That choice was yours, and this choice is mine. I'm going to delete the link to 'Red Riding Hood.'"

Livia appeared behind them. Her eyes widened when she saw me. "You should have let us know you were here, Joanne."

"I just got here," I said.

Flanked by the two women, her poppy shawl clutched tightly across her breast, Livia Brook looked anxious, a mother separating warring twins she can no longer control. She had reason to look uneasy. Naama's reinvention of herself was proceeding apace. Since I'd last seen her, she'd added a triple ear-piercing, a smudge of black eyeliner beneath her lower lids, and a wrist full of delicate silver bangles. She was forty years old. Her transformation of herself into an imperfect imitation of an idol thirteen years her junior was both sad and scary. I wasn't surprised that Solange looked ready to bolt.

"You're obviously in the middle of something," I said. "I came to ask about 'Red Riding Hood,' but from what Solange just said the issue's settled, so I'll let you get back to your discussion."

Solange broke away from the others. "I'll come with you, Joanne. There's something we have to talk about."

"So you've defected," Ann said bitterly.

"A difference of opinion doesn't mean a defection," Solange said. "I'm surprised at you, Ann. Aren't women allowed to disagree? And anyway, what I need to talk to Joanne about has nothing to do with you. Ariel's ashes are being buried at a small service, and her parents have asked me to help with the planning."

Ann Vogel was galvanized. "I'll get on the e-mail. I can make sure every woman at this university turns out for Ariel. I belong to other groups, too. This can be city-wide."

"No!" Solange's response was adamant. "That's exactly what the Warrens *don't* want. When they're ready, they'll have a public memorial service for Ariel, but they want this ceremony to be private. They have a place on an island at Lac La Ronge."

"The Political Science department should be represented," Livia said.

"It will be," Solange replied. "I'll be there, and so will Joanne if she chooses to come." She turned to me. "Will you come?"

"If the Warrens want me there, of course."

"Joanne's invited!" Ann Vogel's words had the biting fury of a child shut out of a birthday party. "Livia and I were both closer to Ariel than Joanne was. Why was she invited instead of us?"

Solange was placating. "You'd have to ask the Warrens. They made up the list, and they had to deal with logistics. The only way to their island is by private plane – the seating is limited."

Livia bit her lip. "I have a right to be there," she said. She seemed close to tears.

"You can't keep us away." Ann Vogel's voice was thick with menace. "Ariel was a Red Riding Hood. We have every right to be there. We have every right to avenge her."

As we walked down the hall towards my office, Solange filled me in on our travel plans. "We'll meet at the airport at seven Thursday morning and fly to Lac La Ronge. Of course, there'll be a couple of stops along the way. From Prince Albert, we take a float-plane to the island. Molly said she thought we'd just spend a little time together with Ariel, then bury the ashes and come back to Regina. We'll be home before dark. Sound okay?"

"Fine," I said. "I'm giving my mid-term Thursday, but I know Ed Mariani will invigilate it for me."

"It's settled then," Solange said, then she looked away. "Joanne, I wasn't honest about the number of seats on the plane. There's room for one more. Molly didn't want a circus, so she told me to use my discretion about whom, if anyone, we ask to take the extra seat. I honestly can't think of anyone who won't make matters worse, but if you know of someone who should be there . . ."

"I do," I said. "But I'll check with Molly Warren before I say anything to him."

When I phoned Molly from my office telling her I needed to talk with her about something that was best dealt with face to face, she was apologetic.

"I hate to ask, but would it be possible for you to come down to my office?" she said. "I'm booking off Thursday, so we've rescheduled patients today and tomorrow. I won't be able to get away."

"I can come down there easily," I said. "Is there any time that's better than others?"

She gave a short, mirthless laugh. "All times are equally bad. And now is as good a time as any."

Parking was usually next to impossible in the streets around the glass tower that housed Molly Warren's offices, but that afternoon I was lucky. I found a spot half a block away, plugged the meter with enough quarters to let me languish in the waiting room for an hour and a half if need be, and took the elevator to the eleventh floor. The Delft-blue waiting room was standing room only, but when I announced my presence to Molly Warren's nurse, Katie, she ushered me directly into Molly's office. I was grateful. That day I didn't have the heart to share couch space with the bountifully pregnant and the anxious-eyed.

"Dr. Warren will be right with you," Katie said. "She's with a patient, but she should be finished soon."

Katie was an attractive woman with brown eyes, dimples, a passion for pastels, and a professional manner that managed to be warm without being cloying. She gestured to a chair in front of the desk. "Make yourself comfortable. There's coffee if you'd like."

"I'm fine," I said. "I've had a busy morning. It'll be good just to sit."

Katie didn't leave. "People think if you work in health care you get used to death. But you don't. At least I haven't. I can't believe Ariel's gone. She was in the office last week. She was going to take her mother out to lunch, but Dr. Warren had an emergency and she had to cancel." Katie shook her head. "I hope the two of them managed to find time to talk."

"They were close?"

Katie hesitated. "They were mother and daughter," she said finally, as if that in itself were an answer.

"How is Dr. Warren doing?"

"She's unbelievable. I know she must be torn apart inside, but she hasn't missed an appointment. If it had been my daughter, I'd be in the basement staring down the business end of a shotgun."

"I'd probably be thinking about that, too," I said.

Katie straightened the edge of the file she was holding. "I'd better get back out front. Dr. Warren will be in as soon as she can get away."

"I'm in no hurry," I said.

I waited a few minutes; then, restless, I began to explore. Two sides of the room were lined with bookshelves upon which framed degrees, awards, and photographs of Molly Warren at meetings of professional organizations had been interspersed artfully among medical texts and bound journals.

I took out a bound journal from the bookshelf. Its table of contents listed articles dealing with the vagaries to which the complex, moon-tied bodies of women are heir: uterine bleeding, chronic pelvic pain, cervical dysplasia, endometriosis, infertility, menopause and peri-menopause, ovarian cysts and cancers, pregnancy (ectopic, hysterical, normal), and birth with its many complications.

I slid the book back into place, and picked up a high-gloss magazine that had been filed next to it. The magazine was really an advertising supplement, trumpeting the wares of a company that manufactured equipment that could produce three-dimensional ultrasounds. I flipped through and found myself looking at a reproduction of a three-month-old foetus, the age Ariel's child had been. I wondered if its presence in this neatly shelved collection of texts meant that Molly Warren had been revisiting what she knew of the characteristics of the grandchild she would never see.

I was staring at the photo when Molly came in. She looked pale and tired, but she was immaculate: fresh makeup, hair carefully tousled, a champagne silk blouse with matching trousers, and her trademark stiletto heels in creamy leather.

She leaned over my shoulder to stare at the page. "The technology is amazing, isn't it?"

"Neo-Natronix's or Mother Nature's?" I asked.

Molly gave me a wan smile. "Both."

She made no move to sit down. There was a room filled with people waiting for her to diagnose, absolve, prescribe, or doom. She was allotting me precious time; it was up to me to use it.

"Did you know that Ariel was pregnant?" I asked.

One of Molly Warren's gold and pearl earrings dropped from her ear and clattered onto the floor. "Damn," she said, and there were tears in her voice. She bent to pick up the earring, then went over and sat in the chair opposite me, the doctor's chair. She slid the earring back through the piercing in her lobe. "I'd suspected," she said. "Ariel and I were supposed to have lunch together last week. I had to cancel on her. Maybe she was planning to tell me then."

"Molly, I came down today because I wanted to talk to you about the baby's father."

Her azure gaze grew cold. "What about him?"

"Solange told me there was room on the plane for another passenger. I think the baby's father should be there." I could feel the chill so I hurried on. "I know him," I said. "He teaches in the Theatre department. He really is a very fine man."

Molly's eyes grew wide, and she leaned forward in her chair. "You mean Charlie wasn't the father?"

"No. Ariel wanted a child, and she asked a man she knew and respected to help her."

Molly's hand wandered to her earlobe to check that her earring was in place. It was, in every way, an uncertain world. "Ariel was always a mystery," she said softly. "I never quite understood what made her tick."

"Would it be all right if I asked Fraser to come tomorrow?"

"Is that his name? Fraser?"

"Yes," I said. "Fraser Jackson. One other thing you should know. Fraser is black."

"I couldn't care less about that," Molly said. "Just as long as he isn't Charlie. I'm glad my daughter found someone else. Charlie was destroying her." Molly's face crumpled. "I guess in that archive room he just finished the job."

CHAPTER

9

I called Fraser Jackson from the public telephone in the lobby of the building in which Molly Warren had her office. Phoning the father of Ariel's baby was the right thing, but it was hard for me to do. I knew that Howard would see the call as a betrayal of Charlie, of Marnie, and of himself, and as I caught my reflection in the mirrored wall by the elevators, I thought that Howard might not be far off the mark.

Fraser Jackson seemed grateful to hear from me, but as I extended Molly's invitation and ran through the travel arrangements, he was mercifully to the point. The trip north would be heavily freighted with emotion, and it was apparent we both wanted the logistics handled with dispatch. After we had arranged the details about where to meet the next morning, I thought I was home free, but Fraser had one final question.

"Is the service a burial?"

"Of the ashes," I said. "Ariel will be cremated later today."

There was silence, then a gentle correction. "Ariel *and the baby* will be cremated later today. When we fly north, we'll be taking them both, Joanne."

As I pulled onto Albert Street, I shrank at the thought of
the next day. There was no getting around the fact that, in the
words of that long-forgotten play, it would be filled with
love, pain, and the whole damned thing, but for me there
would be an extra agony, one that was both personal and
shameful. I would be spending much of the next day in air-
planes of one size or another, and I was terrified of flying. I
went to embarrassing lengths to avoid even the most routine
commercial flight, and the idea of being in a tiny float-plane
hovering over the vast, unforgiving water of Lac La Ronge
filled me with dread.

I had no choice about the flight north, but it was still in
my power to make the next few hours bearable. If I could
manage an afternoon in the sun, a pleasant dinner with the
kids, a stiff drink, and an early night, I might just survive.

I parked in front of Pacific Fish, paid Neptune's ransom
for five tuna steaks, then walked across to the supermarket for
new potatoes, baby carrots, asparagus, and a jar of giant olives.
To complete the meal, I needed a bottle of Bombay Sapphire
and a good Merlot; the liquor store had both. Finally, obeying
my old friend Sally Love's dictum that "Life is uncertain; we
should eat dessert first," I drove to Saje Restaurant, and
bought a chocolate truffle cake. As soon as I got home, I put
the gin in the refrigerator, made a marinade of soy sauce,
ginger, and rice vinegar for the tuna, scrubbed the potatoes
and carrots, snapped the woody parts off the asparagus stalks,
and went out to the deck with a cup of Earl Grey and a stack
of essays from my Political Science 101 class.

For the next two hours, I sniffed the lilacs and wandered
through the maze of freshman prose. It wasn't fun, but it was
familiar turf, and I felt my mind slip into cruise control.
Halfway through the stack, I came upon something that
pulled me up short: a truly original paper titled "Funkional
Politix." The essay took issue with the idea that in our post-

ideological age, it was savvy to be without either ideals or ideas. It called for a new politics, characterized by civility, co-operation, and commitment. I read the paper through twice. It was the work of a student named Lena Eisenberg. Surprisingly, considering I had only met the class twice, Lena's name conjured up a face, that of a whip-thin, tightly wound girl with dreadlocks and clever eyes. I was grateful to her. For almost an hour, her obvious delight in the workings of her mind kept *my* mind from thoughts of hurtling through space in a pressurized metal tube.

I was halfway through a turgid analysis of the role of the Speaker in the Provincial Legislature when Taylor peeled out the back door.

"There's a lady on the phone," she announced breathlessly. "She says she wants to talk to you about Barbies. I told her she must have the wrong number because you hate Barbies, and she said she had the right number and nobody hates Barbies, and I'd better get you lickety-split."

Bebe Morrissey was direct. "Who was that kid who answered the phone?"

"My daughter, Taylor."

"How old is she?"

"Seven."

"Aren't you a little old to have a seven-year-old?"

"Probably," I said. "But I do my best. So, Bebe, what's up?"

"You are," she cackled. "You're up to bat. I've gone through the paper and discovered three garage sales with Barbies."

"Okay," I said. "Give me the addresses and I'll be there first thing Saturday morning."

"You really are a babe in the woods," she said. "By Saturday morning, even the Barbies with their legs chewed off to their kneecaps will be gone. You should get there tonight. The paper says six-thirty, but six would be better. What time do you feed your kid?"

"Kids," I said. "I have three at home." I looked longingly at the refrigerator with its bottle of Bombay Sapphire chilling. The gin would have to wait. "I could be at the first garage sale by six. Can you give me the addresses?"

By 5:55, Taylor and I had inhaled our barbecued tuna and were pulling into Braemar Bay, a swank crescent of shining mock-Tudor homes on the east side of our city. The owner of number 720 told us she had only one Barbie, and it had been sold, but that she had some grapevine wreaths and wicker-ware we might be interested in. Taylor picked out a Thanksgiving wreath with fake Chinese lanterns and plastic turkeys, and a wicker cat-carrying case for Bruce and Benny, who were never carried anywhere except in Taylor's arms.

Our next stop was an estate sale. One glance at the gleaming oak, bevelled glass, and paper-thin teacups and saucers led me to conclude that Bebe was a woman who savoured a practical joke. The woman in charge of the sale was a person of such pearled refinement that I was certain Barbie wasn't even a figure in her cosmos. But she did have a tiny Lalique sparrow for sale. It wasn't a nightingale, but it was the best Lalique bird I could afford, and Ed and Barry had been generous in lending us their cottage.

At number 982, Taylor and I finally hit paydirt: nine Barbies. Their hair showed evidence of brutal attempts at styling, but their toes were pristine. They were four dollars each, but the buxom brunette with the moneybelt said twenty-five dollars could buy the lot.

As I was paying, Taylor arranged the Barbies carefully in a cardboard box that was lying in the corner of the garage. She chattered about garage sales all the way home, and when I dropped her off she leaped out of the car with her wicker cat-carrier and a satisfied sigh. "That was so fun. Let's do it again tomorrow night."

My cellphone was ringing when I pulled up in front of EXXXOTICA. It was Howard Dowhanuik.

"Amazing timing," I said. "I'm on my way to visit Charlie's next-door neighbour?"

"Kyle Morrissey? What the hell's that all about?"

"Unfinished business," I said. "When you had me playing Nancy Drew, I talked to his great-grandmother. She asked me to run an errand for her."

"Still working on stars for your heavenly crown."

"How about you?" I said.

"No crown. No stars," he said curtly. "So what's happening out there?"

I glanced over at the perfect fifties house that Charlie and Ariel had shared. The vision of them happily planning, choosing the colours of paint and trim, the kinds of flowers that would fill the hanging baskets, made me drop my guard. The words tumbled out. "Howard, there's something you should probably know. Ariel's being cremated tonight. There's a service up at her family's place in Lac La Ronge tomorrow morning."

I could hear his intake of breath. "Cremated. God, it's hard to believe that she can just – cease to be." For a beat, he was silent. "Are you going to the service?"

"Yes."

"Say one for me, will you?"

"I will," I said.

The penny dropped. "Jo, if you're going to the Warrens' island on Lac La Ronge, you're going to have to fly."

"That's right," I said.

"Then I'll say one for you."

EXXXOTICA was looking remarkably shipshape. The front window had been scraped clear of the last remnants of the handbills, and two giant pots had been chained to steel poles and filled with those hardiest of floral survivors, dwarf marigolds. When I came through the door, Ronnie Morrissey was at the cash register facing a man in a sports jacket made out of some shiny synthetic. She glanced up, raised a finger to indicate she'd be with me soon, and went back to business. Her customer lowered his head when he saw me, but I had time to notice that his hair was freshly cut, and that he had doused himself with Obsession. The title of the video on the top of his pile was *Hot and Saucy Pizza Girls*. Judging by the way he bolted up the stairs and out the front door the moment Ronnie handed him his movies, he was a hungry man.

Ronnie watched him leave, then came out from behind the counter. Today she was a western belle wearing a denim halter top, matching ankle-length skirt, and hand-tooled cowboy boots. Her hair was almost to her waist and sunstreaked. A skeptic or a stylist might have suspected extensions, but the wild profusion suited her. So did her manicure: each of her nails was painted in a different pearlized colour – I knew the names of the shades were ultra-cool because of Taylor's unrequited longing for them: Bruise, Urban Putty, Raw.

Ronnie caught me staring at her fingers, and she wiggled them obligingly. "Make quite a statement, eh?"

"My younger daughter would love them. She's always wanting to paint her nails."

"It was the same for me when I was a kid," Ronnie said huskily. "Of course, given the circumstances, it was out of the question." She shrugged. "Well, better late than never."

As she had before, Ronnie led me to the back of the video store and unlocked the back door. When she opened it, I found myself face to face with a young man I recognized from the newspapers as Kyle Morrissey. He was soap-star handsome with bulging pecs, a trim waist, a mop of black curly hair, and what we used to call bedroom eyes, languid and long-lashed. He was wearing a T-shirt that cautioned "Think Long and Hard Before You Take Me Home," but there was a vacancy in his sexy eyes that gave the warning an unsettling edge.

"That's quite the shirt," I said.

Kyle smiled obligingly. "Ronnie gave it to me. It's sort of a joke, but not really." He adjusted his features to an appearance of solemnity. "You're here to see Bebe," he said. He looked at the cardboard box in my hand. "I hope there are Barbies in there."

I smiled. "Nine of them."

"Great," he said. This time the smile was as open as a prairie sky. "Bebe will be really happy."

He led me up the stairs, but stopped outside Bebe's room. "Wait here till I get our snack," he said.

"Thanks, but I just ate."

His brow furrowed. "Bebe said we'll need a snack." He looked confused.

"Okay," I said. He disappeared into a room on the right and reappeared almost immediately with a tray upon which were a litre of milk, a bag of Dad's cookies, a cow-shaped plastic container of chocolate syrup, and three glasses. I followed him into Bebe's big front room.

As she had on my first visit, Bebe was sitting in the wing chair by the window. In the early-evening shadows, the sea of bubble-gum-pink Barbies had muted to dusky rose, and Bebe herself seemed softer, an old woman who welcomed the gentle embrace of the gloaming. It was a scene from a Hallmark card, and just as remote from reality.

The second she spotted me, Bebe flicked on the powerful standard lamp beside her, and the illusion shattered. "Let's see them," she barked.

I handed her the cardboard box. She lifted the flaps and examined the dolls with the professional squint and unerring fingers of a veteran customs inspector. When she'd checked out the last one, she smacked her lips. "Not bad," she said. "How much did you pay?"

"Twenty-five dollars."

Bebe made a hissing sound through her teeth: whether it was a hiss of approval or opprobrium was impossible to tell. "Better you than me," she said finally. "Let's visit with Kyle for a bit, then you and I can talk business."

Kyle passed around the cookies and mixed the chocolate milk with exquisite care. When he handed Bebe hers, she turned up her nose. "You know I like a double."

He picked up the plastic cow obligingly and poured syrup into Bebe's milk until she held up a palm to indicate that he could stop.

"That's more like it," she said, then she raised her glass. "To justice," she said.

"That's a surprising toast coming from you," I said. "Has something happened?"

"You bet your sweet bippy something's happened. The cops have finally figured out our boy couldna done it. Proving once again that, as soon as you put a blue uniform on a person, they have a harder time adding two plus two than a normal person does. But I'm getting off track. The point is the cops finally found themselves the truck driver who gave Kyle the wrong directions. Of course, Kyle told them about this lady driver on day one, but they didn't exactly bust their humps looking for her. Anyway, on the morning in question, this lady truck driver was dumping off a load of wiring in the sub-basement – no connection with what Kyle was doing, so of course no one pursued her. Kyle asked this driver where he should go to fix the air conditioning, and she got turned around and pointed him towards the room where, unbeknownst to her or Kyle, that girl Ariel was already dead." Thrilled by the vagaries of fate, Bebe Morrissey rocked back and forth in her chair. "The one lucky thing for Kyle was that the truck driver was a lady."

"Why was that lucky?" I said.

Bebe rolled her eyes. "Because there's never been a woman born who, once they saw Kyle, forgot him."

Bebe's great-grandson lowered his head in embarrassment.

I turned to him. "You must be so relieved," I said. "These last days must have been a nightmare."

Kyle furrowed his brow. "Ronnie always says you have to take the crunchy with the smooth, and it's been crunchy. All the same, I'm not mad at anybody. Not even the police. I know why they thought it was me. Ariel was so pretty and so smart. They couldn't believe she'd want to be my friend."

"She was a good person," I said.

"Whoever killed her didn't mean to." Kyle's voice rang with conviction. "They just loved her so much they made a mistake."

Bebe gave him a thin smile. "Go watch TV," she said. "The Jays are playing, and you like them. Come back in ten minutes and get our snack dishes. If you don't wash the glasses quick enough, all that chocolate gunk sticks to the bottoms."

As soon as Kyle was out of earshot, Bebe shook her head. "A nice boy, but dumb enough to be a cop. He's moved back here now."

"Ronnie told me," I said.

"It's for the best," Bebe said. "He's got a short fuse, and until they capture the real murderer, people are going to be giving him the evil eye." Her head darted like an old tortoise's. "Which leads me to my next point. Did you talk to that African prince?"

"Yes," I said. "We had a long talk this morning."

Her eyes danced with expectancy. "So – could he have done it?"

I thought of the man who had felt ten feet tall and bullet-proof from the moment Ariel asked him to help her have a child. "Not in a thousand years," I said.

"Case closed on him?"

I nodded.

"Good. Not often you see a real man any more. It would be a shame to have to turn him in. How about the one with the face?"

"He's . . . out of town."

Bebe's radar registered my hesitation. "That's not the same as 'case closed,' is it?"

"No," I said, "it isn't."

"Then keep your ears open." She flicked her tongue over her upper lip and captured a drop of chocolate that had caught on a whisker. "I've got another potato to throw in the pot," she said. "What do you know about the girl's mother?"

"Molly Warren? She's my gynecologist. She's phenomenal."

"Maybe not so *phenomenal*," Bebe said mockingly. "She came to visit the girl a few times. They only quarrelled the once in my hearing, but it was the kind of spat that left questions in my head."

"Questions about what?"

"About parents and kids and where you draw the line." Bebe's tone had grown sombre.

"How many kids do you have, Bebe?"

"I *had* three – all dead now. What I've got left is Ronnie, who was my youngest's youngest, and Kyle, who is my one and only great-grandchild. I've had disappointments in my life. Don't kid yourself about that. All the same, I never woulda spoke to one of mine the way that doctor of yours spoke to her girl."

"What did Molly say?"

"All I heard was a snippet. They were squabbling about something the daughter wanted to do. I don't remember what it was, but finally the girl said, 'I have to do what I think is best. I only have one life.' Then the mother said, 'You're wrong. You have two lives, because I gave you mine.'"

"When was this?" I asked.

"Not long ago," Bebe said. "Coupla weeks, maybe three. But the *when* isn't as important as the *what*. In my opinion, that's a helluva thing to say to your own flesh and blood. I never got all the way through grade eight, so maybe I'm not one to judge. But if I was you, I'd be asking myself whether I might've been wrong in thinking my friend, the gyn-e-col-o-gist, was such hot stuff."

By 5:30 the next morning, Bebe's words were still roiling in my mind. Maybe that's why I ended up having a double martini for breakfast, or maybe it was just that, on that particular day, gin seemed as reasonable a way to cope with the vagaries of human existence as any other.

On the day of Ariel's burial, the fanfare prelude to the AccuWeather forecast catapulted my body into full flight-or-fight mode, but I was neither a fighter nor a flyer. I was a fifty-two-year-old woman trembling with the hope that climatologist Tara Lavallee's forecast for the day ahead would be shot through with Old Testament pyrotechnics: skies riven with lightning, torrential winds, bushes exploding into flames. Anything to make travel impossible. But Tara's chirp was lively, and the weather she predicted was picture-perfect, province-wide.

I reached down and stroked Willie. "No exit," I said, but Bouviers aren't hard-wired for existential gloom. When I swung my legs out of bed, Willie's hind end shimmied with joy. As we had every morning of our life together, we were going for a run around the lake. It was the highlight of Willie's day, but that morning the run was for me. I was counting on exercise to dull the edge of the axe that was pounding at my nerve ends.

It didn't work. Neither did the long, hot shower or the series of deep inhalations of Lavender Breeze scented oil that Angus had given me for Mother's Day with the suggestion that aromatherapy might help me chill out.

Molly Warren had been adamant about not wanting us to wear anything "funereal" for the trip to Lac La Ronge. She said Ariel had loved the cottage, and it would be good for us to spend at least part of the day exploring the island's rough terrain. As I pulled on my bluejeans, a turtleneck, and my favourite fleece jacket, I tried to banish fear by imagining the species of wildflowers that might cover the island at this time of year, but I was beyond help. Visualization may make it possible for a tight end to win a Super Bowl ring, but it didn't work for me. The knot of terror in my stomach as I started downstairs in search of something to eat was the size of a bowling ball.

From my pregnancies I had learned that even the queasiest stomach can tolerate soda crackers. I found half a box of saltines in the cupboard and opened the refrigerator in search of something with which to wash them down. When I shook the orange-juice carton and discovered it was empty, my fate was sealed. The bright blue bottle of Bombay gin jumped into my hand.

Remembering the sense of well-being that had enveloped me in Druthers when the first sip of gin and vermouth hit my bloodstream, I mixed a martini that was very dry and very large. The four jumbo olives I added for food value would have made a traditional martini glass pitifully small, and I complimented myself on having the foresight to use a tumbler. I took my breakfast to the deck, where I shared my crackers with Willie and savoured my martini. By the time,

I'd emptied the glass, I could have flown to New Delhi. Gin:
the Breakfast of Champions.

The waiting area for Athabaska Air is at the north end of
the Regina airport terminal. In all, five of us were flying
north: Molly and Drew Warren, Solange, Fraser Jackson, and
me. I was the last to arrive, and as we exchanged greetings I
thought that with our jeans, hiking boots, and air of forced
conviviality, we could have been taken for a group about to
fly to some sort of corporate retreat. Only the rectangular
box in Molly Warren's hand hinted at a mission grimmer
than formulating shared goals or fine-tuning human-
relations policies.

The 8:05 flight to Saskatoon was a favourite of business
people and civil servants. A dozen of them, toting laptops
and insulated coffee mugs, crossed the tarmac ahead of us. I
tried to emulate their confident, purposeful stride, but my
feet dragged. Halfway to the plane, filled with longing for
the safe world I was leaving behind, I turned to gaze back
at the terminal.

The sun was glinting off the windows that separated the
waiting room from the runway, so at first I couldn't be
certain that the woman pressed so close to the wall of glass
really was Livia Brook, but the Botticelli abundance of hair
and the explosion of scarlet poppies on the woman's shawl
were dead giveaways. As I watched, Livia raised her arm in
a gesture that could have been either farewell or benediction.
I averted my glance. The memory of her sad party for one
was still vivid; I didn't need another image of Livia Brook's
painful longing for connection.

Behind me, Solange's shout was insistent. "Joanne, what's
so fascinating? They won't wait for us, you know." Solange,
too, had lingered, anxious for a final smoke before boarding.
She had abandoned her customary uniform for a costume
that was the epitome of urban chic: bluejeans, white T-shirt,

smart black leather jacket, backpack decorated with
Japanese cartoon characters, black ankle-length boots. When
she saw me coming towards her, she took a lung-filling drag,
threw the cigarette to the pavement, and ground it out with
her toe. Then she looked at me with an abashed smile. "No
more delaying tactics," she said softly. "Time to take our
friend home."

In the first days after Ariel's death, I had feared for
Solange. Her grief and anger manifested themselves in a
manic energy that could have consumed her, if she hadn't
found an outlet for it. Luckily, she had. Rosalie told me that
Solange had taken to riding her bike for hours at a time:
twice she had ridden all night. When she had shown me her
shining Trek WSD the previous September, Solange had
admitted the bike cost her a month's salary and then some.
That morning at the airport, it seemed the bike had been
worth every penny. Solange was pale but composed; it was
apparent that somewhere in her solitary journeys along the
bike paths and streets of our city, she had found a measure of
peace. As that seriously undervalued philosopher Frank
Sinatra once said, "Whatever gets you through the night."

When Solange and I fell into step, I touched her arm. "Did
you see Livia in the airport?"

Solange made a moue of disgust. "I would have thought
she'd have more pride. She's been obsessive, as if this trip
were an adventure one longed to be a part of."

"Were she and Ariel that close?"

"Maybe at the beginning. Ariel told me that when she and
Livia met at that women's retreat on Saltspring, they were
both at a turning point in their lives. They supported one
another's choices, the way women are supposed to do, and
for a while there was a bond. I've always assumed Livia was
instrumental in getting Ariel the job here." Solange looked
away. "I'll be grateful to Livia for that as long as I live."

At that moment, the attendant asked for our boarding passes, and we had to climb the stairs and find our seats. The plane was small and airless. I felt a flicker of panic, but the Bombay gin seemed to have long-lasting anaesthetising power, and as Solange led me to the only two empty seats left, I surrendered to inevitability.

After we'd fastened our seatbelts, Solange pointed her index finger towards the place three seats up and across the aisle from us where Fraser Jackson was sitting with Drew Warren. "Now you can answer a question for me," she whispered. "What's he doing here?"

I didn't tell her the truth. The news of Ariel's pregnancy would have caused Solange anguish, and on that grief-filled day none of us deserved another helping of pain. "I guess they were friends," I said lamely.

"Fraser Jackson and Ariel?" Solange raised an eyebrow. "Different types, wouldn't you say?"

"People are full of surprises," I said.

The plane's engines coughed to life. I closed my eyes and grasped the armrests.

Solange leaned towards me, curiosity mingled with concern. "You hate small planes," she said.

"I hate all planes."

Her gaze was skeptical. "The competent Joanne Kilbourn. I don't believe it."

"Believe it," I said. "Right now, it's all I can do to keep from clawing my way past you to get out of here."

"I always thought you were impervious." She reached into her backpack and pulled out copies of the magazines *Femme Plus* and *Lundi*. "Choose," she said. "The human mind can hold only one thought at a time. Work on your French."

"I'll take *Lundi*," I said. "*Femme Plus* is too earnest. I want to hear Pamela Anderson *dit tout sur ses implants*." By the time we'd reached Saskatoon, the gin was wearing off, but as Pamela *parle à coeur ouvert de sa vie*, I'd learned a great deal about true love, forgiveness, and the removal of prosthetic enhancements. We were in Saskatoon just long enough to catch the flight to Prince Albert. Molly was the first of our group to board the plane; Drew and Fraser were right behind her. On the plane from Regina, I'd been puzzled by the fact that Drew had chosen to sit not with his wife but with Fraser. My assumption was that Ariel's parents had decided that the flight north would give at least one of them a chance to come to know the man their daughter had invited into her life. Molly's reaction when Drew tried to sit next to her forced me to re-examine my hypothesis. She tensed her lips as if to trap words she would not allow herself to speak, then she tightened her grip on the rectangular box and retreated into isolation as complete as that of a figure in an Andrew Wyeth painting.

I hurried past and sank into the next seat. When I had seen them at the symphony or the theatre, the Warrens had always struck me as the prototype of the high-functioning dual-career couple; but the death of their child was revealing the fault lines in their relationship. There wasn't much I could do for them, but I could spare them the knowledge that a virtual stranger had witnessed the strain in their marriage.

Solange took the seat beside me. When we were buckled in, she turned towards me. "Ariel and I flew up here one weekend. It was just after we came to the university. There was so much bitterness in the department. The men had closed ranks. Ariel and I felt our lack of locker-room edge most acutely. I think at that point, if we could have found a way out, we both would have taken it."

"But you'd signed contracts," I said.

She shrugged. "Precisely. We'd made our bed."

"Forgive me, Solange, but it was a pretty comfortable bed,

wasn't it? Tenure-track positions at a good university, and you were both inexperienced."

"In retrospect, I know you're right, but at the time the atmosphere was so poisonous. You can't know . . ." She caught herself. "Well, I guess you can. At any rate, Ariel suggested we come up here for Thanksgiving to put things in perspective." For a moment Solange seemed to lose her train of thought. When she spoke again, her voice was wistful. "It's ironic, Joanne. The weekend worked for me. By the time we flew back to Regina, I knew the only sensible course was to do my own work and keep my head down."

"But Ariel didn't get to that point?"

Solange shook her head. "No. She didn't. For her, it just kept getting worse. Every day. It seemed as if the entire situation just ate at her."

"Maybe she wasn't certain she was on the right side."

"Did she tell you that?"

"Not me directly, but another member of the department. She also told this person she was going to have to right a wrong that had been done."

Solange stiffened. "And your source for this fascinating information is . . . ?"

I sighed. "Kevin Coyle."

Solange threw up her hands in a furious gesture of dismissal. "Unimpeachable, of course."

The engines roared to life, and we were in the air. My composure shattered, and my pulse began to race. The gin had worn off, and I had alienated my travelling companion. It was going to be a lousy flight. But angry as she undoubtedly was, Solange didn't abandon me. "Take some deep breaths," she said. "I'm sorry. I lose reason at the mention of that man's name."

"He really isn't that bad."

"You and Ariel," she said. "Always looking for the diamond in the pile of excrement."

Despite everything, I laughed. So did Solange. Then her expression grew pensive. "Ariel was so good to everyone but herself. Did she ever talk to you about the Hippocratic oath?"

"The recitations in front of the mirror when she was little?" I smiled, remembering.

"Not so funny," Solange said. "She took those words to heart. It's a stringent code, Joanne – sensible enough for a medical practitioner, I suppose, but suicidal for anyone simply wanting to live a decent life."

"You think Ariel held herself to unreasonable standards?"

"I know she did." Realizing the closeness of our quarters, Solange lowered her voice. "'First, do no harm.' A *pensée* perfect for framing and prominent display in the office of an idealistic young M.D., but for Ariel it was disastrous. She was pathological about not hurting others. So self-denying. In the historic way of females, Ariel always held on too long. Relationships that should have been severed weren't."

"But at the end, she had changed," I said. "She *did* break away. Remember what you said that night at the vigil? When Ariel died, she was 'fully alive.' You were right. I saw her that last morning. She was radiant."

"And her joy enraged someone to the point where he felt compelled to kill her. A competent, functioning woman is always a threat. If you don't believe that, think back to l'École Polytechnique." Solange's voice was glacial. "Our friend was a gifted teacher, Joanne. Isn't it a pity she wasn't spared? Who knows, given a few more years she might have been able to bring the violent ones to understand the principle that informed her life."

For the rest of the flight, we were silent: Solange lay, eyes closed, with her head against the headrest. I gazed out the window, watching the shifts in light and topography that indicated we were moving from the Interior Plains into the southern edge of the Precambrian Shield and wondering what the world would be like if man, woman, and child alike lived by the dictum "First, do no harm."

At Prince Albert airport, we moved from a public to a private plane, and in an oddly analogous process, we seemed to leave behind our public selves. For Molly Warren, the transformation began the moment she stepped off the plane. From the time we left Regina, Molly had been inching into a carapace of stoicism and self-containment. Her face blood-less, her hands resting on the small wooden box, she seemed beyond words of comfort or gestures of intimacy, and so, in respectful, baffled silence, we left her alone.

But in Prince Albert, the woman who ran across the tarmac towards Molly Warren broke through Molly's terrible self-imposed isolation. The woman was accompanied by a dog who looked like a wolf, and she herself was what my grandmother would have called "an odd duck": bowl haircut, barrel chest, orange windbreaker and matching ball cap. Odd duck or not, she was obviously the one person Molly Warren wanted to see. When she opened her arms, Molly allowed herself to be enfolded; when the two women moved away from one another, Molly handed her the rectangular wooden box. Even from a distance, it was apparent Molly was grate-ful this particular burden was now being shared.

The two women walked arm in arm towards a small bush plane, the wolf-dog following at their heels. Molly climbed inside but the woman and her dog waited to greet us. I liked her on sight. She had a broad Cree face and a ready smile. She embraced Drew Warren wordlessly, then turned to us.

"I'm Gert," she said. "This is my plane and this is my flying service." She pointed to the dog at her feet. "This is Mr. Birkbeck," she said. "He's been with me since he was a

pup. He goes everywhere with me. We always take the
Warrens up to their place on the island." Her voice was
warm and husky. She patted the box with a square-fingered
hand. "I never would have dreamed that I'd be the one to fly
her up this last time." She gestured with her head towards
the inside of the plane where Molly and Drew had already
taken their places. "Hurry up and get in there," she said.
"They'll need to get this over." Then, as if as an after-
thought, she said, "I hope they make it."

As I gazed at the endless, unknowable sky, I wondered if
any of us would make it. Gert's plane was ridiculously small,
but the motto painted on its side was reassuring: GERT GETS
YOU THERE. I climbed on, found my seat, and watched Mr.
Birkbeck amble aboard. The moment Gert closed the plane
door, he curled up and gave every appearance of falling
instantly into a deep sleep. As the engine coughed to life, I
closed my eyes. Mr. Birkbeck would not be sleeping if he
sensed danger. Somewhere in his marrow he knew that
against every law of physics, Gert could keep this small
metal tube aloft until we reached our destination. I had to
believe he was right. I had to trust Mr. Birkbeck's atavistic
wisdom that somehow Gert would, indeed, get us there.

CHAPTER

10

Making the final break with the physical remains of a being who once glowed with spirit is never easy. But those of us who had gathered to bury Ariel Warren were, for a while at least, part of a farewell that was appropriate, honest, and stamped with the acknowledgement of what she had been to us all. Gert proved to be our salvation. At the Prince Albert airport, she had struck me as a person with the crisp compassion of the basketball coach at the girls' school I'd attended. When a player was injured or humiliated, our coach had a way of catching the girl's eye and communicating a message all the more powerful because it was unspoken. *I know you're hurting*, the look said. *But cry later. Get on with the game.*

Gert, too, seemed to be a person with a natural talent for sizing up a situation and dealing with it. After she'd landed her plane beside the dock and we had all climbed out, only Mr. Birkbeck showed evidence of a sense of purpose. He found a patch of sun and then, in what appeared to be a physiological impossibility, flattened himself until his bones disappeared, leaving only his head and his hide. The rest of us looked hollowed out too, like survivors of an accident, dazed and uncertain about what to do next.

Gert took charge. "Misery hates a full stomach." She turned to Drew and Fraser. "There are two coolers stowed in the back of the aircraft. Why don't you get them off while the ladies and I go up and air out the cabin?"

Relieved at being issued marching orders, we set to work.

The cabin was made of logs, and it was very old. "My father built this place," Molly Warren said. "He was a physician, too. He'd seen so many children with polio." Her lips tightened. "He thought he could keep us safe."

Gert knew a bad moment when she saw it. "Better get moving," she said. "That cabin won't air itself out."

The wooden shutters were still nailed in place. When we unlocked the door, we were met with the musty gloom of a room that only rodents had called home during the long winter months. As my eyes grew accustomed to the shadows, I made out a wood stove, a couch piled high with Hudson's Bay blankets wrapped in heavy plastic, and, incongruously, a lipstick-red canoe, hull side up, in the centre of the floor.

When she spotted it, Molly slumped. "Ariel's," she said. For a moment, she was silent, then she turned to Gert. "What was that joke she liked about the canoe?"

Gert swatted at a blackfly. "Not a joke," she said. "A true story. They say that one day God was fooling around, the way He does, and son of a gun if He didn't make a canoe. Well, He'd made a lot of stuff, but that canoe really blew Him away. 'Helluva boat,' he said. 'But where am I going to paddle it?' All of a sudden, it came to Him."

Molly smiled as she supplied the punchline. "'I know,' He said. 'I'll make Canada.'"

Drew and Fraser appeared in the doorway, each carrying an old metal cooler. Drew's eyes found his wife. "Nice to see you cheerful," he said.

"The canoe story hasn't failed yet," Gert said. "Now, the two of you are going to have to do an about-face. It's too dusty to eat in here. Let's get back to the dock."

The men traded glances, then started back towards the water. The easy camaraderie that had sprung up between Drew Warren and Fraser Jackson seemed to strengthen them both. Carrying out the ordinary tasks associated with Ariel's last trip north appeared to give them a way to share the burden of their grief.

Molly Warren, too, was working hard at focusing on the mundane. "I'll get the tablecloth," she said. She went into the cabin and returned almost immediately with a zippered plastic storage bag. "Let's go," she said, and we headed for the lake.

Up the shoreline, the old dock, mugged by one too many winters, bellied low in the water, but the dock we had landed beside was new, a T-shaped structure in which the top bar of the T had been widened to ease the loading and unloading of passengers and provisions. The men had taken the coolers to the end of the dock and were unpacking the lunch in the shadow of the plane.

Molly looked thoughtful as she watched. "Maybe it'll help to eat on the water."

It did. Under a sun so intense it glazed the pebbles on the lake bottom, Molly lay down the box containing her daughter's ashes. Then she removed the tablecloth from its protective case and shook it so that it fluttered down over the new wood. The cloth was astonishing: midnight-blue velvet, appliquéd with gold- and silver-lamé cut-outs of suns, moons, stars, buds, blossoms, fruits, birds, fish, and animals.

Fraser knelt down to scrutinize the cloth more closely. "This belongs in an art gallery," he said. "Where did it come from?"

"Ariel made it," Solange said. She turned to Molly questioningly. "She was how old . . . ?"

"She turned thirteen the day she finished it," Molly said.

Solange looked thoughtful. "Thirteen – a time of great power for girls."

"It was a time of great power for my daughter," Molly said. "When she was working on this cloth, she thought she'd discovered what she wanted to do with her life."

"She wanted to make art?" I asked.

"Something like that," Molly said. "Of course, it was out of the question."

The gaze Solange shot Molly was lancing, but Gert headed off trouble. "Time to eat," she said. "There's a point past which I don't trust homemade mayo." She handed around the sandwiches. The choices were egg salad or bologna and mustard. Both were on white bread, generously buttered, and both were very good. The tea Gert poured from the Thermos was good, too, strong and sweet. Our talk was not casual. The presence of the pine box upped the ante, provided a subtext of *tempus fugit* that made idle chatter impossible.

Fraser Jackon traced the edges of an appliquéd crescent moon on the midnight-blue cloth. "The only other time I saw something like this was at a magic show. My dad worked for the CNR. Every Christmas, the company had a party for employees' families. One year they had a magician. Looking back, my guess is the poor guy was a serious boozer. He kept dropping things, and just before his big finale, his dove escaped." Fraser laughed softly. "For most of the kids that was the highlight of the party, but not for me. He might have been a drinker, but that old man had a cape that had the same quality this cloth has – it transported you into another dimension."

"And you decided to create your own cape by going into theatre." The words were vintage Solange, but the tone was warm and urgent. She wanted this outsider who had somehow been an intimate of her friend to reveal himself.

He did. "I'd never thought of theatre as a magic cape," Fraser said slowly, "but as metaphors go, that one's not far off the mark. I've been able to make a lot of ugliness disappear through my work; I've also been part of some astonishing moments." His eyes never left Solange's face. "How about you?" he asked. "What's your metaphor?"

She surprised me. Solange was, by nature, guarded, but that morning she didn't shield herself. "The Ice Capades." She shrugged. "Ridiculous, no? And ugly, too."

Fraser's expression was grave. "You don't have to elaborate."

"Why not?" she said. "We're looking for truths about one another. And one truth about me is that all of my childhood stories are ugly. This one is particularly ugly because it's about a man. Shall I continue?"

She glanced at each of us in turn, defying us to shut her down. No one did.

"Good," she said. "This is a story that should be heard." The warmth that had been in her voice when she had encouraged Fraser Jackson to talk about his past had vanished. Once again, her mask was in place.

"Most of the men my mother brought home left me alone. I'd always counted that as a blessing, but there was one man I liked. His name was Raymond. He was a milkman, and he brought us treats: ice cream, butter, cheese. One day he showed up with two tickets to the Ice Capades. A customer of his had been unable to go. She gave him the tickets, and he invited me. Raymond told me our seats were up with the gods. Naïf that I was, I thought that meant they were the best; of course, it just meant they were cheap, situated at the very top row of the arena. We had to climb and climb. I'd never been in such a crowd. All those people – like a tide, carrying me along." Reflexively, she rubbed her strong, sculpted arms, her insurance against being a victim ever again. "I was pressed against their bodies. I thought I'd suffocate from the smell – wet wool, cigarette smoke, and cheap perfume. By the time we'd found our seats, the blood was singing in my ears. During the national anthem, I had to put my head between my knees to keep from fainting.

"Then the music started, and a girl came onto the ice. Her costume was covered in silver sequins. As she skated on that smooth, perfect rink, little arcs of ice shavings flew from her skates into the air. I'd never seen anything so beautiful. I'd never been so happy." Solange gnawed her lip. "Then I felt Raymond's hand moving between my legs. I was paralysed. When he made me caress him and he grew hard beneath my hand, I felt a coldness in my heart. I knew that if I didn't get away, I would die, that my heart would just freeze and crack open. So I stopped being me. I willed myself into the body and mind of the girl on the ice. The silver sequins on her dress became my armour, protecting me, drawing the light to me, repelling the darkness. It was the first time in my life that I felt safe. Of course, the feeling didn't last. It didn't take me long to learn that women are never safe."

Solange picked up the crust of her sandwich and threw it angrily towards the water. Mr. Birkbeck rose from his sleep, snapped the bread in mid-air and collapsed. Solange turned to me. "You have to play, too, Joanne. We all must take our turn. What's your metaphor?"

Her fierce vulnerability caught me off balance. "I don't know," I said. I touched the midnight-blue cloth. "I guess I was like Ariel. I wanted it all – the sun, the moon, the stars, blossoms, buds, and fruit – everything. What I got was a marriage that was good most of the time, terrific kids, dogs, a house. Naama would say I was an unevolved woman, but it was enough."

Solange had revealed too much to let me get away with less. "You compare yourself with Ariel, but she wanted more than a house with a picket fence. That's your true metaphor, Joanne, and when your husband died the little fence came down and you had to go out into the big world and become a person in your own right."

"I was always a person in my own right," I said loudly, hoping Solange would mistake vehemence for the ring of truth.

She didn't buy it. "I disagree," she said flatly. "Perhaps I'm wrong. I didn't know you then, but when you're with your old friend Howard Dowhanuik, I see vestiges of the woman you were. You defer to him. You're not the person I saw at Ariel's vigil."

I was at a loss; so was everyone else. There was no way the game could go forward. Three of us had revealed ourselves, three were left. But asking Molly or Drew Warren to come up with the metaphor that encapsulated their early dreams was beyond cruel, and Gert struck me as a woman who would rather gut a fish than float a flight of fancy.

Unwittingly, Solange gave us another focus. When she attempted to toss the rest of her sandwich to Mr. Birkbeck, her throw was clumsy. The crust hit the water, and after a lazy catcher's dive, so did Mr. Birkbeck. The splash he made flushed out a bald eagle that struggled briefly then caught an updraft. Absorbed, we watched as the eagle soared, became an infinitesimal speck, then vanished in the cloudless sky.

"My daughter always said that if we saw an eagle the weekend we opened the cottage, it would be a great summer."

An aching silence followed Drew's words. Gentleman that he was, he recognized his gaffe and tried to put us at ease. He fingered the top button of his golf shirt, straightening the knot of the necktie that wasn't there. "I don't know if you remember back to the mid-sixties when there was such

concern about the bald eagle becoming extinct," he said.
"They discovered that bald eagles that summered here in the
north weren't declining at the same rate as other eagles. It
was because northern Saskatchewan wasn't being sprayed
with pesticides – DDT and the like – so the population of
bald eagles remained constant."

On the day of his daughter's burial, Drew's earnest drone
about why the eagles of northern Saskatchewan had escaped
extinction might have seemed bizarre, but it did the trick.
Despite ourselves, we were diverted. My mind went into free
fall, stopping at a memory from twenty years before. Mieka's
grade-two class had held a career morning. My daughter,
always a foot-dragger when it came to school projects, had
been too late to sign up for a visit to one of the glamour-job
sites like the courtroom or the pizzeria. She and the rest of the
stragglers had been stuck with visiting the offices of Drew
Warren's investment firm, and I had been the parent-
volunteer. Drew had tried hard to engage the children. He
asked them how much allowance they were given and
pointed out that, by depositing even the smallest sum each
week, they could make their money grow. He had shown
them how to make images of their hands on his photo-
copier. He even brought out Monopoly money and some
outdated stock certificates to let the kids build their own
stock portfolios. Nothing worked. The children were eye-
rollingly bored. Crestfallen, Drew walked us to the elevator.
Then inspiration hit. He ran back into his office and returned
with booty: two pencils and a stenographer's notepad for
each child.

Drew's discourse upon eagles on the day of his daughter's
burial might have struck a stranger as insensitive, but it
came from the same impulse as his last-minute gift of
pencils and a notepad twenty years before. He was what my
son Angus characterized as a pleaser – a person driven by an

almost pathological need to avoid wounding others. "First, do no harm." Apparently, the chromosome for stunning blond good looks hadn't been the only inheritance passed from father to daughter.

Eager to put an end to another awkward silence, Gert jumped up and slapped her right hand against her thigh. "Come on. Let's walk off those sandwiches. May's a pretty time for the island. The new moss is soft as a baby's bum. And who knows? We might see another eagle. They're always on the lookout for easy fishing and a nice air current." She leaned towards Molly and lowered her voice. "You'll want to see the rock paintings today."

Molly nodded. "Yes," she said, "I'll want to see the rock paintings today." She pulled herself to her feet, bent and picked up the box that contained her daughter's ashes. Quick as a recruit in an honour guard, Fraser retrieved the cloth, folded it the way flags are folded at military funerals, and handed it to Molly. She looked at him levelly. "I'm glad Ariel found you," she said.

Drew led us single file along a trail that bore the marks of nature's effort to reclaim it over the winter. The path was blocked by rocks and fallen tree branches, and melting snow had eroded the line separating trail and wilderness. New moss was everywhere. Idly, I wondered what Blake, who had seen "a world in a grain of sand/And a heaven in a wild flower," would make of vegetation which, flowerless and rootless, still managed to carpet the harsh terrain of a northern island in a green of surpassing tenderness.

To see the paintings, we had to scramble down an embankment and walk back along the shoreline. The lake was high, so most of the beach was underwater. As I leaned back to look up at the rock face, I could feel the water seeping into my boots, but a soaker was a small price to pay for seeing the rock paintings.

There were three of them. One was of a thunderbird holding a bolt of lightning; one was a circle that appeared to hold clouds and an animal, perhaps a bear; the third was on a part of the rock that had been cleft. The circle that framed the picture inside was broken, the drawing inside beyond interpretation.

"How long have they been here?" I asked.

Gert adjusted her ball cap. "Nobody knows for sure – a thousand, maybe two thousand years." She laughed. "Those old ones, they knew how to make paint."

"What did they use?" Solange asked.

"Ochre," Gert said, "mixed in with whatever oil they could find. It was before the days of Home Hardware."

Fraser stepped out into the water to get a better look. "You can feel the power."

Gert chuckled softly. "It depends on who's doing the looking."

No one spoke, but I sensed we all felt a link to the people who had mixed red ochre with the oils of animals and fish. Their paintings were evidence that, like us, they had grappled with the questions that came in the small hours: what does it all mean, and where do I fit in? Molly Warren was beside me. Cradling the pine box and midnight-blue cloth in her arms, she wore her grief like an amulet. As she stared up at the rock paintings, she seemed mesmerized.

Finally, Drew walked over and took his wife's arm. "Time to leave," he said. "Time to do what we came here to do."

Molly shook him off and turned to address the rest of us. "Drew and I have decided on the place for Ariel – not here, although she loved this spot, but closer to our cabin in this clearing that looks out on the water."

We walked back to the cabin in silence. Gert undid the

padlock on a small toolshed and took out a shovel. Drew walked to a spot under a spruce tree and, in a lonely act of love, began to dig. After a few minutes, Fraser took the shovel from him and continued. Each of us took our turn. It was surprisingly hard work, but we managed, and when the hole was deep enough, Molly knelt and put in the box. Gert dropped to her knees, took a cigarette from the package in her breast pocket, broke it open, and placed the tobacco beside the pine box. "It's tradition to give something back," she said simply.

After that, it was over quickly. We handed the shovel around, replaced the earth, and knelt in a circle. Molly Warren smoothed the dirt and covered it with the midnight-blue cloth. "I've been trying all morning to think of the right words," she said. She held out her hands, palms out, empty. "Does anyone have any?"

The sun picked up the gold- and silver-lamé appliqués of the moon and the stars, blossoms, flowers, fruit, fish, animals. Against the midnight blue, the figures that Ariel had cut out seemed to pulse with independent life.

"There's a line from Dante," I said. " 'Oh, the experience of this sweet life.' "

Every face in our circle betrayed a tightening of the throat, but the silence was absolute. We were enveloped in a moment as fragile and self-contained as a teardrop. And then – horribly – the sound of a plane's motor sliced the silent air.

Mr. Birkbeck howled. Solange breathed a curse and a single name. "Naama."

That was the name on my lips, too. As I watched the small plane descend and its pontoons slap the surface of the lake, I remembered Naama's fury in Livia Brook's office. *You can't keep us away. Ariel was a Red Riding Hood. We have every right to be there. We have every right to avenge her.* As I waited for the plane's door to open, I knew I had no resources left to deal with Naama and her unquenchable rage. Neither did anyone else. Faced with this new challenge, we stumbled to our feet. We were all running on empty.

Not surprisingly, it was Gert who made the first move. She snapped her fingers, brought Mr. Birkbeck to heel, and the two of them set off to meet the plane taxiing towards the old dock. When the motors cut, the door opened and a short, grey-haired man emerged. He and Gert pumped hands, then turned towards the open plane door. I steeled myself, waiting for the assault of Naama and her cohorts. But the passengers who stepped onto the dock were even more of a nightmare than Naama would have been.

Howard Dowhanuik and his son were both in full mourning: black suits, white shirts, dark ties. They looked like the Blues Brothers on vacation. Shocked, I almost laughed, but as they came closer the anguish on Charlie's face killed the laugh in my throat.

It didn't take Charlie long to read the situation. His eyes passed over the mourners and rested on the gravesite, then he went straight to Molly and Drew. "You can't leave her there," he said simply. "She shouldn't be in the dark. Let me take the canoe out on the lake. I'll scatter her ashes."

Molly's face was bloodless, her lips a line thin as a surgical scar. "It's a bad idea, Charlie. Ashes from a human body are dense. If you try to scatter them, they get under your fingernails, into your skin. You can't get them out."

"I don't want to get them out," Charlie said.

Solange's pupils were pinpoints of loathing. "Are you hoping her ashes will cover her blood?" she said.

"You were the one she was afraid of," he said.

Solange's mouth shaped itself into a cartoon-like O. "Never," she said. "I never would have hurt her."

Howard grabbed his son and pulled him away from

Solange. "Coming here was a mistake, Charlie. Let's just get back on the plane and go home."

"Your father's right." Fraser Jackson's voice was powerful and assured. "This has been a terrible day for all of us. None of us should do anything to make it worse."

Charlie looked at Fraser without comprehension. "What are you doing here?"

Fraser didn't flinch. "Like everyone here, I just came to say goodbye. It's time to let Ariel rest in peace, Charlie."

"*Peace.*" Charlie repeated the word as if it were a noun from an unknown language, then broke from his father's arms and sprinted towards the plane.

Howard's voice in my ear was urgent. "You gotta come back with us, Jo. I don't know how to handle this."

I didn't hesitate. I walked over to Drew and Molly Warren. "I'm going to fly back with them," I said. "I hope you understand."

"Do what you need to do," Drew said. And then, a prisoner of his immaculate manners, he patted my hand. "It was good of you to come all this way, Joanne. I hope it wasn't too hard on you. Molly and I keep telling people we're all right, but we're not, you know. I don't think we could have handled this alone."

I embraced Molly. When Fraser Jackson kissed my cheek, I promised I'd call him later in the weekend. Gert was over on the old dock talking to the pilot of the other plane, so the only farewell left was to Solange. When I reached out to her, she spun away.

"Not so evolved after all," she said. "A man asks, and Joanne Kilbourn scurries after him."

"Not every encounter between a man and a woman is a power struggle," I said.

I tried to walk away with a purposeful stride, but Howard had long legs and a determination to get the hell out. As usual, once he'd exacted the agreement he needed, he was dealing with the next problem. I could feel Solange's eyes burning into my back as I ran along behind him. It was going to be a long flight home.

The plane we flew back to Prince Albert on was called the *Silver Fox*, after its owner, who on closer inspection turned out to be a banty rooster of a man with vulpine features, hair moussed into a silver sweep, and dentures that dazzled. Gert handed me over to Silver without any time-wasting sentimentalities.

"I noticed you're a nervous flyer," she said, "but Silver here has been in the business as long as I have."

Silver took his comb and perfected his sweep-back. "Haven't lost a passenger yet. At least not a good-looking one."

Gert shot him a dismissive glance and held out her hand to me. "It's been a pleasure," she said. "Happy landings."

Charlie was slumped against the window in the seat behind the pilot. He was wearing the earphones from a Discman and, as I walked past him, I could hear the tinny overflow of rhythm that comes when someone is listening to hard rock at full volume.

Except for the two seats opposite Charlie, the plane was filled with cargo. I sat down next to Howard, and I didn't cut him any slack. "What in the name of God were you thinking of, bringing him up here?" I said.

"Jo, I've been a lousy father his whole life. He wanted to come. Marnie said it was my turn."

"*Marnie!* Howard, you know Marnie's judgement hasn't exactly been reliable since her accident. Did she understand what she was saying?"

Howard balled his hands into fists. "Jesus, Jo. Will you lay off? I know I made a mistake. Do you want to see what I was dealing with? Here." He reached into the inside pocket of his funeral suit, pulled out a hand full of photographs and thrust them at me.

"These are for you," he said. "From Marnie. She liked the picture you sent from the old days so much she had me stick it up on the wall next to her bed."

The image deflated me. "I'm glad she liked it," I said weakly.

"She loved it," Howard said, "and of course the sisters at Good Shepherd are getting a real kick out of those words of wisdom you wrote on the bottom of the picture."

Remembering, I cringed. "'Screw them all!' Howard, it never occurred to me that the photo would be on display."

"It doesn't matter. Actually, not much of anything matters any more in that quarter."

He was right. The pictures in my hand were of Marnie. There were vestiges of the Marnie I had known in this woman's face, but she was a stranger. Her hair had grown back grey and surprisingly curly. She was carefully made-up – another surprise, since the Marnie I had known said makeup was for clowns. She was wearing a pink tracksuit. Someone had put a matching pink ribbon in her hair. Suddenly I was furious.

I turned to Howard. "How could you let them do that to her?" I asked.

"Do what?"

"Turn her into a doll."

"The sisters are very kind to her, Jo. They try to make her happy. I don't give a good goddamn if they want to play dressup with her. To be honest, she doesn't seem to mind."

"I'll bet."

The Silver Fox revved the engines and we skimmed off the lake. I leaned across Howard to look out the window. We were moving across the cobalt-blue waters, lifting above a hundred islands. Once, a glacier had covered the whole area; when it retreated, this was the topography it had left behind. I thought of the misery at the Warrens' cottage, and in our plane. "Maybe we were better off when all this was a glacier," I said. "Better off frozen solid, before the big melt-down when somebody had the bright idea to climb out of the slime."

Howard gave me a look of disgust. "Save the existential crap for somebody who cares, Jo. We gotta figure out a way to deal with what's happening. How much trouble is Charlie in?"

"You tell me. The woman he loves to the point of obsession leaves him, and she's pregnant with another man's child."

Howard rubbed the bridge of his nose. "I take it the baby's father was that black guy who was at the service today."

I nodded. "His name is Fraser Jackson. He teaches in the Theatre department at the university.

Howard didn't flinch. "So Ariel met him at work and fell in love with him."

"It wasn't like that," I said.

"What was it like?"

"She wanted a child, and she chose Fraser Jackson as the biological father."

True to form, Howard travelled straight to the heart of the matter. "She needed to make a choice where there was no turning back," he said. He leaned across me to look at his son. Charlie was sprawled across the seat, with his eyes closed and earphones in place, blasting their tinny sound, shutting out the world. He seemed closer in age to Angus than to Mieka. There was an adolescent narcissism about his grief that I found unsettling. It couldn't have been easy for Ariel living with that juvenile intensity.

Howard straightened, leaned his head against the headrest, and stared at the plane's ceiling. "Did she hate him that much?" he asked.

"I don't think she hated him at all," I said. "I think she

just needed to break away." Suddenly, the plane dropped through the sky and spun. Howard draped an arm around my shoulders. "Just an air pocket, Jo. Our pilot is responding with a little loop-de-loop. My guess is it's for your benefit."

"He doesn't need to impress me," I said tightly. "If he can keep this in the air, I'll be dazzled." The plane regained altitude, and I removed Howard's protective arm.

"Okay?" he asked.

"Yeah," I said, "I'm okay."

"So," he said, "she didn't hate him. She just needed to break away, and he couldn't let her."

I nodded.

"Was she afraid of him?"

"I don't know," I said.

"*I know.*" At the sound of Charlie's voice, Howard and I both snapped our heads towards him. Charlie's dark hair was tangled, and the earphones dangled from his neck. "She wasn't afraid of me," he said. "How could she be? She was the centre of my life. She *was* my life."

"You were smothering her, Charlie." I could feel my blood rising. "She wanted her own life. Why couldn't you get it? The day she died, you recited a poem by Denise Levertov. Remember it, Charlie? 'Dig them the deepest well,/Still it's not deep enough/To drink the moon from.' Anyone who heard your show that day knew how angry you were."

"Leave him alone, Jo." Howard was angry, too.

"No," I said. "Howard, you dragged me into this. You said you needed my help. If I'm going to help, I need some answers. Another thing – the police are going to want to talk to Charlie. He has to be prepared for the kinds of questions they'll be asking."

Howard's face sagged. "She's right, Charlie," he said quietly. "You need to level with us."

"About what?" Charlie voice was wary.

"For starters, about the baby," Howard said. "You did know Ariel was pregnant, didn't you?"

Strangely, Charlie seemed almost proud. "You can't love a woman the way I loved her without being aware of every nuance in her voice, every change in her body. Of course, I knew."

"And you knew it wasn't your child."

Charlie tightened. "It wasn't a concern for me," he said.

"Was it a concern for you when Ariel moved out?" I asked.

"She would have come back," Charlie said. "It was only a matter of time." He put his earphones back on and cranked up the sound on his Discman, sealing himself away, closing us out.

For a few moments, Howard and I were silent as strangers. Then he turned to me. "Maybe you were right," he said.

"About what?"

"Maybe we *were* better off when all this was frozen solid," he said, rapping on the window of the plane. "Maybe we were happier before the big meltdown when that first wise guy had the bright idea of climbing out of the slime."

I glared at him. "Save the existential crap for someone who cares," I said. "We gotta figure out what to do next."

CHAPTER

11

"I can't offer you a lift," I said. "I took a cab this morning."

Howard looked at his watch. "It's almost five. Do you want to go someplace for a drink?"

Rumpled, weary, and blinking in the sunshine, Howard, Charlie, and I were standing outside the main entrance to the Regina airport. We were home, but there was no cause to break out the ticker tape. Coming home meant facing up to the hard questions we'd been able to dodge from the moment the Silver Fox had deposited us on the tarmac at Prince Albert airport, and we had boarded the first of the two public planes that flew us out of the boreal north back to the short-grass prairie. Surrounded again by coffee-carrying bureaucrats and business people, Howard and I had talked listlessly, and Charlie had wrapped himself in a blanket of impenetrable solitude. Circumstances had demanded discretion, but now circumstances had changed. The prospect of a drink and a private conversation in a dark restaurant was appealing, but it was also unrealistic. In our province, drunks and idealists still considered an ex-premier fair game, and Charlie's blood-marked face made his anonymity unlikely.

"It might be easier to talk at my place," I said. "Why don't you come back for dinner?"

"What's on the menu?" Howard asked.

"Gin," I said.

"Sold," he said, grinning wearily. Charlie smiled, too, and I felt a faint stirring of hope.

When we got there, the kids and the animals were in the family room watching an Adam Sandler movie. Howard was a familiar figure in our home; normally, his presence wouldn't have merited much beyond a glance and a grin. But Charlie was another matter entirely. Taylor, who knew enough not to stare, said hi, then busied herself pretending to check her cats for fleas. Angus offered Charlie a laconic wave of acknowledgement, but Eli was transfixed. His idol was in the room.

"I don't think you've met Eli Kequahtooway," I said to Charlie. "He's the nephew of a good friend, and he's a big fan of yours."

Charlie extended a hand and Eli took it.

"I'm sorry about your girlfriend," Eli said softly.

"Thanks," Charlie said. There was an uncomfortable silence, then Eli gestured towards an empty armchair. "This movie's pretty cool if you haven't got anything better to do."

"I haven't got anything better to do," Charlie said. He sprawled in the chair and, within an instant, seemed wholly absorbed.

Howard looked at me. "There was a mention of gin."

After considerably more than a mention of gin, we ordered take-out from Peking House. Howard's treat. It was, he said, the least he could do, and I didn't disagree.

Our order was extravagantly large and expensive. When the last of the cardboard containers had been emptied and Willie and the boys had run off their dinner, Angus and his girlfriend, Leah, went to hear the newest, hottest band, and the rest of us gravitated towards the backyard. Eli asked Charlie if he wanted to swim, and Charlie surprised me by accepting the invitation. He came back wearing one of Angus's suits. His skin was the blue-white of skimmed milk, and his body was very thin; he projected an aura that was both vulnerable and achingly sexual. The exposure of self was disturbing, and I was relieved when he dove into the pool and his pale body disappeared beneath the water. Without exchanging a word, he and Eli began to swim laps, moving through the water with the methodical rhythm of channel swimmers headed for a distant shore.

Taylor plunked herself next to Howard. My old friend was only marginally better with children than he was with women, but he had one party trick that Taylor loved. He told Tommy Douglas's old political parable about Mouseland with immense panache. Taylor had always been fascinated by the story about the little mice who, every four years, walked to the polls and blithely cast their ballots for an all-cat slate of candidates. That night, however, as Howard moved towards the story's climax, my daughter was squirming. Howard had barely described the scene in which one little mouse proposes electing a government made up of mice and is locked up as a Bolshevik when Taylor streaked out of the room.

"Losing your touch," I said to Howard. "She didn't even stick around for 'You can lock up a mouse or a man, but you can't lock up an idea,' and that's the best line."

"Maybe Bruce and Benny got to her," Howard said gloomily. "Any more of that gin left?"

Luckily, my daughter was back before I had to tell Howard that, as far as he was concerned, the bar was closed. She was struggling under the weight of a canvas almost as big as she was. Howard jumped up to help her, and she sighed dramatically. "This was supposed to be a surprise, but when you told the story I knew I couldn't wait." Her eyes caught mine. "Jo, I won first prize in that Social Studies contest. Ms. Cousin wanted to tell you, but I thought it would be so neat if you thought you were just coming to the Legislature as a parent-helper, but it was really because I'd won." She looked up at Howard. "Could you turn the painting so we can see it?"

Howard dropped to his knees and held the canvas out in front of him. "Jesus," he said. "It's Mouseland. Look, Jo, there's the Legislature and there are all the mice, running the show. It's great, Taylor, but who's that old mouse – the tough-looking one with the snarl?"

"You!" Taylor crowed. "You're in charge."

"Maybe I'll do a better job this time," Howard said. He turned to me. "So fill me in. What's this all about?"

"Actually, it was an idea Ben Jesse had to get kids thinking about studying government. All the grade twos from the city were eligible to submit projects. Livia chaired the committee that judged the entries. I knew she was going to be at the presentation tomorrow, but she didn't breathe a word about Taylor winning." I looked at my daughter. "Neither did you. I can't believe you didn't spill the beans."

Taylor clenched her fists in triumph. "Angus says I can't keep a secret. I kept this one right till the day before you were supposed to find out."

"A record," I said.

She ignored me. "The prize is you get to meet your Member of the Legislature and then you and your parent have refreshments with her or him."

Howard hooted. "So, Jo, you'll be breaking bread with Bev Pilon. That'll be nice for you."

I had tried hard to defeat Bev Pilon in the last election. She was smart, rich, and unswervingly committed to the proposition that the sleek should inherit the earth. In a real-life Mouseland, she would be Queen of the Mean Cats.

"My cup runneth over," I said.

Taylor scrunched her face. "But you are glad I won."

I reached out and touched her cheek. "I couldn't be more proud. Now we'd better get that painting in the house before the mosquitoes splat into it."

When I returned, I thought for a moment that Howard was asleep. He was stretched out on the lazy lounge with his eyes closed, but when he heard my step, he turned his head towards me. "There *are* good times," he said.

I reached over and took his hand. "Plenty of them," I said. "And there will be more."

Across the yard, Charlie and Eli were getting out of the pool – Eli picked up a towel, tied it around his waist in the way of teenage boys, then threw another towel to Charlie. Charlie wrapped himself in his, instinctively covering as much of his body as he could.

When Eli started towards the house, Charlie called out after him. "Thanks," he said. "That helped. It really did."

Instead of following Eli, Howard's son veered towards us and squatted cross-legged on the ground, turning his face so that the birthmark was away from us. "Not many people are smart enough to know that sometimes the best thing you can do to help is just be there and be quiet," he said.

His tone was wistful and reflective, but Howard didn't get past the words. "Goddammit, Charlie, do you think the cops are just sitting there being quiet, or do you think they might actually be out there asking questions and getting answers?"

"I just meant I was grateful to Eli, Dad." Suddenly, there was an edgy danger in Charlie's voice. "I understand that you need me to work out answers for the police's questions before they ask me," he said.

"I need you to tell the truth, son." Howard's words had a simple Biblical force.

So did Charlie's response. "I'll tell the truth," he said.

The darkness had settled. It was a relief to listen without the distraction of Charlie's face. Nightfall seemed to free him, too, allow him to become a truer self, one in whom I began to discern flashes of the boy Marnie had raised and, for a time, Ariel had loved.

Howard breathed deeply. "Okay," he said. "Let's start with the big one. Did you kill Ariel?"

"No."

Howard nodded, seemingly accepting his son's one-word answer as sufficient. It wasn't enough for me, but I could feel myself moving towards belief in Charlie's innocence.

"Then the next step," Howard said, "is to find out if you know anything that will help the police find out who did kill her."

"All right," Charlie said.

There was an awkward silence. Howard shot me a look that called for help. "So, Jo. You've been closer to this than we have. Any thoughts?"

"That was smooth," I said. Charlie laughed quietly. Encouraged, I continued. "I guess my first thought is Solange," I said. "Charlie, when you two clashed today, you told Solange that Ariel was afraid of her. Was that just a heat-of-the-moment accusation or was it true?"

Charlie made a gesture of dismissal. "There's so much about the past that just doesn't seem relevant any more," he said. "Solange is going through her own hell."

"I know," I said. "But that doesn't exempt her, and it doesn't make what happened in the past irrelevant. We're not just talking about being dumped here; we're talking about murder. If Ariel really was afraid of Solange, it matters."

Charlie drew in his narrow shoulders and looked down at the grass. "Ariel and Solange had an unusual relationship."

"Unusual in what way?"

He looked thoughtful. "In its voltage," he said finally. "It was far too intense – at least on Solange's side. It wasn't always like that. At first, Ariel and Solange were just friends, the way any two people who work together are. Solange even came by the house and had a drink with us a couple of times, but after they went to Mount Assiniboine it was different."

"Solange told me that Ariel found herself on Mount Assiniboine."

Charlie shook his head with the weariness of a man forced to explain a self-evident truth. "Ariel found herself *with me*. I gave her everything she needed or wanted. She'd lost sight of that, but we would have worked it out if Solange hadn't come along with her *insights*."

"So you don't believe that Ariel was liberated by her experience on Mount Assiniboine."

Charlie's eyes widened in disbelief. "*Liberated*. That has to be Solange's word, and it couldn't be more wrong. Joanne, we're not talking about girl power here. It's something more complex."

"Then explain it to me," I said.

"Solange loved Ariel," Charlie said. "Ariel felt that brought certain obligations."

Howard's reaction was a sputter. "You mean Solange and Ariel were . . . ?"

"They were *nothing*." Charlie's voice was low with fury. "Solange was temporary. An abberation. Ariel's destiny was intertwined with mine from the day we met. She was just confused."

"You and Ariel talked about this confusion?" I asked.

"We didn't have to," Charlie said. "I didn't need flaming letters in the sky. When you're as close to someone as I was to Ariel, you learn to read the signs. After Mount Assiniboine, the signs were there. She didn't want to be with me. There was never an angry word, but one night I brushed her arm and she flinched. It wasn't calculated. It was the response a person has to touching something they find repugnant, like a snake or a slug. I ignored it. I knew that if I just kept loving her . . ."

"But loving her wasn't enough," I said. "She wanted out."

"She *thought* she wanted out. But even when she was saying we had to break it off, her real feelings were apparent. She told me that her life had been immeasurably enriched by knowing me, that she couldn't have asked for more in a lover or a friend." He rubbed his eyes with his fists, like a child fighting sleep. "That's why I couldn't let her go. I knew neither of us could have a life without the other."

"Jesus!" Howard's curse was an explosion in the tranquil air. "I can't listen to this."

When Howard jumped from his chair, I grabbed his arm. "Let Charlie talk," I said.

Howard's son continued like a man in a trance. "So she stayed. I tried to anticipate everything she could possibly want: food, flowers, music – even Fritz. She'd always wanted a dog, so we went to the Humane Society and got Fritz. I thought our relationship was working." He hunched into a position that was almost foetal. "Two weeks ago I came home, and she was moving out."

"Fraser Jackson was with her," I said.

"He was just incidental," Charlie said wearily, closing the topic.

I reopened it. "So you came home by chance . . ."

"When it came to Ariel, I never left anything to chance," he said. "Everything about her was too important. I knew her habits, her routines. She always folded her nightgown and left it under her pillow. That morning, I checked. The nightgown wasn't there. That's what alerted me. So I asked Troy to finish the show, and I came home early. Of course, she'd hoped to avoid a confrontation."

"Did it get violent?" Howard asked.

"Do you mean apart from the fact that she was ripping our lives apart? No, Dad, it didn't get violent. It was just sad – really sad – for both of us. She seemed so tired, but I couldn't help myself. I lost it . . ."

"Lost it how?" I asked.

He winced at the memory. "I cried. You know, that thing real men aren't supposed to do. She just seemed to slump. It was as if I'd hit her. That's when she told me she'd broken it off with Solange, too."

Suddenly, Howard was all lawyer. He leaned forward. "What did Ariel say exactly?"

Charlie's face tightened. "She said, 'I can't go through this again. I thought *she* at least would understand. She's always insisted that all she wants is for me to be happy . . . but she was so angry. I'm frightened. She's done some terrible things.'"

"And she mentioned Solange by name?"

"Not by name," he said, "but who else could it be?"

Howard pounded his fist into his palm. "Why the hell didn't you mention this before?"

Charlie looked at his father in amazement. "How anxious would you be to revisit the worst day of your life?"

They left early, not much past eight o'clock. Charlie insisted on staying at the home he and Ariel had shared, and Howard insisted on not leaving his son alone. I watched their cab pull away, then went upstairs to check on the kids.

Taylor was already in bed, eyes squeezed shut, courting sleep, but when she heard my step, she bolted upright. "I'm so excited," she said. "Are you?"

"Very," I said. "Now, I want to take a closer look at *Mouseland*. The light wasn't very good outside, and we were all a little distracted."

"By that boy," she said.

"By that *man*," I said, correcting her. "Charlie's twenty-seven years old. The same age as Mieka."

Taylor took in the information. "He seemed more like a kid." She shrugged. "Let's look at the picture. You didn't even notice that I put you and me in there."

I picked up *Mouseland* and carried it over to the bed. It really was a terrific piece: the Legislature was Crayola-bright and surreal, but Taylor had drawn the duly elected mice and the sulky displaced cats with a cartoonist's eye for detail. At the top of the marble steps leading into the Legislature, a matronly mouse in sensible shoes raised her paws in delight as a shining-eyed young mouse with braids twirled on one toe.

I pointed the figures out to Taylor. "Us?" I asked.

She nodded happily. "This is going to be so fun, Jo."

"You bet," I said. Then I leaned across her and turned out the light.

Eli's door was closed, but when I knocked, he invited me in.

"I just wanted to thank you for helping Charlie tonight." I said.

"I didn't do anything special."

"You were there," I said, "and that was what he needed."

Eli matched the fingertips of his hands and flexed them thoughtfully. "My uncle used to tell me this was a spider doing push-ups on a mirror," he said.

"Funny guy, your uncle." I said.

Eli smiled. "I wish he was here."

"Me, too," I said. "But I'll tell you one thing. Even your uncle couldn't have done a better job than you did tonight."

For a moment, I stood outside Eli's doorway thinking about all the things I should do: phone Ed Mariani and ask him if there had been any problems with the mid-term; take the dishes out of the dishwasher; mark some of the essays that seemed to breed in my briefcase; iron a blouse to wear to the Legislature the next morning. There was no shortage of worthy projects awaiting my attention. I rejected them all in favour of a hot shower and clean pyjamas.

Fifteen minutes later, I was in bed. As a sop to my conscience, I took *Political Perspectives* with me. I was trying to make sense of the concept of sovereignty-association when the phone rang. A sixth sense told me the news would not be good, and the sixth sense was right.

Kevin Coyle's voice was a breathy rasp. "Trouble's brewing," he said.

"Kevin, you're starting to sound more and more like a character in a Sam Peckinpah movie."

"You think you're insulting me – implying I'm marginal and obsessed with the dark side – but Peckinpah knew things about the human psyche that you and I would do well to remember."

"Such as . . . ?"

"Such as the fact that violence doesn't just pop up like a mushroom. It's character-driven. If you don't believe that, check out what Ann Vogel and *her* wild bunch are doing on Ariel's Web page. There's a fresh list of atrocities and new plans for retribution. Incidentally, there's a reference to you that's less than favourable. Apparently, you're guilty of a sin of omission or commission that's moved you from the circle of the elect to the circle of the damned."

"Kevin, I'm so sick of this."

"There's more," he said, but his tone was both gentle and apologetic. "There was someone sniffing around your office earlier tonight. When she saw me she ran."

"Who was it?"

"I was down the hall but, unless I'm very much mistaken, it was our friend, Solange."

"What was she doing?

"Sliding something under your door."

"Swell," I said.

"I'm sure Solange draws the line at letter bombs," Kevin said.

Remembering the scene Charlie had described, I was silent.

"That was supposed to cheer you up," Kevin said. "A Sam Peckinpah joke."

"I think I'm beyond cheering," I said.

There was a pause. "This gives me no pleasure. I hope you know that, Joanne."

"I do. It's hard for all of us. Now, I guess I'd better check out that Web site."

"You'll need fortification."

I didn't have to be told twice. I walked into Angus's room with a glass containing two fingers of Crown Royal. When I saw the Web page I was glad I have broad fingers. Someone had managed to get the autopsy photographs of Ariel and had posted them on the site. Whether the thief had been bribed or had simply shared Ann Vogel's monomania would be a question for the police to answer. All I knew was that the last private place in Ariel's life had been invaded, and I was sick at heart.

Oddly, except for the fact that she was lying on a metal autopsy table, the photographs of Ariel were not disturbing. She was, of course, very pale, but otherwise unmarked. I remembered Rosalie quoting her ever-quotable Robert on the fact that Ariel had died from a surgically precise wound in the back. She hadn't been mutilated; in death she was as lovely as ever. With her trailing hair, her perfect profile, and her translucent skin, she looked like a Maxfield Parrish illustration of Sleeping Beauty, waiting for the kiss from her prince.

But the additions the Friends of Red Riding Hood had made to Ariel's Web page were not the stuff of fairy tales, and their statistics conjured up a world in which princes were in mighty short supply. One hundred women murdered each year in Canada by a male partner; 62 per cent of all women murdered, victims of domestic violence; a Canadian woman raped every seven minutes; 84 per cent of sexual assaults committed by someone known to the victims; almost half of all women with disabilities sexually abused as children; number of sexual assaults reported to Canadian police growing exponentially.

Horrifying as they were, the statistics were simply prologue. The real focus of the Web page was a letter addressed "TO ALL WHO SEEK JUSTICE." It began:

Some of you will question our decision to post autopsy photographs of Ariel Warren on this page. You want to remember Ariel as the vital, evolving woman she was, not as a corpse with a toe-tag. You will find the pictures disturbing. You will resent us for forcing you to confront images so stark and so real that to contemplate them is to feel the knife in one's own back. Events in the past week have made it necessary for us to act.

In the days before her death, Ariel attempted many times to leave her Intimate Partner. He refused to let her go. Now she is dead; her ex-lover walks the streets; one of her colleagues joins forces with her killer's father; the police shrug. The Friends of Red Riding Hood refuse to abandon Ariel to the vagaries of a patriarchal law system, a system created by men to protect their own. Charlie Dowhanuik (a.k.a. Charlie D of CVOX radio) must be brought to justice. Hunt him down the way Ariel was hunted down. Phone him. E-mail him. Fax him.

A list of the numbers and addresses through which Charlie could be reached followed. The letter's final paragraph was a call to arms.

Jam the switchboard at his radio station with demands that he be fired. Phone him at home every hour on the hour. Make his life hell, the way he made her life hell. Join the Friends tomorrow night as we march to the house he shared with Ariel and demand answers to our questions. We will meet at 5:00 p.m. in front of the library where Ariel was murdered and march to the house on Manitoba Street that she tried so often to leave.

I dialled Howard's cellphone. "Trouble," I said. "I just checked the Internet. There's an open letter there you should see. Do you have access to Charlie's computer?"

"It wouldn't do me any good. I don't even know how to turn one on."

"Get Charlie to do it."

"He's not here."

"Where is he?"

"I don't know. Just out."

"You've got to do better than that," I said. "You have to stay with him."

"Jo, you sound a little hysterical."

"I *am* a little hysterical. Listen to this letter, Howard." As I read, I tried to keep my tone flat, to defuse the words. It was impossible.

When I finished. Howard uttered an expletive that even he should have been ashamed of using. Then he muttered, "Lynch-mob mentality."

"They're grieving, and they believe they'll never get justice. It's a dangerous combination. I think Charlie should lie low for a while."

"Stay at my place?" Howard said.

"You're not exactly an unknown quantity yourself," I said.

"Where then?"

I didn't welcome the answer that presented itself. But Charlie was Marnie and Howard's son and, whatever else he had done, I now believed he would have cut off his hand before he raised it against Ariel. "Charlie can stay with us," I said. "There's an extra bed in Eli's room."

"I'll bring him over as soon as he gets back," Howard said.

"I'll leave the key under the planter on the front porch," I said. "You may be late, and I've had enough today."

"You and me both, kid," Howard said. "I wonder if this is ever going to end."

I slept fitfully, waiting for the sound of the key in the lock or of Charlie's footstep. Neither came. The next morning when the alarm went off, I padded down to Eli's room; the twin bed next to his was empty. Charlie hadn't spent the night. In the pit of my stomach, I felt the stirrings of anxiety. When I looked at my reflection in the bathroom mirror, I remembered Duke Ellington's famous response to someone who had commented on the bags under his eyes. "Those aren't bags," said Duke. "Those are stored-up virtue."

It took a few passes with the concealer to mask my stored-up virtue, but by the time Taylor came in to show me her outfit, I wouldn't have drawn attention in a crowd. Taylor, on the other hand, would have – for all the right reasons. On many days she was an eccentric dresser, but today she had obviously considered the solemnity of the occasion. She was wearing her Nova Scotia tartan kilt, matching cream turtleneck and tights, and the beaded barrettes Alex had bought her at last summer's powwow at Standing Buffalo. The all-Canadian girl, and she was as excited as I could ever remember seeing her. I drove the two blocks to the Legislature with the *Mouseland* canvas, carefully wrapped and balanced against the back seat. Taylor and I carried it up the steps of the Legislature together.

Bev Pilon and Livia Brook were waiting for us by the commissionaire's desk in the first-floor lobby. Livia appeared less haggard than she had in a week. Her skin was faintly pink, as if she'd spent some time outdoors, and her mass of grey and chestnut curls was pushed neatly back with a tortoiseshell hairband. Mercifully, she had decided against wearing the poppy-spattered shawl that Ariel had made, and her outfit was both simple and attractive: tan cotton jumper, white T-shirt, and Birkenstocks, the uniform for female academics of a certain age.

Bev Pilon's look was corporate cool: a smart spring suit in apple green, honey hair artfully styled to look artless, makeup smoothly subtle. She beamed when she spotted Taylor, introduced herself, then took my daughter's hand and headed for the stairs. Just as the ancient commissionaire noticed me struggling with the picture and came out of his booth, a cameraman from NationTV came through the front door. Kim took in the optics and waved off the commissionaire with a dazzling smile.

"Thanks, but we can handle this," she said. Then, as co-operatively as the citizens of Mouseland, Bev Pilon, Livia Brook, and I carried Taylor's canvas towards the rotunda where Marie Cousin and the grade-two class from Lakeview School were waiting for the presentation.

The ceremony didn't take long. Livia presented Taylor with a plaque, then spoke gracefully of Ben Jesse's commitment to making young people believe politics was an honourable profession. She quoted Ben's comment that it was good for government when schools bring kids to see the Legislature in session, because when real children are present, our legislators are, occasionally, shamed into acting like adults. Bev accepted the jibe with a tinkling laugh and an impressive display of teeth. She gave Taylor a tiny Saskatchewan flag and a lapel pin, then summoned the cameraman from NationTV to get his interview. After my daughter had delivered her opinions on socialism, mice, and art, I went over to Marie Cousin.

"That was terrific," I said. "And your subterfuge was brilliant. Anyway, I signed up as a parent-helper, so what's next?"

Marie's eyes were concerned. "You look a little weary," she said. "Since the real purpose of your coming today was to see Taylor get her award, how about giving the tour a pass?"

"To use a word that Taylor tells me you believe should be kept in reserve, that would be *awesome*."

The corners of Marie's mouth turned up slightly. "Taylor told you about Cheops."

"She did," I said, "but at the moment, the idea of having the next hour to myself beats the prospect of seeing the pyramids by a country mile."

We said our goodbyes, and then I joined Livia. She and I made our way back through the shadowy halls to the brilliant sunshine. After the chilly recycled air of the building, the warm outdoor air was seductively sweet. When Livia started towards her car, I was tempted to let her go, and head home to the lazy lounge on the deck, but the message of Ariel's Web site was too urgent to ignore.

I went after her. "Livia, do you have a few minutes to talk?"

She shrugged. "I'm not going anywhere."

"There's a bench over there where we could have a little privacy," I said, pointing to a green space between the Legislature and Albert Street.

We strolled along a path flanked by flowerbeds. In high summer, the area was a riot of colours and scents, but that

May morning the spectacular beauty was still to come. Only the first tender green shoots of perennials and bedding plants were visible in the fresh-turned earth. The bench and the simple bronze memorial to Woodrow Lloyd opposite it were less than a minute's walk away.

"I had no idea this place was even here," Livia said. She moved closer so she could see the poem inscribed on the bronze. "'The Road Not Taken,'" she said. "I haven't thought of Robert Frost in a hundred years."

"Most of us leave him behind after freshman English," I agreed, "but I still like him."

She came over and took a place at the other end of the bench, as far away as possible from me. "I assume you want to talk about the march tonight," she said.

"Among other things," I said. "Livia, do you have any idea who wrote that open letter?"

"'To All Who Seek Justice'? I've come up with some possibilities. Nothing definite."

"I thought at first it might have been Ann Vogel," I said, "but she was a student of mine. I'm familiar with her writing. Even with the spell-checker and grammar check, she couldn't have managed this. The constructions are too sophisticated."

"I would have said Solange. She's the one who travels in the really radical feminist circles. The women she knows wouldn't stick at publishing an autopsy photo." Livia ran a hand through her hair distractedly. "Why does it matter?"

"Because that letter is an incitement to mob action, and mobs are unpredictable and dangerous. This march would be a lousy idea even if Charlie Dowhanuik were guilty, and I don't believe that he is."

"Do you know something the rest of us don't?"

"Just that Ariel had another close relationship that was causing her concern."

Livia gnawed her lip. "Solange," she said finally. "We should have been more careful."

"*Who* should have been more careful?"

"Those of us on the committee that appointed her." Livia's face was etched with regret. "Her references were . . . questionable."

"The files for the short-listed candidates were circulated. I read them all. Solange's letters of reference were glowing. Ariel's letters were the ones that seemed doubtful. All her referees were positive, but, as I recall, at least two of them expressed reservations about her commitment to academic life. They picked up on the same ambivalence the committee sensed in her interview."

"There were other considerations," Livia said crisply. "I phoned all the referees, pressed them to give me more detailed profiles than a letter would permit. The people with whom Ariel had studied spoke so eloquently about her potential that I knew we had to have her."

"Even if she wasn't certain this was where she wanted to be," I said.

"This *was* where she wanted to be. Joanne, when I met Ariel at the women's retreat at Saltspring, there was an immediate kinship. Despite the difference in our ages, we were at parallel stages in our lives. We were both at that point where . . . what was it Frost said?"

" 'Two roads diverged,' " I said.

"That's it exactly, and because each of us knew how the other felt, we were able to support one another. That was the mandate of the retreat: women empowering women."

"And you empowered Ariel to continue to her studies."

Livia's eyes were shining. "Yes, and she empowered me to find my essential self."

"So that's why you supported her candidacy when she applied here."

"It was a good decision. Solange wasn't. As you say, on paper she was perfect. But when I spoke to her referees, all three of them alluded to psychiatric problems in her past."

"Livia, if universities went through their faculties and fired everyone who'd ever seen a shrink, post-secondary education would grind to a halt."

"Solange's difficulties go well beyond trouble dealing with a stressful environment. She's obsessive. She was obsessive about Ariel when Ariel was alive and she's still obsessive about her. Wouldn't you characterize as obsessive all the hours she's spent riding that bike of hers? Even our students are concerned. A young man who was in one of Solange's classes was at a loft party in the warehouse district a couple of nights ago. When he came out, he saw Solange riding her bike. It was two-thirty in the morning, Joanne. Our student offered to put the bike in his trunk and drive Solange home, but she just rode away. The student said Solange looked, and I'm quoting, 'as if she needed professional help.'"

"Grief isn't guilt," I said.

"I'm not saying Solange is guilty of anything." Livia's voice was tight. "I'm just saying she's unbalanced, and that means there's no way of predicting what she is or is not capable of doing."

I thought of the girl at the Ice Capades, so determined to survive that, even as her body was being violated, she was able to find refuge in imagining that the cheap sequinned costume of a professional skater could be protective armour. Solange had spent a lifetime creating a persona that would make her impervious to assault. Not many of us had seen the woman beyond the persona, but Ariel had. Solange had allowed Ariel Warren into her private world. How had she reacted when Ariel announced that she no longer wanted to be a part of that world, that she wanted a different kind of life, one that didn't include Solange? Charlie's words echoed. "She's done some terrible things." How terrible was "terrible"?

"I think we have to talk to Bob Hallam about this," I said. "If he knows how fragile Solange is, he'll be gentle with her. I can call him if you like."

"No." Livia's response was swift. "I'll handle this, Joanne. It was my mistake. I'll fix it." Her voice had been so decisive, I expected her to head straight for the parking lot; instead, she stopped before the cairn with the copper plaque. Then, in a small, private voice, she read the third stanza of 'The Road Not Taken.'

And both that morning equally lay
In leaves no step had trodden black.
Oh, I kept the first for another day!
Yet knowing how way leads on to way,
I doubted if I should ever come back.

The gesture seemed stagy, theatrical, but when Livia turned, her eyes were filled with tears. "Why is it that we never know how 'way leads on to way' until it's too late?" she asked. Then, without waiting for an answer, she walked away.

CHAPTER

12

"To paraphrase my favourite old lizzie, Gertrude Stein, 'a cage is a cage is a cage.'" Ed Mariani and I were standing in front of the pastel silk and bamboo pleasure dome that housed his nightingale, Florence. "Barry and I can't bear to come into this room any more. It's so depressing." Ed shot me a sidelong glance. "Taylor was quite taken with the whole set-up. I don't suppose you'd be interested in . . . ?"

"Not for all the tea in China. Willie is already grinding me down, and if you think a caged Florence is a bummer, consider how you'd feel if Bruce and Benny decided to make her the blue plate special."

Ed laughed grudgingly. "You're sounding chipper."

"I'm faking it," I said. "It's been one hell of a week, and it's not showing signs of improvement."

A shaft of sunlight hit the corner of Florence's cage, and Ed adjusted a plum-blossom silkscreen to diffuse it. "I've been keeping up with the Web page," he said. "Ann Vogel is pulling out all the stops. If she's not careful, she's going to find herself in court. That letter is libellous."

"Livia doesn't think Ann Vogel wrote it," I said. "According to Livia, Solange is the one who travels in circles so ideologically pure they would have no compunction about making autopsy photos public if it served the cause. I tend to agree with Livia about Ann, but not for the same reason. When she was my student, even subject-verb agreements strained her thought processes, and that letter is elegantly written."

"The phrasing may be elegant, but it reflects an ugly mind."

"Or a troubled one," I said. "This morning Livia told me that Solange has a history of psychiatric problems."

Ed frowned. "And this just came to light?"

"Livia knew," I said. "Apparently when Solange applied for the job here, Livia called her referees and encouraged them to open up."

"The new and improved Livia is a thorough woman," Ed said dryly. "I've always believed that needlepoint she hung in her office when she became department head was intended as a warning to us all. 'No Surprises.'" He shuddered. "So what was Solange's surprise?"

"Livia says clinical depression."

Ed winced. "That's a nasty one. More to the point," he said thoughtfully, "it doesn't fit."

"Meaning?"

"Meaning I remember what it was like when the vulture was hovering. Thanks to Barry and Prozac, my bouts with depression are in the past, but when it was at its worst, I could barely manage to put on my socks in the morning. If she truly is suffering from depression, I don't think Solange would be capable of organizing this latest campaign."

I took a deep breath. "Would she be capable of committing murder?"

Ed's eyes widened. "Are you serious?"

"I don't know," I said. "Charlie told me last night that when Ariel told Solange she was moving on, there was a lot of anger."

Ed's face registered surprise. "Did Solange's relationship with Ariel go beyond friendship?"

"I don't know that either." I threw up my hands in defeat. "Even if it did, it's no one's business unless . . ."

"Unless the breakup ended violently," Ed finished for me. "It happens, you know."

"I know," I said. "I just hope it didn't happen in this case." I picked up the stack of mid-terms from the coffee table. "Thank God for marking," I said. "It keeps the fingers busy and the mind semi-engaged. And I owe it all to you. I really appreciate your proctoring the exam, Ed. Promise me you'll let me return the favour."

He gave me a smart salute. "Scout's honour."

When I reached into my purse for the car keys, my fingers hit the small box I'd been carrying around since Wednesday. I pulled it out and handed it to Ed with a flourish. "And here's your merit badge for hospitality. Our family had a sensational Victoria Day weekend at the lake."

Ed took out the sparrow and held it to the light. "Lalique," he said. "I won't say you shouldn't have done it because I love her already, but these don't come in Frosted Flakes."

"Luckily, they can be found at high-end garage sales." I said. "Like Florence, your Lalique sparrow has already known another home. You seem destined to own second-hand birds."

Ed ran his finger over a crystal wing. "Then perhaps Barry and I should accept our fate with grace," he said. "I can almost hear Livia intoning that this is our way of acquiring good karma."

The first thing I did when I got home was check Eli's room. Charlie still hadn't shown up. There were no messages on the voice mail. It was obvious there had been a change of plans; it was equally obvious that neither Howard nor his son had seen any point in telling me. Howard's failures to communicate were legendary, and I was neither worried nor nettled.

The day was getting lovelier by the moment and, while I did have work to do, there was no reason I couldn't do it out-doors. I made myself a pot of green tea and took the mid-terms out to the sunshine of the back deck; by lunchtime, I'd made a small but measurable dent in the pile. After I'd eaten, I took a swim. As I was changing out of my wet suit, my bed looked so inviting I put on my pyjamas and slid between the sheets.

I woke to the sound of Charlie Dowhanuik's voice, but when I opened my eyes it wasn't Charlie standing beside the bed, it was Eli. He was wearing khaki shorts and a T-shirt and holding a portable radio.

"I'm sorry to wake you up," he said, "but I thought you should listen to this."

Charlie was in full rhetorical flight. "The word 'mob' is a shortened form of the Latin *mobile vulgus*, 'fickle common people,'" he said. "For the Romans, the mob was harmless enough, a bunch of boys and girls with a fondness for bread and circuses. Your basic WWF crowd. But mobs have changed. Today, right here in our city, there's a mob forming. And the people in it aren't just good old boys and good old girls. They're sophisticated. They even have their own Web site. Their name may sound innocent but, make no mistake, the Friends of Red Riding Hood are not fairy-tale characters. They're beasts who feed on the stupid, suck up the gullible, then move along, leaving nothing behind but a reeking spoor of self-righteousness. Fight them. Now . . . back to the Dave Matthews Band."

Eli sat on the edge of my bed. "That's the only music he's playing. It's his theme, 'Ants Marching.'"

"I've heard it before," I said. "It's a good song, but I'm not sure how many repetitions I could take."

Eli nodded. "Charlie D's taking calls, too. Some of them are really scary. Threats. He doesn't seem to care. CVOX has been running announcements all day saying they're standing behind Charlie D. On the news just now, a guy said the Friends of Red Riding Hood are renting buses to take the Friends out to the station tonight so they can protest. Charlie D told them to come ahead."

I looked at Eli. "I'm going to call Charlie's dad," I said.

I tried Howard's apartment. There was no answer. I tried his cellphone. A female voice told me, in both official languages, that the customer I was calling was unavailable at the moment. The news was hardly surprising; in order to have been 'available,' Howard would have had to activate his phone, and that was something he seldom did.

"No luck," I said to Eli.

"What are you going to do?" Eli asked.

"Get dressed and go up the university. Howard knew there'd be trouble, and he's always believed in attacking trouble at its source. The march is scheduled to start from the library. Even if Howard isn't there, I'll be able to see first-hand what's happening." I glanced at the clock on my night-stand. "Incidentally," I said, "it's two-thirty. How come you're home from school."

"Half-day teacher in-service," he said. "I told you about it last night."

"Sorry," I said. "I'm playing with an incomplete deck these days. Does Taylor have the afternoon off, too?"

"Nope, it's only the high schools. Taylor's class is on garbage patrol in her schoolyard, so she won't be home till after four. She mentioned that, too," he said gently.

"How would you like to move in permanently?" I asked.

"We've never had a kid around here who actually *delivered* messages."

"Cool," he said. "Talk to Uncle Alex. I think we're a matched set."

I threw my pillow at him. "Get outta here," I said.

He left with a grin, but the strains of 'Ants Marching,' Dave Matthews's indictment of mindless conformity, lingered.

As I drove to the university, my nerves felt as if they were connected by piano wire. I couldn't slap a label on what I feared, and so, nameless, the fear grew. It took an act of will to insert the key in the lock of my office. When I saw the envelope lying on the floor, my heart sank. Any message Solange had considered critical enough to slide under my door the night before wouldn't be good news. The envelope I picked up was the kind our office used for business letters. Inside was a single sheet of university stationery. The note was handwritten, two lines long:

Joanne,
    The heart has its reasons, and they're not always imme-
diately apparent to others. Forgive me,
    Solange

The remorse was apparent, but the note's ambiguity gnawed. The two lines could be read as either an apology for a temperamental outburst or an admission of complicity in something more sinister.

I walked down the hall and knocked on Solange's door. There was no answer, and when I tried the knob, the door was locked. I had no better luck at the main office. It was 3:30 – Rosalie's coffee time. Even Kevin Coyle wasn't in.

I went back to my office and tried Solange's home number. There was no answer. I pulled the mid-terms from my brief case and began to read. Five minutes later, I gave up. I would not have wanted one of my kids to have their paper marked by an instructor whose concentration was as fragmented as mine. I reread Solange's letter. It didn't yield any answers. All I knew for certain was that there had been a radical shift in Solange's feelings. The question was, *Why?*

Luckily, the time frame during which the change took place was a narrow one. Fraser Jackson had been with Solange on the island and on the flights back. He had struck me as a man with keen powers of observation and a good ear for detecting variations in the emotional pitch of others. I packed up my mid-terms, locked my door, and walked to the elevator. I needed information, and Fraser seemed as good a place as any to start.

His door was open, but when I stuck my head around the corner, I saw that he was on the telephone. As soon as he saw me, he hung up. "Synchronicity," he said with a grin. "I was just calling you. Molly told me on the way back that it was your idea to invite me. I'm grateful, Joanne. I found it very comforting to be part of the ceremony." He gestured to the chair opposite his. "But you came to see me. . . ."

"I wanted to talk about yesterday, too," I said, taking the chair he'd offered. "Fraser, I was hoping you could tell me about how Solange was after I left."

He took a breath. "Well, at first she was very angry. Of course, you saw that."

"It was pretty hard to miss," I said. "But sometime last night she slid this under my office door." I gave him Solange's note.

As Fraser read the note, his face was sombre. "I can't say that I'm surprised," he said.

"Then something *did* happen."

"No *single* thing," he said slowly, and I could see my own concern reflected in his dark eyes. "Solange took me aside as soon as you left with Howard and his son. She was . . . distraught. She asked me about my relationship with Ariel. There didn't seem to be any point in lying, so I told her the truth. She took the news calmly; in fact, she seemed almost indifferent. I've thought about it since, and I think I just had to establish my bona fides before she asked the one question that really mattered to her."

"Which was?"

"Which was if Ariel had ever suggested, in any way, that she feared her."

"Had she?" I asked.

"Never. She always spoke of Solange with the greatest affection and respect."

I felt the piano-wire tension of my nerves lessen. "So Charlie was wrong."

"One hundred per cent wrong." Fraser was adamant. "Solange was a hero to Ariel. She believed Solange had given her some sort of key to living her life fully."

"And you told Solange that."

He shook his head in amazement. "She was so grateful, Joanne. She told me I couldn't have given her a greater gift. Then the penny dropped."

"What do you mean?"

"I wish I knew. All I know is that the light went out of her face, and she said, 'If it wasn't me, then who *was* Ariel afraid of?' After that, she just withdrew. I made a point of sitting beside her on the flights home, but she didn't say another word till we were about to land in Regina. Then she asked me something I'm still puzzling over. She wanted to know if I'd ever studied *Murder in the Cathedral*."

"T.S. Eliot," I said. "I don't get the connection."

"Neither did I, but I wanted her to keep talking. I told her the summer before last I'd seen a terrific production of the play in London, and that I'd done some work on it and was considering doing a student production here. That's when she asked me if I knew Thomas Becket's line about the greatest treason." Fraser leaned towards me. "Are you familiar with the play?"

"Very," I said. "When my husband was in politics, that particular line came up a time or two. 'The last temptation is the greatest treason: to do the right deed for the wrong reason.'"

Fraser nodded approval. "It's a provocative line for idealists," he said. "I wasn't surprised that Solange had been taken with it, but it seemed she was more interested in the inversion. 'It's treason the other way, too,' she said. 'If a person does the wrong deed for the right reason.'"

"And she didn't elaborate?"

"Not another word on that subject or any other. The plane landed; we shared a cab from the airport. I got dropped off first, and I haven't seen her since. I've been uneasy enough about her state of mind to try her office and her house a half-dozen times. No luck."

"I'm sure she's fine, just out riding her bike somewhere," I said, with what I hoped sounded like conviction. "I'll call if I manage to connect with her."

"I hope one of us finds her soon," he said. "Because all the bike-riding in the world doesn't offset the fact that that note was written by a deeply troubled woman."

When I got back to the Political Science office, Rosalie was at her desk. She was wearing a white silk blouse, a single strand of pearls, and delicate pearl and diamond drop earrings. She looked lovely, and I told her so.

"One of the tips in my bridal book is that a bride should try out her jewellery for the wedding beforehand. It says a bride doesn't want to be walking down the aisle when she discovers that she should have had her grandmother's pearls restrung."

"No," I said, "I guess she doesn't."

Rosalie picked up the flatness in my voice. "Am I talking too much about my own life these days?"

"Of course not," I said. "I love hearing the details. You know that. I'm just a little preoccupied. You haven't seen Solange, have you?"

"She was waiting outside the office when I got to work this morning."

"Is she around now?"

"No. She wanted some information, and when I gave it to her, she left."

"What was the information?"

Rosalie fingered her grandmother's pearls pensively. "You know that I try to keep my dealings with every faculty member confidential. . . ."

"This is important," I said quickly.

"I guess there's no reason not to divulge this," Rosalie said. "Solange wanted to know if we had a current phone number for Maryse Bergman."

The name was familiar but I couldn't make a connection. "Is she a student?" I asked.

"She *was* a student," Rosalie said. "She was the one who accused Dr. Coyle of rape."

"Right," I said. "How soon we forget."

"I'll bet Dr. Coyle hasn't forgotten," Rosalie said tartly.

"I'm sure he hasn't," I said. "So, did you have a current number?"

"The last listing we had was in care of the Political Science department where Ms. Bergman went to do her M.A."

"You mean some university actually *accepted* her into their graduate program? Kevin showed me her transcript when all his problems with her started. She barely made it through her undergraduate degree. Who took her?"

Rosalie named the university.

"That doesn't make any sense," I said. "Their program is first-rate. They've rejected students of ours who had a lot more potential than Maryse Bergman."

"Maybe she didn't have that much potential after all." Rosalie's blackberry eyes sparkled with secret pleasure. "Solange wasn't able to reach Ms. Bergman through the Political Science department there. She must have flunked out. Anyway, Solange came back and asked if we had anything more current."

"And we don't."

"We don't, but I knew Dr. Coyle would. He makes a point of keeping track of all the people involved in his defence. He calls them his 'players.' I guess he was able to give Solange what she needed because I haven't seen either of them since. Funny. Dr. Coyle didn't even drop by to tell me where he could be reached. That's not like him at all."

"Rosalie, do you have Tom Bradley's number? He's . . ."

"Head of the Political Science department that accepted Maryse Bergman?" she said. "Of course, I have it. He was one of Dr. Jesse's closest friends."

"I'd forgotten that, too," I said.

"I haven't forgotten anything about Dr. Jesse," Rosalie said wistfully. "When he was head of this department, we had standards." As if to stop herself from elaborating, she snapped her lips shut and reached for her Rolodex. The conversation was over. I walked to the filing cabinet, found Maryse Bergman's file, and pulled it.

When Rosalie handed me the paper on which she'd written Tom's number, I noticed her manicure. "I like that shade of nail polish," I said. "What's it called?"

"Bridal Pink," she said, but for the first time an allusion to her wedding didn't bring a blush and a smile.

I went back to my office and opened Maryse Bergman's file. What I saw confirmed the need to call Tom Bradley. Not only were Maryse's grades mediocre, the file was fat with letters of protest she had written about grades. Maryse had never been my student, but her litany of aggrieved entitlement was a familiar one. "I spent three weeks working on this paper and I know for a fact that X wrote hers the night before, and I don't think it's fair that she got a better grade . . ." I closed the file and picked up the phone.

I'd met Tom Bradley several times when Ben had been alive, and we had liked one another enough to keep up the acquaintance through e-mail. I was glad we were on good terms because the question I had to ask Tom was a humdinger.

His pleasure when he heard my voice filled me with guilt, but there was no turning back. "I need to ask you about Maryse Bergman," I said.

When he spoke again, there was a distinct chill. "What about her?"

"Is she still in your M.A. program?"

"She didn't last."

"That can't have been a surprise. I've just been looking at her file. What made you accept her?"

The silence between us grew painful.

"You did it as a favour to Ben, didn't you?" I said.

"To Ben and to your department," he said finally. "Joanne, you remember the atmosphere then. It was a war zone, and the press was panting over every lurid rumour. Finally, when it seemed as if the worst was over, Maryse Bergman came along with her charges against Kevin Coyle. They would have been proven false. I want you to know that. If there had been even the slightest chance that Maryse Bergman was telling the truth, Ben wouldn't have called me."

"And asked you to accept Maryse into your graduate program to get her out of the way," I said.

"It was a decision I didn't lose a moment's sleep over," Tom said. "By accepting an unqualified student who, logic suggested, wouldn't make it through her first year of studies, I was able to spare an innocent man more public humiliation and give your department a chance to reflect and regroup. Most importantly, I was able to take some of the heat off Ben. He'd already had one heart attack. I could see the price he was paying for trying to be fair and decent to a small group of people who were neither. I didn't want to lose him. As it turned out, we lost him anyway, but I take comfort in the fact that I did my best for him."

"You should," I said. "Ben Jesse was one of the finest men I've ever known. Unfortunately, that's not a factor here. I still need to get in touch with Maryse Bergman. Do you have a number where she can be reached?"

"So Ben's obituary is going to be rewritten after all," Tom said coldly. "Like Neville Chamberlain, he'll be remembered as a man with a fatal need to appease."

"If I'm lucky, Ben's name won't even come up," I said. "All I need to find out from Maryse Bergman is if she acted alone or if she had a little help from her friends."

"Joanne, does all this have something to do with that instructor who was killed out there last week? There hasn't been much about it in our media, but I assumed it was a case of random violence. It never occurred to me till this minute that there might be a link with that mess two years ago."

"There may not be," I said, "but if there is, Maryse Bergman may be able to shed light on the connection. Will you give me her number?"

"Sure," he said. "But if you were of a mind to, you could

hop in your car and be talking to her face to face in less than an hour. When her studies didn't work out here, Maryse moved back to Saskatchewan. She works on the front desk at the Big Sky Motel in Moose Jaw."

I thanked Tom, rang off, then dialled the number he had given me. My call was picked up on the first ring. I was obviously dealing with a five-star establishment.

"Big Sky Inn," a male voice said, "Kelly speaking. How may I help you?"

"I'd like to speak to Maryse Bergman, please. She's an employee."

"Maryse is no longer with us."

"As of when?"

"As of this morning. She walked off in the middle of her shift without a word of explanation to anybody."

"Do you have a home number for her?"

"It's against company policy to give out the phone numbers of employees."

"But she's no longer an employee."

He laughed. "You've got me there, ma'am. Hold on."

He gave me the number, but when I dialled, all I got was Maryse's voice mail telling me that she'd been forced to relocate and her friends would hear from her soon.

Too restless to work, I headed for the café in the Lab Building where Ann Vogel and her group hung out. It was empty, and the metal accordion screens had been pulled across the serving area. It seemed everyone but I had left for the weekend. I'd started back to my office when I heard someone call my name. I turned and saw Kristy Stevenson, the archivist who had sung at the vigil for Ariel.

"Have you got a few minutes?" she asked. She was wearing a lavender-blue silk blouse; the colour matched her eyes, but her oval face was pale and miserable. "I hate this Friends of Red Riding Hood stuff," she said. "I keep thinking of the lines from that song by Beowulf's Daughters that you used in your talk."

"Darkness is our womb and destination, Light, a heartbeat glory, gone too soon," I said.

"Well, no one at this march has any interest in turning back darkness. Ann Vogel and her gang are getting ready in the library quadrangle, and it makes me sick." Kristy bit her lip in frustration. "Joanne, I've loved libraries since I was a little kid. That's why I chose to be an archivist, making certain that all the pieces of the puzzle were there for anyone who was seeking answers."

"People like Ann Vogel don't need archives," I said. "They don't even need libraries. They already have the answers."

Kristy's eyes flashed with anger. "You bet they do. Simplistic ones. Women who don't share their views are bad; books that don't reflect their philosophy are bad; art that doesn't mirror their reality is bad; literature that doesn't tell their story is bad. Why would they need a library?"

We had reached the glass doors that opened onto the quad. Outside, perhaps a dozen women were working on placards: attaching wooden pickets to poster-board, filling the blank faces of the signs with words or with painted sunflowers or ferocious cartoon wolves. The finished placards were propped against a low wall to dry, and their messages were designed to foment: NEVER FORGET; WOLVES BELONG IN CAGES; ARIEL WARREN — THE BEST AND BRIGHTEST; REAL MEN DON'T KILL; REVENGE THE RED RIDING HOODS; MURDERERS DESERVE WHAT THEY GET.

"There seems to be a certain lack of focus," Kristy said dryly.

"No lack of firepower, though," I said. "I'm going to go out and ask them to tone down the rhetoric."

Ann Vogel was on her knees stapling rectangles of poster-board back to back. Despite her falling-out with Solange,

Ann appeared to be sticking to the combat look: head-to-toe black, and hennaed hair shirred to a buzz cut. When she recognized me, she stood and waved her staple gun in mock menace. "You're not wanted here," she said.

"That makes us even, because I don't want to be here," I said. "So I'll just ask one quick question. What if you're wrong about Charlie, too?"

Ann narrowed her eyes. "What else was I wrong about?"

"Kevin Coyle," I said. "I talked to Tom Bradley, he's the head of . . ."

"I know who Tom Bradley is," Ann snapped.

"Good. So you'll know that, while the idea of a trustworthy man may be an oxymoron to you, it's not to a lot of other people. When Tom says that Ben Jesse believed the charges Maryse Bergman made against Kevin were false, I believe him. Other people will, too."

Ann tilted her chin defiantly. "Kevin Coyle deserved what he got," she said. "He's unfair to women. He marks us too hard. He's dismissive of the answers we give in class."

"Oh, for God's sake, Ann. Kevin's unfair to everybody," I said. "He marks everybody hard, and he's dismissive of everybody. That doesn't make it right, but that's the truth. He's an anachronism. When I was an undergraduate, the universities were full of profs like that."

"We don't have to take that kind of crap from men any more."

"I know," I said, "and amen to that. But I still don't get it. Why did you target Kevin? He's rude, he's abrupt, he's probably misanthropic. But he's not a misogynist. Why did you get Maryse Bergman to lie about him? Why did *you* go after him?"

"You never get the point, do you?" She looked around to check if anyone was in hearing range, then she lowered her voice. "We needed an example. If we showed how bad he was, everybody would see that we needed women in the department."

"There were women in the department," I said.

"Women like you," she said. "Women who were no better than men. Look at what happened yesterday. You're given the honour of going to a funeral for a Red Riding Hood."

"For Ariel Warren," I corrected her quietly.

"Whatever. But when Ariel's killer crashes the party with his father, you just leave with the men. Now you tell me, what does that make you?"

"A loyal friend?" I said.

"A traitor," she said. "Not just to Ariel but to all women, and no matter what Maryse is saying now, what we did then was for all women. Our department needed gender parity."

"And that was worth risking a man's career?"

"It was worth everything," she said.

"'The last temptation is the greatest treason: to do the wrong deed for the right reason,'" I said.

She looked at me sharply. "What?"

"Solange has defected from your group, hasn't she?"

"She had issues," Ann said coldly. "And I have signs to make, so if you'll excuse me . . ."

"I'll excuse you," I said. "But I won't forgive you."

She stepped close to me and placed the staple gun so that the business end was flat against my cheek. "Go fuck yourself," she said. Then she turned on her heel, strode over to a stack of placards, and began stapling them to pickets.

Very scary. As I walked back into the library, I thought with gratitude of the solid complement of police officers who would be accompanying Ann on the march and who were charged with the duty of keeping her and the other Friends of Red Riding Hood from discovering just how scary they could be.

CHAPTER

13

Taylor and Bruce and Benny were waiting for me on the front step when I got home. Taylor had a new skipping rope, and she was making a lazy crack-the-whip movement with it through the grass so the cats could chase its iridescent rainbow handle. All three were blissed out, and I thought, not for the first time, that being a cat must be one of the all-time great gigs.

Taylor held out the rope to show me. "I got this for helping with garbage patrol."

"Very fancy," I said. "I used to get a new rope every spring."

She looked at me with amazement. "Can you skip?"

"Can Wayne Gretzky score goals?"

"I don't know," she said, "can he?"

"Not so many any more," I said. "But I haven't retired. Why don't you give Bruce and Benny a rest and let me have a turn?"

The moment I began to skip, the tensions of the day dropped away. Salvation through muscle memory. Taylor watched, saucer-eyed, as I not only skipped, but rattled through my store of old skipping songs.

When Angus pulled up, he took in the scene, jumped out of his car, and yelled, "You go, Mum." And I did. I skipped until there wasn't a breath left in my body and my heart felt as if it was about to exit through my chest wall. By the time the kids gave me a round of applause and I quit, my ears were singing, but I'd banished my memory of Ann Vogel and her staple gun, and increased my odds of getting through the evening.

"Okay," I panted. "Show's over. I'd better go in there and act like a mother. Taylor, since you're the headliner today, you get to choose dinner. Make it simple. I've already done my star turn."

"Sloppy Joes the way Nik Manojlovich makes them on TV. He's so funny."

"Good choice," I said. "I can manage Sloppy Joes. Besides, they're portable, and I thought we'd watch the news while we ate supper tonight. I want to tape you winning your prize."

At 5:30 on the button, we were sitting in the family room with plates filled with Sloppy Joes, potato chips, and raw vegetables balanced on our TV tables, the perfect fifties family – minus the father. Unfortunately, our television wasn't showing "Leave it to Beaver" or "Don Messer's Jubilee." The news began with brief accounts of the investigation into Ariel's murder and the battle that had erupted between the Friends of Red Riding Hood and their popular host, Charlie D. There was a live shot of the concrete and glass boxes that housed the station's deep-discount neighbours, then the camera closed in for a tight shot of the CVOX call letters, lingering on the lascivious Mick Jagger tongue that wagged from the red-lipped open mouth of the O. The first of the buses that had been scheduled to arrive in time for live coverage pulled up, and the Friends of Red Riding Hood piled out.

In all there were perhaps twenty-five protestors, and the NationTV reporter, a dark-haired beauty named Jen Quesnel, struggled to keep the report lively as the Friends handed out their placards and milled about, trying to decide on their next move. As Jen reported that the turnout was surprisingly small, Ann Vogel muscled her way into camera range and began a chant that was picked up by the others. The words were simple and cruel. "Show us your face, Charlie D. Show us your face."

But nothing happened. Not even a bird disturbed the eerie calm at the entrance to the radio station. No buses arrived carrying reinforcements, and the meagre crowd of protestors, embarrassed by the ragged quality of its cry, grew silent. Caught in the middle of what was clearly a non-event, Jen Quesnel began to wrap up her story.

Throughout the newscast, Eli had been as motionless as if he were carved in stone. Now he relaxed. "It was a bust," he said. "And I'm glad because what those people are saying is really shitty." He darted a glance in my direction. "Pardon my language."

"No pardon necessary," I said. "What they're saying really is shitty."

Eli laughed. When he was happy, his face became animated and open. It was a sight in which I always took pleasure, but that night the pleasure was short-lived.

Suddenly, he leaned forward, his eyes riveted once more on the screen. "Charlie's coming out," he said. I turned my attention back to the television in time to see Charlie walk through the front doors of CVOX. He was alone, and he moved deliberately from the shadow of the building into the light. A slight figure in bluejeans and a T-shirt, he stood with his hands clasped behind his back. He made no attempt to cover his face or hide it.

Jen Quesnel ran over to him with her microphone. They exchanged glances, then she said, "So, Charlie, people want to hear what you're thinking right now."

Before he had a chance to answer, Ann Vogel leaned into the microphone. "Tell the truth, Charlie D. Tell the truth."

Charlie shrugged his thin shoulders. "You already know it," he said. "I loved a woman. She's dead. The beauty in my life is gone. I don't care what happens next." Charlie turned to the crowd. "I'm here," he said, raising his arms in a gesture of surrender. "Do what you want."

For a few seconds, the camera stayed on Charlie; then it moved to Ann Vogel for a reaction shot. Her face registered disbelief, then anger.

"This is a trick," she said. "We won't let you get away with it." She turned to her supporters. "Will we?" But her dispirited followers were already straggling towards the bus.

Jen Quesnel looked into the camera. "Apparently the Friends of Red Riding Hood have decided on a change in strategy. That's it from our location at CVOX. Now back to Kathy in the studio."

Kathy did an item on a house fire in the inner city, then one on the robbery of a convenience store. After the announcement from the City's Department of Parks and Recreation of the dates for the opening of outdoor swimming pools, it was our turn. Bev Pilon and Livia Brook were on the screen.

"Hit record on the VCR," I said to Angus.

He grimaced in exasperation and waved the remote control in the air. "I already have, Mum."

Beside Bev's polished Technicolor sheen, Livia looked wan and schoolmarmish, but NationTV did include Livia's anecdote about Ben, and they spelled her name right. They spelled Taylor's name right, too, and I squeezed my daughter's hand when I saw that she had asked to be identified as

Taylor Kilbourn. As she explained her work to the interviewer she was poised and polite; equally important from my perspective, her turtleneck was spotless, her kilt untwisted, and only one of her braids had come undone. In all, it was a virtuoso performance, and the phone began to ring the minute it was over.

The first call was from Mieka in Saskatoon. "I hope you taped that," she said. "Maddy was hollering, so I missed the first part, but Taylor looked sensational and her painting is terrific. *Mouseland*! Any other day, Uncle Howard would have been bursting his buttons."

"Yeah," I said. "Any other day."

Mieka's voice was concerned. "Mum, what's going to happen to Charlie?"

"I don't know," I said. "I expect he doesn't, either. When I hear from Howard, I'll fill you in. Now, Taylor's at my elbow, longing to hear you tell her how fabulous she was, so I'm going to hand you over. Give everybody a hug for me."

As soon as Taylor hung up, the phone rang again. My younger daughter chatted happily for five minutes, then handed the receiver to me. It was my old friend Hilda McCourt, calling to say she was proud of Taylor and worried about Charlie. The third phone call was from Ed Mariani, who was also proud and worried. By the time the fourth call came, my Sloppy Joe was lukewarm and soggy and I'd had enough interruptions.

"Leave it," I shouted, but Taylor had already answered. She held out the phone to me.

"For you," she said brightly.

It took me a moment to identify the voice on the other end. Bebe Morrissey was a woman who didn't waste time on preamble, and obviously she worked on the assumption that once you'd met her, you wouldn't forget her.

"I need to talk to you," she said.

"Bebe, can I call you back? We're just in the middle of dinner."

"Don't put me off," she said. "This is important. On the news tonight, that little kid with the drawing was your daughter, right?"

"Right," I said. "But why is that important?"

"I'm ninety-five years old, and I need to make sure I've got everybody straight in my mind," she said irritably. "Now, the bottle blonde who gave your kid the flag and the pin was that right-winger, Bev Pilon."

I smiled to myself. "Right," I said.

"And the other one, the pasty-faced one, was – hang on, I wrote it down – Livia Brook, head of the department of Political Science."

"Right again. Look, Bebe, I don't mean to be rude, but my dinner is stone cold. Why don't you let me nuke it, eat it, and call you back?"

"Because I live with a silent killer, high blood pressure, and by the time you call back, I could be dead. Now listen, I've made a serious mistake. Remember when I told you I saw Ariel Warren having that fight with her mother?"

"I remember," I said; then, in an attempt to speed her along, I provided Bebe with a quick recap of the incident. "After Ariel said that she had to do what she thought was best because she only had one life, her mother said, 'You have two lives because I gave you mine.' You and I agreed that it was a pretty ugly thing to say to your own flesh and blood."

Bebe cackled triumphantly. "Except – and this is my point – the woman who said that wasn't Ariel's flesh and blood. It was the other one, with the pasty face."

"Livia?" I asked.

"Yes," Bebe said, "Livia Brook, head of the department of Political Science. She was the one who told Ariel that she'd given her her life."

The pieces of the puzzle rearranged themselves, falling into place to reveal a truth that was as ugly as it was inescapable. Livia had been the woman Ariel had feared, the woman who, while insisting that all she wanted was Ariel's happiness, had been unable to accept Ariel's choice of a life that didn't include her. Livia was the woman who had done "terrible things." Unbidden, a memory surged into my consciousness: Ann Vogel in the Political Science office bragging about her role in getting Solange her job. Ann had said, "What Livia and I did wasn't pretty, but it was necessary," and Livia had silenced her. At the time, I had believed Livia was trying to put an end to a quarrel; now, it was clear that her motivation was far from altruistic. She had, I realized, been trying to shut Ann down before she said too much.

For a beat, shock froze me. Then I felt the lash of panic. This wasn't over. Solange wouldn't let it be over until she found the woman Ariel had feared. The fact that Solange had been looking for Maryse Bergman suggested that the pieces of the puzzle were coming together for her, too.

By now, I knew Solange's home and office numbers by heart. When there was no answer at either place, I grabbed my car keys.

Angus had just rewound the tape, so that Taylor could see herself again. "I'm going to make a quick trip to the university," I said. "There's something I have to check on."

"What's up? You haven't even finished supper."

"Just stick it in the fridge for me, will you, Angus? I'll get it later."

Taylor was wholly absorbed in watching herself, but my son was on his feet. "You look kind of weird. Is everything okay?"

Eli, always sensitive to problems, shifted position so he could check out the situation as well.

I took in their worried faces and decided against setting off any alarms. "Just university politics," I said. "A problem involving a couple of colleagues."

Angus grinned. "I'll bet you a loonie that one of them is Dr. Coyle."

"You lose," I said.

Ten minutes later, as I pulled off the Parkway, I thought I'd give a bag full of loonies to see Kevin's old boat of a Buick in its usual spot. My bank account was safe; the parking lot was deserted. I was deflated but not surprised. It was a gentle Friday night in spring. There was no reason for anyone to be at the university. But when I walked towards the main door of College West, I saw that someone was. A solitary bike was chained to the rack. The apprehension that had been shadowing me like the black cloud over the head of Joe Bfstplk in the old "Li'l Abner" cartoons deepened. I wasn't an expert on bikes, but I knew this one. It was Solange's Trek WSD.

I began to run. My footfalls echoed as I padded down the empty corridors and through the silent halls. When I got to the Classroom Building, I decided against taking the elevator. It had been unpredictable all week, and I couldn't do much for Solange if I was trapped between floors. I raced up the stairs. By the time I got to the third floor, my heart was thumping harder than it had when I'd completed my triumphant skipping exhibition. This time there was no applause.

I went straight to Solange's office and began pounding at her door. "It's Joanne, Solange. Let me in." There was no response, then, very faintly, a sound halfway between a moan and a cry. I tried the door. It was locked. I put my mouth to the door edge. "It's going to be all right," I said. "I'm getting help." Then I ran to my office to call for an ambulance.

I couldn't seem to get the key to catch. Finally, its teeth gripped the lock and the door opened. I rushed to my desk and reached across to pick up the phone. My back was to the door. An arm shot past me from behind. The knife was at my throat before I had time to be afraid. And that was a blessing, because the person holding the knife was shaking so violently it seemed possible she might sever my throat accidentally. It would have been a Sam Peckinpah death: stupid and brutal. Oddly, the sheer craziness of that image calmed me enough to think about my next step. I knew that I had to slow my assailant's rhythm to match my own. The question was, *How*? I managed to inhale; the scent of Pears soap, so familiar and so reassuring, gave me the answer. My best hope lay in a pattern of behaviour Livia herself had perfected. Ed Mariani had always called it coercion by compassion, and at the moment it was the only game in town.

"This must be a nightmare for you," I said.

Livia shivered and I felt the cool brush of silk against my bare arm. From the corner of my eye, I saw that she was wearing the poppy shawl that had been Ariel's parting gift to her.

"It is." Livia's dreamy New Age nuances made her sound like a woman in a trance. The woman whose byword was "No Surprises" had been surprised once too often. "No one ever comes to the office on a Friday night in the spring," she said.

"Everything's going wrong," I said. "And all you ever wanted was to do what was best for everybody."

"That's right," she agreed. "And that meant I had to start with myself. I needed to regenerate, to stop allowing experiences from the past to intrude on new relationships. I had to learn to trust again, and that was hard because . . ."

"Because your husband had betrayed you."

"Kenneth almost destroyed me," she said.

"But Ariel gave you a chance to begin again."

"Our relationship was not parasitic, it was symbiotic. I could give Ariel the things she needed, too: a place to regenerate, a mentor who would foster her personal growth. From the first night we talked at Saltspring, I knew she belonged in our department. Having her here was worth every risk." Suddenly, Livia tensed. "There was never anything sexual, you know."

"That never even occurred to me," I said. "I knew you were just two women being loving and supportive."

The hand holding the knife dropped from my throat and rested on my breast. "It could have been perfect," she said. "For both of us. I would have done anything for her. Why wasn't it enough?"

"'Some people,/No matter what you give them/Still want the moon,'" I said.

Livia whirled me around to face her. "I offered her the moon," she said furiously. "She didn't want it. She wanted to move away, have a child, grow things, make art, make choices. After she'd taken away all *my* choices."

"Not all of them," I said. "Livia, you can still decide how this will end."

For what seemed like an eternity, we looked into one another's eyes. It was the most terrible intimacy I had ever known.

Finally, she said, "I *can* decide, can't I?"

"Of course," I said.

My intent, that she spare me and give herself up to the authorities, was so clear in my own mind, it never occurred to me that Livia had seen another answer in my words.

She took a ring of keys from her pocket and handed it to me. "This one opens Solange's office," she said, indicating the key marked with Solange's office number. "She's bleeding heavily. You should go to her. I'll call 911 myself."

Relief washed over me. "You won't regret this," I said.

Livia reached out and, with a hand that was as cold as death, she touched my cheek. "Even when I turned against you during Kevin's case, you never told."

"Told what?"

Her face crumpled with shame. "How I debased myself the night my husband left me."

Clear as a Polaroid print, the image of Livia drunkenly attempting to light the candles on her birthday cake flashed before my eyes. "Every life has some terrible moments," I said. "But there's always a new moment, another chance to regain our dignity."

Livia's eyes never left my face. "That's true, isn't it?" Her lips brushed my cheek. "Sisters forever," she said, and I felt something inside me shrivel.

I held Solange's hand as we waited for the ambulance. She floated in and out of consciousness, moaning, talking a little. Once she whispered, "'God says, "Take what you want. Take it, and pay for it."' Don't forget the fat priest, Joanne. Livia has to pay . . ." She closed her eyes then, drifted into the twilight sleep of one whose pain is too great to be borne in any other way. As we heard the sirens that announced the arrival of the police and the ambulance, Solange's eyelids fluttered. "We killed her with our love," she murmured, and I shuddered at the truth.

As the attendants strapped Solange to the stretcher and took her away, the police streamed into the hall. I directed them to Livia's office, and then returned to my own. For a few moments, I drank in its ordinariness: the pictures of my kids and of Alex and Eli, the familiar spines of my books, the comforting roundness of my Brown Betty.

The officer who burst through my door didn't look much older than Angus. "Livia Brook's not there," he said, and his voice cracked with frustration. I followed him into the hall.

Uniformed police were everywhere. Robert Hallam, strid-
ing smartly towards me in a blue blazer and grey flannel
slacks, was a welcome emissary from the everyday world.
"Do you have any idea where she could have gone?" he asked.

I shook my head. "She said she was going to call 911. I was
so anxious to get to Solange, it never occurred to me that
Livia would try to escape. There's nowhere she can go,
except . . ." I touched my cheek, remembering Livia's wintry
kiss, the way she had leaped at my words when I said she
could still decide how the nightmare would end.

I touched Bob Hallam's arm. "She may have decided to
choose her own way out," I said.

His face showed nothing. "Do you know her home
address? Usually, that's where they go."

"I can't imagine that would be Livia's choice," I said.
"After her marriage broke up, she moved into a condo, but
I think it was just a place to go at the end of day. This was
her home."

"You think she's still here?"

I held up the ring of keys Livia had handed me. "Let's
check Ariel Warren's office."

I let Robert open the door and walk in ahead of me. The
office was shadowy, but I could see that she wasn't there. I
tried to put myself in Livia's place; where would I go? The
answer was not long in coming. I led Robert down to the wide
concrete walkway that runs along the outside of our building.

The evening was soft and filled with birdsong. Livia's body
had landed on the little hill where Ariel had taught her last
class. I wondered if she had known, if she had planned it that
way. In death, Livia seemed too insignificant to have planned
anything: a broken doll, as lifeless as one of Bebe's Barbies.
The poppy shawl lay on the grass beside her. One of her
fingers touched its edge, pinning it to the ground. As we
watched, a gust of wind came up and lifted the shawl into

the air. For the briefest of moments, it swirled, a flash of pure beauty, an emblem of what might have been.

The Monday after Livia's suicide, Kevin Coyle became acting head of our department. The decision had been unanimous, but his appointment gave new meaning to the term "hollow victory." No one wanted to be department head. It was the end of May: holidays had been planned, arrangements had been made to deliver learned papers at conferences in exotic places. Like grade-school kids, we were all sick of school. The last thing any of us wanted to do was hang around the office.

But Kevin revelled in his new status. He moved his shining new computer and his coffee-maker into the department head's office and plunged into his duties. There weren't many. Livia had left our affairs in order, but Kevin managed to keep busy. Every afternoon, he visited Solange in hospital. He told me they talked little but played endless games of cribbage. Somewhere between hands, Solange convinced Kevin to enrol in a Women's Studies class that was being offered that summer. Eager as a freshman, Kevin went straight to the bookstore and purchased his texts. When I came to pick up my mail, I often spotted him reading one of them, underlining and harrumphing at some fresh oddity about the lives of girls and women.

Charlie was back on the air. Eli kept me posted. Apparently, Charlie had lost none of his edge, but one day the sadness in his voice had become so overwhelming that Eli called the station and invited Charlie to meet him and his psychiatrist, Dan Kasperski, for coffee. The two men had hit it off so well that, when Charlie asked, Dan accepted him as a patient.

Alex came home with a fresh tin of hemp oil that we managed to empty by the end of his first week back. After

one particularly gratifying hour of lovemaking, Alex lay back
on his pillow and grinned at me. "As Truman Capote once
said, 'Home! And Happy to Be.'"

I rolled over and snuggled in. "Imagine a kid from
Standing Buffalo quoting Truman Capote."

Alex kissed the top of my head. "You forget," he said.
"I've been to the big city."

Busy with Alex, plans for the boys' graduations, Taylor's
endless end-of-term activities, and my own marking, I never
seemed to get around to calling Bebe Morrissey. Character-
istically, Bebe took matters into her own hands and invited
me over.

Rain was threatening the afternoon I pulled up in front of
EXXXOTICA, but the marigolds in Ronnie's iron pots were
cheery, and Kyle, who was installing a cinder-block front
walk, was cheery, too. As soon as he recognized me, he
threw down his shovel. "Great to see you," he said. "I'll take
you up to Bebe. There's a ton of customers in the store.
Rainy days and full moons are good for business, at least
that's what Ronnie always says."

Business was indeed booming. Ronnie was at the cash register, ringing up a stack of videos. She waved when she saw
me. "Come talk to me before you leave," she said.

"Absolutely," I said. Then I followed Kyle up the narrow
stairs to Bebe's room.

There were fresh circles of rouge on Bebe's wizened apple
cheeks, and her white hair was brushed into an aureole as
insubstantial as dandelion fluff. "Well, we got her," she said
by way of greeting. "We got our murderer, that Livia Brook.
I've made a whole scrapbook on the case. It's over there on
the chest. I thought we could look at it together while we
had our snack."

As I drank my chocolate milk and perused Bebe's album, I thought there were worse ways to spend a rainy afternoon. The milk was comforting and, mounted in the scrapbook, the grainy newsprint pictures of people I had known so well already seemed distant, part of a painful but receding history.

When I closed the book, Bebe's blue eyes were bright with interest. "So what d'ya make of it?"

"You did a terrific job," I said. "Not just on the book, but on identifying Livia. You probably saved a woman's life. After you called that night and told me it was Livia who had quarrelled with Ariel, I went straight to the university. Solange Levy – you have her picture in your book – was already bleeding badly. She might have died if I hadn't made it in time. She has you to thank for the fact that I did."

"So she's going to be okay?"

"Yes," I said. "It'll take her a while to recuperate, but she's going to be fine."

Bebe burrowed through the basket of dolls on her knee. Finally, she found what she was a looking for: a Barbie with platinum hair piled high, a tiara of bubble-gum-pink hearts, and a ballgown with a bodice comprised of two hearts that covered Barbie's breasts like shields and a skirt of stiffly crocheted flowers. "Give Miss Hearts and Flowers to that Solange," Bebe said. "It doesn't matter how old a girl is, she always feels better if she gets a new doll."

Ronnie was reshelving videos when I got back downstairs. She was in a checked shirt and bluejeans, and she was very tanned.

"Have you been away?" I asked.

"Nah," she said. "Just a tanning salon. I'll never be beauty-pageant material like her," she said, pointing to the Barbie I was holding. "I figure the least I can do is look wholesome."

"It works for you," I said. "I like the way that gingham ribbon in your hair matches your shirt – very Doris Day."

Ronnie swished her ponytail. "You know, Joanne, one of the things I like about you is that you never once asked me about the gender thing."

I smiled at her. "That's because I know it's tough being a woman."

Ronnie clapped her massive hands together and roared with laughter. "You've got that one right, friend," she said. "But I'll let you in on a little secret. It's no bowl of cherries playing for the other team either."

If you enjoyed

BURYING ARIEL

treat yourself to all of the
Joanne Kilbourn mysteries,
now available in stunning new
trade paperback editions
and as eBooks

McCLELLAND & STEWART

www.mcclelland.com
www.mysterybooks.ca

DEADLY APPEARANCES

When Andy Boychuk drops dead at a political picnic, the evidence points to his wife. Joanne takes her first "case" as Canada's favourite amateur sleuth as she seeks to clear Eve Boychuk, discovering along the way a Bible college that isn't all it seems . . .

"A compelling novel infused with a subtext that's both inventive and diabolical." – Montreal *Gazette*

Trade Paperback 978-0-7710-1324-9   Ebook 978-0-7710-1322-5

MURDER AT THE MENDEL

"TENSE, MASTERFULLY WRITTEN. . . . BOLD AND POWERFUL."
– PUBLISHERS WEEKLY

Joanne's childhood friend, Sally Love, is an artist who courts controversy. When Sally's former partner turns up dead, Joanne discovers the past they shared was much more complicated, sordid, and deadly than she ever guessed.

"Classic. . . . Enough twists to qualify as a page turner. . . . Bowen and her genteel sleuth are here to stay."
– Saskatoon *StarPhoenix*

Trade Paperback 978-0-7710-1321-8   Ebook 978-0-7710-1320-1

THE WANDERING SOUL MURDERS

"BOWEN GETS BETTER WITH EACH FORAY."
– EDMONTON JOURNAL

Joanne's peace is destroyed when her daughter finds a young woman's body near her shop. The next day, her son's girlfriend drowns, an apparent suicide. When it is discovered that the two young women had at least one thing in common, Joanne is drawn into a twilight world where money can buy anything.

"With her rare talent for plumbing emotional pain, Bowen makes you feel the shock of murder."
– *Kirkus Reviews*

Trade Paperback 978-0-7710-1319-5   Ebook 978-0-7710-1318-8

A COLDER KIND OF DEATH

When the man convicted of murdering her husband six years earlier is himself shot, Joanne is forced to relive the most horrible time of her life. But it soon gets much worse when the prisoner's menacing wife is found dead a few nights later, strangled with Joanne's own silk scarf . . .

"A terrific story with a slick twist at the end."
– Globe and Mail

Trade Paperback 978-0-7710-1317-1   Ebook 978-0-7710-1316-4

A KILLING SPRING

The head of the School of Journalism at Joanne's university is found in a seedy rooming house wearing only women's lingerie and an electrical cord around his neck. When other events indicate that it was not a case of accidental suicide, Joanne finds herself deep in a world of fear, deceit, and danger.

"A compelling novel as well as a gripping mystery."
– Publishers Weekly

Trade Paperback 978-0-7710-1315-7   Ebook 978-1-5519-9613-4

VERDICT IN BLOOD

The corpse of the respected – and feared – Judge Justine Blackwell is found in a Regina park. Joanne tries to help a good friend involved in a struggle over which of Blackwell's wills is valid, and those who stand to lose the inheritance may well be murderers willing to strike again.

"An entirely satisfying example of why Gail Bowen has become one of the best mystery writers in the country."
– London Free Press

Trade Paperback 978-0-7710-1311-9   Ebook 978-1-5519-9614-1

BURYING ARIEL

Ariel Warren, a young colleague at Joanne's university, is stabbed to death in the library, and two men are under suspicion. The apparently tight-knit academic community is bitterly divided, vengeance is in the air, and Joanne is desperate to keep the wrong person from being punished for Ariel's death.

"Nearly flawless plotting, characterization, and writing." – *London Free Press*

Trade Paperback 978-0-7710-1309-6   Ebook 978-1-5519-9615-8

THE GLASS COFFIN

Joanne's friend Jill is about to marry a celebrated documentary filmmaker, both of whose previous wives committed suicide – after he had made films about them. When the best man's dead body is found just hours before the ceremony, Joanne begins to truly fear for her friend's safety.

"Chilling and unexpected." – *Globe and Mail*

Trade Paperback 978-0-7710-1305-8   Ebook 978-1-5519-9616-5

THE LAST GOOD DAY

Joanne is on holiday at a cottage in an exclusive enclave owned by lawyers from the same prestigious firm. When one of them kills himself the night after a long talk with Joanne, she is pushed into an investigation that has startling – and possibly fatal – consequences.

"A classic whodunit in which everything from setting to plot to character works beautifully.... A treat from first page to final paragraph." – *Globe and Mail*

Trade Paperback 978-0-7710-1349-2   Ebook 978-1-5519-9617-2

THE ENDLESS KNOT

After journalist Kathryn Morrissey publishes a tell-all book on the adult children of Canadian celebrities, one of the parents angrily confronts her and as a result is charged with attempted murder. When the parent hires Zack Shreve, the new love in Joanne's life, to defend him, her own understanding of the knot that binds parent and child becomes both personal and very urgent.

"A late-night page turner. . . . A rich and satisfying read." – *Edmonton Journal*

Trade Paperback 978-0-7710-1347-8   Ebook 978-1-5519-9246-4

THE BRUTAL HEART

A local call girl is dead, and her impressive client list includes the name of Joanne's new husband. Shaken that Zack saw the woman regularly before they met, Joanne throws herself into her work and is soon embroiled in a bitter and increasingly strange custody battle of a local MP, who is simultaneously trying to win an election.

"Elegant. . . . Joanne rules the narrative. [*The Brutal Heart*] slips along with grace and style." – *Toronto Star*

Trade Paperback 978-0-7710-0994-5   Ebook 978-1-5519-9233-4

THE NESTING DOLLS

Just before she is murdered, a young woman hands her baby to a perfect stranger and disappears. The stranger is the daughter of lawyer Delia Wainberg, and soon a secret from Delia's youth comes out. Not only is a killer on the loose, but the dead woman's partner is demanding custody of the child, and the battle threatens to tear apart Joanne's own family.

"The underlying human drama of love and good intentions gone very, very bad make the novel a compelling read." – *Vancouver Sun*

Trade Paperback 978-0-7710-1276-1   Ebook 978-0-7710-1277-8

Edward Willet

GAIL BOWEN's first Joanne Kilbourn mystery, *Deadly Appearances* (1990), was nominated for the W.H. Smith/ Books in Canada Best First Novel Award. It was followed by *Murder at the Mendel* (1991), *The Wandering Soul Murders* (1992), *A Colder Kind of Death* (1994) (which won an Arthur Ellis Award for best crime novel), *A Killing Spring* (1996), *Verdict in Blood* (1998), *Burying Ariel* (2000), *The Glass Coffin* (2002), *The Last Good Day* (2004), *The Endless Knot* (2006), *The Brutal Heart* (2008), and *The Nesting Dolls* (2010). In 2008 *Reader's Digest* named Bowen Canada's Best Mystery Novelist; in 2009 she received the Derrick Murdoch Award from the Crime Writers of Canada. Bowen has also written plays that have been produced across Canada and on CBC Radio. Now retired from teaching at First Nations University of Canada, Gail Bowen lives in Regina. Please visit the author at www.gailbowen.com.